Based on True

Events

The Fire of Fortitude

Melissa Scott

The Fire In Fortitude: The novel By Melissa Scott
Original Concept: Melissa Scott

Cover Illustration by David Gunstone

This book is a work of fiction
All the names, characters, places and incidents are the
product of the author's imagination and are used
fictitiously. Any resemblance to actual events, locales, real
persons living or dead, is purely coincidental.

This First Edition Published in December 2021

A CIP catalogue record for this book is available from the
British Library.

Hardback ISBN: 978-1-7399752-1-0
Paperback ISBN: 978-1-7399752-0-3

Dedicated to

My Dad, Dave

Thank you for always being there for me, inspiring me and standing by me through my journey and life. You mean everything to me. I need you to know how thankful I am to you for everything you have done for me. You helped me look into my heart and gather the courage to write my story. You are phenomenal, and I thank you for encouraging and motivating me every day. Thank you. Dad, I Love You, Millions.

My Mum, Julie (Juls)

Where to even start, Mum? I could not have done any of it without you right from birth to now. I need you to know that I Love You with my whole heart. Thank you for always Loving me and being there for me no matter what. I would not be where I am today without you. Thank you for being my rock and being my Mum. I want you to know how special you are to me and how much I Love and appreciate You.

My Step-Dad, Nigel

It takes a great man to step up and be there for a child that's not his blood, so I want to thank you for accepting me and always seeing and treating me as your daughter. We have a strong bond, and I want to thank you for being my inspiration to join the military and leading me down the path that led me to where I am today. I Love You, and I want you to know that I am so thankful for all you have done for me.

My Husband, Sidney

I never knew what true Love was until the day I met you. You are my fairytale come true, my world and my dream. Thank you for always being there for me. You stand by me while I follow my dreams, and I truly appreciate you for that, and now it's my turn to stand by you as you follow yours. Thank you for all you do for me and for Loving me. Some people never find their soul mate, but that day I met you, I knew I had found mine. You are my true Love, and I Love You more than any words can say. Always & Forever.

My Son, Joshua (Joshi)

I have no words, to even begin to explain how much I Love You and how much you mean to me. Thank you for being an amazing son. You are compassionate, caring, and understanding, and I know you will follow your dreams one day, and I will always be there for you, helping you achieve them. Thank you for motivating me with my story. Although you are young, your kind words inspire me to reach my dreams. I Love You, Josh, more than anything, and I promise I will always be there for you.

My Sister, Tanya

Thank you for being my sister and my friend. I want you to know that no matter what, I will always be there for you. We have been through so much together. And even though our paths have taken different turns, I want you to know how much you mean to me. I Love You, and whenever you need me, I'll be there.

I Thank you all for always being there for me, believing in me, loving me and most of all, for always having faith in me,

I want to say an extra special thank you to my dad for all the time and work he put in to complete my cover art. Thank you Dad it means so much to me.

Part One

Chapter Zero

Nothing Comes For Free

What is a phoenix? Is this epic creature simply magical stuff movies are made from, making way for a beautiful, powerful and immortal legend to be born? Some say that every one of us holds the key to that same power.

The power of this legendary creature, the power of immortality.

What makes it so easy to fall once life becomes less than you wanted it to be? Maybe things have gone seriously wrong for you, or you are genuinely broken-hearted or terrified, and you want to start over, make it all stop and banish your pain. Maybe there could be a way.

What if I told you that you could just burst into flames in all the glory and the majesty of the phoenix? In one simple breath-taking moment, as you close your eyes, you see total darkness, a deep everlasting nothingness with no end in sight. Then just as quickly as it was to close your eyes, making it all stop, you snap them open. With a quick blink of your eye, you come back the same you, but you are no longer travelling on the road full of darkness, and you find yourself no longer in pain.

If only it were that easy.... To have a free pass, to escape the dark, winding dead end, you have found yourself travelling down. To find a new HOPE and a new reality.... But it's just not that easy, and NOTHING comes for free....

If you DARE.... I invite you to join me now, to witness actual pain, loneliness, struggle, sacrifice, commitment, and loyalty. But most of all, to witness fear. A FEAR, so real that you feel it deep down to the dark depths of your very core. Embark with me on this journey, and you will learn the deepest darkest places a lost soul can take you.

I ask you, what is the soundtrack to your life? What music is playing in your most epic moment, and what is the perfect setting in which you find yourself wanting to be? Life is precious. People say we only have one chance to be someone, make a difference, and make dreams come true. But I ask you, is there a way to change it all and deviate from your given path. After this experience, don't waste a single moment and have no regrets. But most of all, make sure you LIVE your life.... Don't just survive.

. . . .

Darkness, what is the dark? We all have ideas and notions of what we perceive the darkness to be. The sun goes down, and all the LIGHTS go out. Then there is nothing, just the absence of LIGHT. Some say it's the perfect time for the other side to awaken. Society has come up with many reasons as to why we should sleep at night. But why? Is there more to this? What is the real reason we lay there so vulnerable with our eyes closed, blind to what's going on around us whilst we dream? Are we simply replaying events and significant moments from our lives? Or is it something more, and why do we sometimes relive scary moments from the past? Could it all be wrong? To understand might be far more challenging than anyone can comprehend. Think about those times when you were asleep, and there was just **NOTHING**. What if when our time comes to an end, that's it, and there is **NOTHING!**

What happens when you can't sleep at night, and you are completely alone in the dark? When the LIGHT is no longer blinding you, do your eyes play tricks on your brain? Or do you see forbidden things that you should never see? Do you now witness your actual reality and what's genuinely there, lurking in the deep depths of the dark? How do we know the difference? How do we know what is true and what we believe to be true? What are we meant to see, and what do we see by accident? Beyond the line of perceived reality, lying in this unmarked territory, do we witness events and untold things that we are not allowed to see? Are things that should have never crossed our path now becoming part of our reality? How do we know when we have found ourselves in the presence of the **UNSEEN**.

Chapter One

The Old Keevil Bridge

The music continuously plays, but it's the same tune playing repeatedly. It's coming from my yellow music box. My mum always sets it up before she tucks me in to go to sleep. This simple, innocent nursery rhyme goes on and on like a never-ending spiralled tunnel with no end in sight, nothing except a final destination of **DARKNESS**….

The old Keevil bridge will not stay up,
Will not stay up,
Will just not stay up,
The old Keevil bridge will not stay up,
Trapping us inside….

The old Keevil bridge will not stay up,

Will not stay up,
Will just not stay up,
The old Keevil bridge will not stay up,
Trapping us inside....

As I lay here, I close my eyes and listen to
THAT song, THAT song coming out of THAT
box! This room is full of darkness. It's so dark that
not even a single beam of LIGHT can get inside. I
pray for a tiny spec of LIGHT to attack my fear
and expose reality. I pull the covers up over my
head in a fast, elegant movement, trying my hardest
not to disturb the UNSEEN. I don't want to
witness the darkness, the deep, never-ending dark.
But most of all, I do not want to see what hides
waiting for me in the darkness, in the nothingness.

As far back as I can remember, my fear of the
dark kept me awake at night, just a normal childish
fear, some would say. But this theory was short-
lived because this quickly became more than just a
silly fear of the dark. This fear is very REAL, and
it's been here all along, only it was dormant, biding
its time until the opportune moment. It waits for
me in the deep dark depths of the night. It remains
hidden, waiting for my brain to become developed

just enough to understand what's truly out there. The very things that remain **UNSEEN** will one day become **SEEN**, and the covers can **NOT** and will **NOT** protect me.

From this point on, I lie awake each night listening to **THAT** song coming out of **THAT** box whilst drifting down a deep dark tunnel to an unknown destination of darkness. An old tree stands right outside, but it has a rouge branch that points towards our house and always hits my window. It's been out there for as long as I can remember, and it constantly crashes into the glass pane. It collides with it, leaving its image on one of my curtains. I begin to see a long, bony finger **TAPPING** on my window. This old and wrinkly finger continuously tries its hardest to be **LET IN**, in the deep dark of the night.

TAP,

TAP,

TAP,

TAP!

TAP,

TAP,

TAP,

TAP!

It persists and does not STOP. It gets louder and louder, making it seem like it will break through the window pane and shatter the glass. The TAPPING continues, ON and ON, but there is still some HOPE that it might come to a HALT. Thankfully I can faintly hear my sister coming up the stairs, and just as she touches the door handle, the TAPPING from the branch suddenly STOPPED. Whilst I lay here alone in the dark, it felt like years passed by as I waited for her to come upstairs. It's almost like that TAPPING on the window is a warning that must be heard by me and me alone.

But every night, as soon as my sister falls asleep, it

all **BEGINS!**

Chapter Two

It Begins

The human brain is very complex. People state that humans are more likely to remember big or bad moments over small ones. Memories are the information that we store, encode and retain. Memories influence our lives every day, but could it be possible for false memories to exist. Could it be possible to think about something so much and genuinely believe in it that this then becomes a memory? But this is not a real memory. It's simply a thought or a desire that has become a memory, developed from a true belief. The brain stores the situation as it is. But when we recall this information, it becomes merged with past experiences, and then it's identified as an actual memory. How do we know what is real and what is not?

Have you ever felt that intense throbbing and the extreme pounding in your head that comes hand in hand with an unbearable pressure that's trying to crush your brain, or so it would feel? I'm referring to headaches and migraines. Are they just a pain in your head, from lack of sleep, overworking, or too much stress. Or are they so much more?

I look towards a picture that I drew of my family, which my mum kindly put on the wall. I see my mum, my dad, my sister, me and our cat Speckles. In my drawing, we all stand outside our home in this small village that we call Keevil. I look at the front door and notice I have labelled it with a significant gold number four that sits right in the middle, above the letterbox. As I look to the bottom of the page, I see the year 1994. I wrote the year there using a blue crayon, so I will never forget when I drew this image. I thought, wow, I'm still only six years old. Time is passing by so slowly. I drew our house to be entirely accurate, *(well for a six-year-old anyway)*. We have always lived here in this small village, which is an old and historical place. It's said to be the stuff from which legends are born. Although Keevil is a settlement with less than fifty houses, I only drew our house. Some say it dates back to the 11th century. However, there is no solid proof, only an old Keevil rumour. My picture made me remember hearing that at school, and just looking at it also reminded me, it is not always about what can be seen, but how what we see can make you feel.

We live on Ember-Shadow Road, just a short walk from The Church of the Holy Spirit. This small village looked like any other place before dusk. During the daylight hours, there were family's out walking, and children would be outside playing. I'm even sure the cows over at Big Foot's Farm, which is just around the corner from our house, moo louder than usual to get people to remember they are there. However, this village changes once the sun goes down.

A light mist begins creeping through the streets. It happens so elegantly that before you can see it coming, it's just there filling the roads and drifting up to the sky, as far as your eyes can see. The village becomes ominous as if it's come to life, as though it has a heartbeat all of its own, wanting to be seen and wanting to make its presence known. It releases its dark, isolated soul in perfect rhythm with the sun as it begins to go down.

Our house, number four, sits prominently on Ember-Shadow Road. We are a three bedroomed detached house, which gives us privacy from the neighbours, not that this is needed, but it is just nice to have. Just as I drew in my picture, our house is gorgeous. We have a beautiful big garden out the back with a pond sitting at the end that my dad has worked very hard on. We have a shed and a red swing set, which my dad cemented down to keep it secure. Within the cement, my sister and I imprinted our handprints to be forever locked in time, a treasured memory that remains today. I recalled all of this just from looking at my drawing and spending some time thinking about my life.

As I lay in my bed still looking at my picture, my mum suddenly comes in, pulls open the curtains, and instructs us that it's time to get up. My attention immediately turns to the window. I know today will be a cold day because I can see frost stretching right across the glass. I also hear the roar of our car's engine outside, where my dad has already begun defrosting the vehicle. I look across the room towards my sister Talia. She just woke up because we must get ready for school. Even though we have three bedrooms in our house, I share a room with my sister. However, I'm glad about this at this point in my life because at least I'm not alone at night.

We have a fairly big room, and we are lucky because our mum and dad let us choose our own wallpaper. We love the one we selected because it's full of cute, cuddly bears. Everywhere you look, you can see a different bear in a different colour. We also both have cute trolls that hang from the side of our beds. They make squeaky noises if you shake them. It's kind of funny in a cute way, but they are not your regular trolls. They are fluffy and round, with a troll face positioned in the middle. We both have one, and I like that there are two of them because it keeps the room's balance.

We share this room because my dad is using the third room for his art and music. Besides, I like that Talia and I share a room. It's helped us become closer because now it feels like she is my friend and my sister. That is how I think about us and what I hope for anyway. Talia is a beautiful girl with long brown hair and matching brown eyes. She is three years older than me, and it's clear that we are already so different and destined for opposite paths. We are both born of the same parents, but we have very different personalities. I genuinely believe she will be there for me forever as I will be for her because family is truly important. When all else fails, who would you turn to for help? No matter what, family is FOREVER.

We have a few things in common though, we both love to play with toys of many types and figurines of all sizes. We also have these tiny, miniature figures. They are not even the size of your little finger, the pinkie as many people know it. We play with these small figures all the time because they have long and beautiful coloured hair. They come in many varieties, and there are so many different colours to choose from, we would get one each time we went to the toy shop. We would always play with them on our long and winding stairs that spiralled around from top to bottom, but I never knew what made us choose to play here until much later on.

Chapter Three

Routine

Please take a moment and see how far back in your life you can remember. What is the earliest memory you can recall? Was it an everyday moment, a bad one, a scary one or simply a significant one?

At this point in our journey, I am six, and Talia is nine years old. Neither one of us have any idea where our lives will lead us. We both attend The Old Oak Tree School, which is around the corner from The Church of The Holy Spirit and a short walk away from our house. Today our mum is walking us to school because our dad has to go to work.

I'm in the same class as my best friend Paisley at school, and luckily we sit at the same table. We are inseparable and the best of friends. When the time is right, we have great fun and enjoy doing crazy dances to rock songs. We laugh so hard while doing those silly little dances. I sit here patiently waiting for the day to end so I can go home because I've found today incredibly dull. The lessons were not fun at all. We have spent most of the day in silence because the teacher has been reading aloud. But Paisley and I didn't waste any time before we began looking at each other and bursting out laughing. After repeatedly being told to behave, we began to pay attention.

My teacher was reading us a story about a bunny rabbit who is afraid of the dark. Once I began to pay attention, I realised that I could relate to this rabbit. I started to feel very strongly towards this story and found myself wishing I had paid attention in the first place. The clock soon struck half-past three, and this meant it was time to go home. I was glad to go home, but I felt sad at the same time because now I wanted to know what happened to the rabbit in the end.

Our mum always gets me from my classroom first, and then we go and collect Talia. Once our mum has us both, we walk home. Sometimes we are allowed to go to the shop to get some sweets.

We eat them on the way, whilst talking about our day at school. I feel delighted and cheerful today because the story at school seemed to lead to a happy ending where dark and fear gets conquered. But despite my happiness, I had no idea that today would be the day that my nights would never be the same ever again.

Once we arrive at home, Talia and I play with our toys for a little while on the stairs, then our mum calls us for dinner. Today we have fishcakes. We always cut them up into pieces and pretend it's cake. It's easier to eat that way, and we thought it was more fun. Well, I know I thought so anyway. Our mum always makes delicious food for us to eat at mealtimes and she always plays music whilst we eat. She plays songs that we enjoy, and I thought nothing of it because it's just harmless music.

After dinner, I took a bubble bath, got into my pyjamas, and then brushed my hair. Now that I'm ready for bed, I can play for a bit longer because I have some time to spare before my dreaded bedtime. I decide to use this time to wind Talia up, so I chase her around the house and pretend to be BEEBLEDOSH.

Now, Talia has an imaginary friend, and his

name is BEEBLEDOSH. I don't know much about him because she does not disclose much information regarding him. I only know that he visits her and is her very best friend, but no one else can see him. I sometimes put my mum's tall laundry basket over my head and put my arms out vertically and follow her around the house, saying,

BEEBLEDOSH,

BEEEEEE BLE DOOOOOOSH,

BEEEEEE BLE DOOOOOOSH,

BEEEEEE BLE DOOOOOOSH,

BEEBLEDOSH....

But once she gets annoyed, she chases me upstairs to make me stop, this sounds mean, but it's just harmless fun. My mum would even join in sometimes. It really is just a bit of playful fun, and even Talia plays along for a little while. Tonight she played along with me, so I chased her around the house, then she ran back at me, and I ended up

19

landing on the sofa, and she landed on the floor, but we were both laughing so hard.

Bedtime was drawing in fast, I always go to bed before Talia because of the age gap, but I have things to help me fall asleep. Well, they are supposed to help me. I have THAT music box that plays THAT song. It's a wind-up tv, a music box that has an image of The Old Keevil Bridge and a girl in a boat sailing under it on the front. It's a cartoon and plays music based on the old nursery rhyme from the bridge. It plays only music, though. There are no lyrics. I also have a cassette (tape) player, which has professional readings of fairy tales on the tape, ready to play if I feel I need it. But the best thing of all is the live show, produced and performed by my dad. The production is called PIPPY at the door, starring PIPPY and friends.

PIPPY at the door is a spectacular show that my dad created from his love for us because he loves to see us smile. It really is the best time of the day, and the show star's PIPPY, my favourite stuffed animal. PIPPY is an orange and yellow rabbit with long ears and red sunglasses. Some of our other friends are also the main stars of the show. Dino, my blue dinosaur, is among them, and

Talia's bear, called Born, also takes part in the show. Sometimes different bears would guest star on random nights, and my dad uses the characters to tell remarkable bedtime stories above the door, just like a puppet show.

We always enjoy my dad's stories because they are full of good morals and life lessons, but most of all, we enjoy the fact that the animals are always having a good time. I always cherish these moments because it demonstrates the amount of love my dad has for us. He shows us this because he gives his complete effort and attention just to see us smile. With all the effort my dad puts in and the detail of the stories, it really does make my dad's, PIPPY, at the door spectacular, a truly priceless legend in the making.

Tonight's show has ended, so my dad hands PIPPY back to me as Talia goes downstairs. My mum and dad then come over to my bed to tuck me in and say goodnight. My mum then starts to wind up THAT music box for me because she thinks I enjoy it. She's an amazing mum, and she can't possibly know something unless I tell her, and I haven't told her what happens in the dark. I know I will never forget the clicking noise it makes as she winds it turning the red dial around and around until it reaches the end. Once it comes to an end, it suddenly lets out a grinding noise letting us know it's as far as it can go and it can't be wound any further, then THAT song begins to play,

The old Keevil bridge will not stay up,
Will not stay up,
Will just not stay up,
The old Keevil bridge will not stay up,
Trapping us inside….

It continues to play THAT song in what seems like a never-ending cycle. My mum gives me a hug and a kiss and then she tells me she loves me and I reply to tell her that I love her more than anything. On her way out, she turns OUT the LIGHT and closes my door, and as I lay here, I can hear her footsteps as she walks across the hall to go down the stairs.

THUD,

THUD,

THUD,

THUD,

Thud,

Thud,

Thud,

Thud....

The further away she gets, the quieter her steps become, and I notice that I can no longer hear her. I suddenly become very aware that I am now alone in the dark. I feel my eyes burning. They feel so heavy, and I'm struggling to hold them open. I'm sure I will drift off to sleep in no time, even if it is only for a short while. I realise I can't stop rubbing my eyes, and then I feel them close. I try my hardest to force them open, but it's almost impossible. They are just so heavy. I continue to try, but I know I'm going to fall asleep soon.

TAP,

TAP,

TAP,

TAP!

I open my eyes in a fast burst and look out into my room. I can't see anything except never-ending darkness, and all I can hear is THAT,

TAP,

TAP,

TAP,

TAP!

I take a moment to compose myself and think. I ask myself, ok, how long have I been asleep? I don't know because I have no concept of time in the dark, but I'm pretty sure Talia's not up here yet, so this means I haven't been asleep for very long.

TAP,

TAP,

TAP,

TAP!

The **TAPPING** on the window will not stop, it's all I can focus on, and the darkness Is creating a shadow on my wall. The harder I stare, the more it looks like a long arm with a bony long pointing finger. What could it be pointing at in the darkness? Is it pointing towards me? I do not know, but I feel every hair on my neck stand, and I begin to sweat and feel cold simultaneously. I start to feel goosebumps appear at the top of my back and spread all the way to the bottom, and I also feel them crawling up my arms and legs. What does it want with me?

It seems like it will break through the window, so I pull my blanket over my head and press play on my cassette tape. Maybe the sound would deter the finger, and I will be safe. I feel like it's pointing at me, unleashing something and sending it towards my bed. I close my eyes and listen to the story on my tape player, but the TAPPING only gets louder.

TAP,

TAP,

TAP,

TAP!

I feel like IT'S speaking to me. Saying, hear me, you can't hide from me, play your tape, hide under the covers, but I am still here. I just lay here, keeping entirely still, trying with all my might, not to move a muscle and not to breathe aloud! I just listen to my story, focus on the words, and not focus on anything else.

I have no idea what fate has planned for me.

FINALLY, I can hear Talia coming up the

stairs. I listen to her open the bathroom door to go and brush her teeth. Now that I know she is about to come in here, I press stop on my tape player, and I listen out for the TAPPING....

But the TAPPING has abruptly STOPPED. It stopped dead as if something swiftly snapped THAT branch. I tell myself now that Talia is in the bathroom, it should be safe to pull the covers down slightly and investigate....

My heart is pounding, and my whole body has become numb. My heart starts to race even faster as I see THAT shadow arm pointing. To my dismay, it is still there, only now it's completely still like a solid object fixed in place. It's not even blowing with the wind. Some would say this was a coincidence, but I can feel something is not right in this room. Talia then comes in and climbs into her bed. She very quickly falls asleep, just as she always does. I dislike how easy Talia finds it to sleep. I envy her because I would do anything to be able to go to sleep and stay asleep as easily as she does. I wish that I could fall asleep with all my might, then I would be naïve to all the occurrences of the night. However, tonight once Talia falls into a deep sleep, to my horror,

IT BEGINS!

Chapter Four

The Unseen

As Talia remains fast asleep, I can hear her breathing lightly. She looks so peaceful and happy. I look over at her, wishing I was fast asleep and having pleasant dreams. I wonder how she sleeps so soundly. As I led here, looking out into the darkness, I began thinking, what if I get my dad to cut down THAT tree outside my window? THAT tree just sits there motionless, waiting in an ominous silence masked in the light mist that creeps through the streets, stretching as far as any eyes can see. It is said that this village comes to life at night. They say if you stay quiet and really listen, you can hear a heartbeat. What twisted soul possesses THAT tree? It's so dark, so isolated. I can't help but wonder what tragedy or horrors this tree has witnessed in all the years it has stood here, trapped in a long web of loneliness. If THAT tree could speak, what horrors would come from the words it spoke. Would the lonely soul left behind still tap on my window, insisting that it is heard or would it cease to exist, and I would finally be free to sleep at night?

TAP,

TAP,

TAP,

TAP!

It continues TAPPING....

I snap my head away from looking out into the darkness and look over towards the window. I feel my heart start to race, and the goosebumps begin to spread all over my body once again. All I can see is THAT shadow. It's pointing its long, bony, old finger directly towards me. I immediately pull the covers over my head and squeeze my eyes shut as hard as I can. I close them so tight that the shade of black I usually see when my eyes are closed turns into a YELLOWY, GOLDEN sort of colour. I then make sure I tuck my legs under my duvet, hooking the covers under my feet to protect them from the darkness. I then place my feet as close to the wall as physically possible, and I squeeze PIPPY so tight.

I repeat aloud to myself,

Nothings there,

Nothings there,

Nothings there,

NOTHINGS THERE,

NOTHINGS THERE,

NOTHINGS THERE,

NOTHINGS THERE,

NOTHING IS THERE!

I hold my breath and choose to take a look because I need to know that we're still safe in this room. I think about how I was in this room earlier with the LIGHT ON, and nothing was in here. So how can there be anything in here now? I slowly pull the blanket down from my head, but it's so dark that I can barely even see Talia asleep in her bed. I look over to the window where THAT long, bony finger still points towards me and right there on the curtains is a face. I struggle to make out much detail, but I can see enough to know IT is a face.

I stare straight into ITS deep black eyes that glare right back at me, and as I look around, I see a nose, a mouth and a jawline. THAT face is entwined, locked in and stuck within the material of my curtains. I know this, but how trapped is IT really? Could it indeed free itself from the curtains grasp with some kind of cosmic energy and follow whatever purpose IT'S here to achieve? Does IT plan to hurt me? Is THAT face even real, or is it just the darkness playing tricks on me?

I can barely make out the wardrobe door even though it seems to glow. But wait, what's happening? I see it emerging, shining through the night, almost pixelated. It's highlighted with a haze of LIGHT, seeping through the darkness. The harder I stare into it, the clearer I see it. As I continue to stare hard at the wardrobe door, I focus only on the door and nowhere else. My heart's racing faster than ever before. My breathing has become erratic. I can't help but hold my breath, forgetting to breathe, as I am unable to do anything else but watch as the door slowly opens,

CREEEEEEEEAAAK!

I look away, closing my eyes to refocus them and immediately look straight back. The darkness has taken over. I need to look hard for my eyes to readjust to the dark once more. The door is moving, but the movement is so slow that I have to look closely to see a sign that it's swaying. It's drifting back and forth as if a light wind is catching it. I snap my eyes closed and tell myself that this is not possible. All of this is in your imagination, and none of these things are actually there. I open my eyes, and once the pixelating darkness comes into focus, I clearly see the wardrobe door, only now the door is wide open. I know in my heart that this is not possible. But that does not stop me from immediately pulling the blanket back over my head. No matter what happens, my thoughts will not deter me from demanding to know why this is happening? Has this been going on every night? What is occupying my room, hiding in the day and lurking at night? I lay here waiting, waiting for a LIGHT, waiting for some HOPE, waiting for the mist to clear and the sun to rise, or something, anything.

I need to go and tell my mum and dad what's happening in this room, but as I try to move, I realise that I'm stuck to my bed, glued there, unable to move. I try to lift my arm, but it feels like it's tied down. It will not budge, and I feel paralysed. I convince myself, maybe whatever is out there will stay out there, I am under here, so maybe I'm safe. Perhaps it's best if I try and go to sleep. So I close my eyes and continue to lay here, unable to move.

I suddenly became aware that something was tugging on the right side of my sheet because the part draped over my mattress became tight and stretched out. My covers are somehow slightly lifted, and I can now feel an ice-cold draft coming through the gap. I find that I'm still unable to move, which means I have to admit to myself that it's not me creating that draft. The pressure on the mattress feels like the same kind of force that a cat's paw would apply as it walks across your lap. I start to feel more and more pressure as each second passes, and a horrifying thought crosses my mind, has someone put their hand on my bed?

I feel pressure slowly slithering underneath my covers, creating indentations on my sheet. I'm still unable to move yet fully aware that something has made its way under my covers and is now under here with me. I feel a long cold shiver journey down my spine. I have a terrible feeling that it's a hand, similar to THAT one pointing at me from outside the window with old, wrinkled, long bony fingers. I can feel it reaching down across the sheet, creating creases and indentations as it slowly glides along my mattress. Finger by finger, moving slowly across my bed like a spider trying to creep over a wall whilst remaining undetected. It's scurrying at just the right speed to make progress but go unnoticed.

Only I can feel every move it makes. This unidentified, uninvited THING has entered my personal space with no permission. IT has slowly moved along my sheet and found the way to its resting place. This old and wrinkly hand has succeeded. IT'S wrapped each long bony finger one by one around my right ankle. IT bends and entwines each finger around my skin. IT followed the shape of my ankle to enable its fingers to fit into each other and lock into place. This THING now has hold of my foot tight, and a terrible feeling rushes over me. What if IT has no interest in letting go? I'm trapped, locked in this moment with this THING, but most of all, I'm locked deep into my own fear with nowhere else to run.

Is this the UNSEEN, the cruel monsters that live in the dark? I try my hardest to call out, shout, or scream, but I make no noise no matter how hard I try. I'm completely stuck, but worst of all, my covers are somehow being pulled down from my face in a slow but swift movement. I am now completely exposed to the dark. I try to close my eyes, only I'm held here. Why am I unable to move? I have no option left other than to look out into the darkness. Barely able to see anything, I try to look out of my peripheral vision to see what this unwelcome UNSEEN is. I am only able to see an outline of someone sat squatting by the side of my bed. ITS back is towards me, but I can see long white, matted hair that holds an eerie glow in the darkness. I can also see what looks like old black clothes. But, no matter how hard I try, I can't see IT correctly. My eyes keep going in and out of focus, making IT seem pixilated, then blurred, then IT'S just an outline. But, even in the darkness, this UNSEEN looks like a real person only faded, sort of like a dark hologram.

I suddenly thought of my parents because if this THING, this UNSEEN, is genuinely here making sure I don't move, what is my parents' fate? Are they hurt, or do they have no clue about any of this? What does this UNSEEN want? Wait, my sister, is Talia ok? I strained my eyes, forcing them to look across to her bed. But she is sleeping soundly. How? Does this mean that the UNSEEN are after me and me alone? It does not speak a single word, and I still can't see ITS face. IT just sits there still and staring into space like IT'S judging someone or something or maybe even me. IT abruptly changed ITS deminer and began to look like IT'S laughing, but IT has no sound like IT'S muted. I do all I can to calm my breathing, but my heart's beating faster than I have ever felt

before, and my whole body tingled cold from
goosebumps that by now had spread right across
me.

I decide to look away from the UNSEEN,
hoping that IT will leave. I look up to the ceiling
and find myself looking at what I can only describe
as two small children dressed in very old clothing. I
have never seen these types of clothes before.
There appears to be a boy and a girl. I can only
make this out because one of them has long hair,
and the other has an old-style hat on top of their
head with what looks like very short hair. They
appear to be jumping on the end of my bed as if it's
a trampoline. But they are not causing the bed to
move because they are not even making contact
with it. It's as if they are going straight through it.
They are not fully solid, and I can barely see them
in the dark. But I know I can see them enough to
know they are there. They are almost translucent
yet solid enough to make them out. I'm not getting
a bad ominous vibe from them, they seem
innocent, but they give me a strong sense of dread
and sorrow. This feeling is so strong that I almost
forgot about the UNSEEN!

They seem to be younger than me, but I still

find myself just lying here watching them in fear because there is nothing else I can do. No matter how hard I try, I can't move or speak. Suddenly the atmosphere changes, and I immediately begin to feel uneasy and unsafe, in a kind of threatening manner. Why are there children here, and why are they jumping on my bed? They are just jumping up and down, up and down, with no emotion and no voice. Through the darkness and the pixellation caused by my eyes, I can barely make out the faint look on their faces. It is not a look of happiness. They look empty and soulless. They look like an empty shell, and that look held deep in their glaring eyes is worrying to me, like they are missing something and that they have suffered immensely.

I want to know what is happening and why this is happening to me? Are my family ok, and why is Talia not seeing any of this? Why do they leave her alone? I want it to STOP, I want them to GO away, I want to make sure my mum and dad are safe. I want this UNSEEN to let go of my foot. I can't move or yell out. I am a prisoner to the UNSEEN, and I am TRAPPED.

I can hardly see Talia. The more I try and move, the more I see a dark figure out of the corner of my eye. It's moving so fast that it's never in the same place twice. I don't know if it's actually there or not. But what I do know is that I can now see the outline of the furniture in our room. I take a moment because my eyes keep going in and out of focus. One minute I can see things, then it becomes blurred, and I can't see anything but darkness. Are my eyes playing tricks on me? I'm sure the stuff in my room is now moving. Am I going crazy? How is any of this even possible?

Then for some reason that I do not know, it decided to show itself. The UNSEEN was about to become SEEN. The darkness filled the room with a thick black nothingness. I am completely isolated with no way to escape. I have no option other than to be stuck here in this moment. I never thought anything could get any darker. But then, in a single moment, complete silence filled the air around me like a breeze of wind blowing gently past my face. In the black of the night, out of the darkness, a tall, dark, black figure emerges, then stands before me at the end of my bed. IT does not move. IT just stands there staring at me, watching me. I feel a strong presence like IT'S eternally judging me. I feel IT staring deep into the depths of my soul, my very being, seeing all my deepest darkest thoughts and my untold fears.

The only thing I can feel is the beating of my heart. It has never been so fast. I feel every hair on my neck stand on end, and I know I can't leave, but most of all, I have no way to scream. I want to move my arm to wipe away a tear that's rolling down my cheek. PIPPY rolled onto the floor, and it kills me inside that there is nothing I can do to rescue him. I want to get up so much to grab him because he means everything to me. I tell myself aloud,

I MUST GET HIM, I NEED TO MOVE!

I compose myself, and with this, I finally close my eyes. Once my eyes are closed, I squeeze them shut until I see that YELLOWY, GOLDEN colour to prove to myself that they are closed. It feels like a sign of HOPE. Now I know my eyes are closed to the darkness and the UNSEEN, I begin to tell myself....

It's not real,

It's not real,

IT IS NOT REAL,

IT IS NOT REAL,

I open my eyes….

It still stands there in a wave of nothingness, stood at the end of my bed with no movement staring deep into my very core. It did not leave. Nothing changed. PIPPY is still alone on the floor, and that THING still has a hold of my foot. But the boy and girl from the end of my bed have moved aside. They have given up their space for this UNSEEN to be SEEN. The black figure is still just lingering right there before me.

But then, just as I thought all HOPE was lost….

I see a sudden beam of LIGHT glow around the edge of my door. FINALLY, the hallway LIGHT has come on. Before I can even comprehend the fact that there is finally a LIGHT, the UNSEEN vanished. Just as fast as they arrived, they left. My ankle is free, and I can finally move. I immediately grab PIPPY in one swift movement from off the floor and run out of my room as fast as my feet will move. I run straight to my mum and dad with tears pouring out of my eyes, streaming down harder than rain in winter, I begin trying to get my words out, but I'm only able to make noise.

My mum can't understand what's wrong. I'm trying to tell them what has just happened to me. I can hardly believe what I am even saying. It sounds so crazy now that I'm saying it out loud. My mum really does think that I just had a bad dream, but perhaps she just wants to calm me down, make me feel better and reassure me that I am safe. It makes a lot of sense because of the way I'm explaining it to them. How could they possibly understand without the whole story? I can only get out every other word. I can't possibly tell them about all of this. How can I tell them what I've been through? I can't explain something that I don't even understand myself.

Then it suddenly dawned on me....

An unwelcome thought!

What if it was all a dream, a bad moment, a nightmare, a terrible situation constructed in my subconscious? Did I make this up in my dreams? I have never experienced anything like this before, and I've never seen that THING anywhere until tonight. I know I would remember if I had seen THAT before. I definitely haven't ever seen the type of clothes the two children were wearing, and as for the dark black figure, I have no idea. Was this Talia's imaginary friend whom I previously mocked? I don't know, and I don't want to find out. I want so much to believe this was a nightmare, just as my mum called it. I'm not ready to find out. I could never prepare myself for such a fate again. With everything I have in me, I choose to believe that this was indeed a nightmare created out of some childish fear brought on by a spooky branch tapping on my window. It has to be. It must be. No, IT WAS JUST A NIGHTMARE.

I ask my mum to stay with me until I fall asleep, and I insist that the hallway LIGHT stays ON with the door slightly open for the rest of the night. Despite what I have just been through, I am relieved to know that my mum and dad are safe. On this occasion, my mum stays with me, she sits down next to me and plays my cassette tape, and we listen to a fairy-tale together. I lie here hugging PIPPY so tight, but for a split second, right before I close my eyes, I'm sure I just saw the black figure stood right behind my mum. It was only there for a second, and then it was gone. Are my eyes playing tricks on me again, or was this a gentle way of letting me know it was all REAL? I'm not sure, but it has left me with a very uneasy feeling. My mum is making me feel SAFE, so I focus on her. I hold her hand, close my eyes and try to fall asleep. I know my mum will wait until I fall asleep before she goes to bed because I haven't ever seen her leave any other time she sat with me when I was scared. I do my best to keep opening my eyes to make sure she's still there, but my eyes just become so heavy, it becomes harder and harder to open them....

Chapter Five

Bad Dream Or Bad Reality?

Today is Saturday, so we don't have to go to school. I try and explain to Talia what happened last night. I tell her about my bad dream. I describe it like this not to convince her but to make myself believe my own words. Talia wants to know what happened, but I don't have any comments because I'm not even sure myself, now that I think back to it. But I tell her that I thought **BEEBLEDOSH** was there. Talia doesn't understand why I thought it was him because she had never described him to me. The only answer I have for her is that I just got a feeling it was him.

I grab PIPPY, and we go downstairs to eat breakfast. He always comes with me everywhere he can because I don't like leaving him behind. We sit down at our table, which is next to the kitchen and under the stairs. Our stairs are winding, so they come down over the table and off to the side, creating a boxed area where the table fits nicely. Our table is very cosy and comfortable to sit at as a family, and sometimes whilst my mum is cooking I sit here and play whilst talking to her.

I always have a cereal called Star-dust for breakfast because it's my favourite one. My mum has fruit because she is trying to be healthy, and my dad always has a cup of tea in his favourite beige coloured mug. The one he loves the most has a sketch of some horses and a house on the side. He always has this cup of tea with a bowl of cereal flakes. Talia has cereal with me, and we nearly always have Star-dust. But the best part about breakfast is when we need to open a new box to dig deep and find the prize.

I'm especially feeling an emptiness deep to my very core on this particular morning. Maybe it's because of my nightmare or the experience I endured, but I feel like I have lost something. I can't help it, but I have a desire, a dying need to ask my mum what happens when we die? She responds how any mum would, and the answer I get is that we go to heaven and exist in a great peaceful place filled with the things and people we love. For some irritating reason, this answer is not good enough for me. I really feel like there is more than just heaven. For some painful reason, I get an overwhelming feeling rush over me, and I suddenly really feared for my mum. I felt as though she would vanish one day and just disappear with no explanation and for no specific reason. This thought made me feel very uneasy and worried. What would I do without my mum? Where would she go? What would happen to her, and why would someone or something take her?

The fear of my mum suddenly disappearing, never to return, led me to think about what existed before life began. Where were we located before we were born? I can only remember as far back as being about three or four years old. I was outside in the back garden in front of the double patio doors playing with toys whilst looking inside at Talia watching television. I need to know where I came from before I was here with my parents? What else was there? What else is there?

I begin to feel very uneasy, my stomach starts to turn, and I begin to feel sick to my stomach. But not the kind where you need to be sick but the type brought on by deep thoughts of worry. Worry is that type of sickness that you can't get rid of so easily.

Talia invites me to play on the stairs, and I agree, thinking maybe this would deter my mind, but I decide that first I would go and give my mum and dad a hug and tell them that I love them. I meet Talia on the stairs, where she has already set up her toys and is sitting down talking to BEEBLEDOSH. I walk up a few stairs and sit on the stair below her. I reveal to her that I genuinely want to know where BEEBLEDOSH comes from and where he goes when he leaves. But Talia is always very minimalistic when it comes to talking about BEEBLEDOSH. The response I get from her is that he comes from within the walls, but he's gone, for now, so we can play. So I thought I better just go along with it because I'm trying to divert my focus from last night and my fear of our mum disappearing.

Lunchtime soon came and passed, but I suddenly became very aware of bedtime as the evening drew near. I found myself not wanting to go to bed. I was dreading it. I felt cold, then sweaty, then just worried, and then that sick feeling quickly returned. My appetite has completely disappeared, which has given me an idea, maybe if I refuse to eat my dinner, my mum will see something is wrong and won't send me to bed.

Dinnertime quickly came around. My mum put her music on as she did most days whilst everyone sat down to eat their food. I just sit here playing with mine for the longest time, but then I decide it will be better just to explain how sick I feel instead. My mum listens to me, but she tells me that I still need to take a bath and go up to bed. So I accept my bath without a fuss, but then right before it's time to go up to my room, I refuse. I begin explaining how I do not want to go into THAT room. There is SOMETHING in there, and it comes from THAT tree, the nothingness and out of the darkness!

My mum and dad go upstairs to look inside the wardrobe, under the beds and behind the curtains. But they develop no conclusion because there is nothing in my room. I beg them to let me keep the hallway LIGHT on, with the door open. My mum says ok for tonight but only until Talia comes up. I begin to plead with her by explaining that the

UNSEEN only come out once she is asleep. I must sound so crazy because my mum and dad explain that there is no one in my room or this house and that we are all safe.

My mum gives me a hug and a kiss and says goodnight, and I make sure to tell her I love her. She says it back, and then she goes back downstairs. Talia climbs onto my bed, and my dad begins tonight's episode of PIPPY at the door. My dad wants to make me feel better, so he performs an adventure based on bad dreams. PIPPY and friends would fight away any monsters who tried to hurt us. My dad's moral was that GOOD conquers EVIL and will defeat the harmful monsters by doing the right thing. FORTITUDE, you only have to be brave and make sure you believe in yourself and have courage in difficult situations.

After PIPPY at the door, Talia goes back downstairs, and my dad then gives me a hug and a kiss, tucks me and PIPPY in and says goodnight. He wound THAT music box and placed it on the end of my bed, and then as promised, he left the LIGHT ON in the hallway and the door open. Before he goes, I tell him I love him, and he says it back.

I notice that there is no TAPPING on the window. I can see the shadow of THAT long pointing finger, but it's not moving. It's just there immaculately still as though it's sitting in cement or clay. It's not TAPPING, and it's not making a single sound. A terrible thought interrupts my mind, had I indeed had a bad dream? Had I made all of this up or is this simply because tonight I have LIGHT and I'm not alone in the nothingness, the darkness? Could it be that the UNSEEN can only come to life in the dark? Does the LIGHT banish them?

My thoughts suddenly turn to THAT music box as it continues to play THAT song,

The old Keevil bridge will not stay up,
Will not stay up,
Will just not stay up,
The old Keevil bridge will not stay up,
Trapping us inside….

As it continues to play, I turn towards the window, holding onto PIPPY as tight as possible. I will not stop. I will not release my eyes from

52

THAT long pointing finger that tonight stands immaculately still, not even blowing in the wind. I stare at it harder and harder, almost willing it to move just to prove that I'm not crazy. I continue to stare intently at it, giving it all my attention, so I no longer hear THAT song playing out of THAT box. Then silence falls over me as if someone pressed a stop button on the sound of the world, only I continue to stare, waiting for it to make its move, but nothing,

Nothing happens.

I must have drifted off to sleep because now I hear Talia running water in the bathroom and brushing her teeth. I really don't understand why I always wake up at this point of the night. She is not loud at all and never makes any noise. She turns off the hallway LIGHT and closes our door, she climbs into her bed, and as she always does, she quickly falls asleep. I begin to feel worried. Although I convinced myself it was all just a bad dream and that none of it was real, I suddenly got a wave of fear come across me and that same familiar shiver down my spine.

I continue to lie here, looking out into the darkness. I look around the room at the shapes of our things because I can barely make anything out. But I can see something, so I look closer to focus on it. I see what looks like the shape of a man in the corner of our room. A head peered out from behind the dresser, but it remained still, only moving enough to ensure I saw it. Then just as fast as it appeared, it was gone.

It was SEEN out the corner of my eyes, so I tell myself that I'm just seeing things and scaring myself. Just as I think this, I look back towards the window and instantly become horrified. I see THAT face beginning to appear in the curtains. IT'S emerging through the fabric with a truly horrifying grin, a smile from one side of its face to the other just like a clowns smile. I continue to stare at the face, and I decide not to take my eyes off it. Perhaps then it would disappear, and I can tell myself I've imagined it again. Hopefully, my mum was right, and I'm just dreaming....

Tap,

Tap,

Tap,

TAP!

TAP,

TAP,

TAP,

TAP!

There it is. That TAPPING from THAT pointing finger. Was I truly not having a bad dream? Was this all indeed REAL? I know for a fact that I'm not asleep, but then it quickly dawned on me,

That THING....

I do not want IT to grab my foot or even show up. But just encase, I bend my legs at my knees and hook the covers under my feet, hoping this will protect me and keep my feet away from that THING. I make sure to keep my legs bent and my feet away from the edge of the bed, and I always make sure to face towards the side where that THING sits squatting. I also make sure that I can always see the window. The other side of my bed is thankfully against the wall, so I don't need to worry about that. Then I lay here waiting and listening to that TAPPING, hoping that the worst is not coming tonight, that the UNSEEN would stay away because this is not a bad dream. It's a bad reality.

I look around at each corner of the room back and forth from the wardrobe door to the window to Talia's bed and then back to PIPPY. I keep doing this whilst keeping my wits about me. I think that maybe if I see it coming, I can be brave. I'm a sitting duck, and my fate is already written and decided for me. I know deep down inside that THING is going to show up. I can feel it. IT'S here in this room hiding, waiting for its opportunity to creep over and squat by my bed. Then IT will reach out to grab my ankle and never let go. But, when and what direction will it spawn from to come for me? The darkness creates so much unknown. What UNSEEN is lurking here tonight? I think I see things, then I look back with better focus but there gone. I can't see it, but I know that THING is here.

CREEEEEEEAAAAK!

The wardrobe door slowly opens, I immediately turn my eyes towards it, and I just stare. I look but remain completely still, not moving a muscle. Then I wait. I don't take my eyes off the door, I freeze, and this wave comes over me once again, leaving me unable to move. I keep my eyes on the door, thinking that I can be more prepared if I expect it. I convince myself of this, but then I feel THAT familiar draft coming from outside my covers. Then I feel pressure on my mattress, and someway somehow, I feel the old, long bony fingers wrap around my ankle. It got me anyway despite my effort to keep IT away.

The door was a trick. I became so focused on it coming out of there that I didn't even see IT coming. I pause and try to catch my breath. I want to look towards that THING, but I fear the unknown. What will I see? Would it be the same? Would it still be laughing silently, or will I see something far worse? I decide not to look at all. Instead, I actually manage to CLOSE MY EYES and try to will that THING to go back to wherever it came from....

No one's there,

No one's there,

NO ONE'S THERE,

NO ONE IS THERE.

It didn't work. THAT thing is still there, and I can still feel THAT hand firmly gripped around my foot. I remain frozen, locked in this position, unable to move. I'm trapped.

The two children start to emerge from the darkness, slowly becoming highlighted with a type of aura about them. This time, they were hollow yet solid but also transparent. But they are definitely here. They still jump up and down, with that same look of dread and horror on their faces. They look dead, and their eyes are looking straight through me as though I'm not even here. But I'm still getting a strong feeling that they have suffered greatly.

I decide to close my eyes and ignore it all, pretending that none of this is happening. I squeeze PIPPY tightly and tell myself to lay here and keep still because it won't be long until this is all over. The sun will soon rise, and then they will leave. I think I can move this time, but I don't dare try because I fear that if I move, they will react, and something terrible will happen. They have me trapped, and now my fear of moving is preventing my escape. I believe I'm free to move if I choose to, but if I move, that THING will know, and I don't want to find out what the UNSEEN is capable of doing? I feel a tear roll down my cheek, and there's a wave of fear that lingers over me. I am a prisoner of the darkness and the monsters who are the UNSEEN.

Keeping my EYES CLOSED makes it possible for me to shut it all out and tell myself they are not there. This pungent smell floods my room. I can't name the scent because I've never smelt it before. It's an awful, musty smell and very unfamiliar to my nose. The smell seems very strong, as if it's been sprayed right next to my bed. I open my eyes and, once again, I see THAT black figure with no face and no detail, only a black outline standing at the foot of my bed. There is no movement at all. IT just stands there watching me, spreading an eery ominous feeling across the room. I stare at it harder and harder, but it feels as though it is getting closer and further away both at the same time. I know in my mind that's impossible. But it's happening. THAT shadow man, this figure is moving away and towards me simultaneously. It makes no sense, but most important of all, I know I am NOT SAFE.

I know all too well that I can't tell my mum and dad about any of this in the morning because they will think I really am going crazy. They already put it down to a bad dream. Maybe if I just do nothing and say nothing, they will go away and leave me alone for good. I will wait for the sun to rise, then I can sleep. But until then, I hope PIPPY and my CLOSED EYES will keep me SAFE.

Chapter Six

Halloween

A couple of months later!

I stuck to my plan and said nothing, and each night has been the same. The **UNSEEN** come out of the nothingness and the darkness to torment me, trap me and stare into my soul. What do they want? I still have no idea? I sleep before Talia comes up to bed and then again at sunrise until my parents or Talia wake me up. I figured out that if I stay very still and keep my eyes closed, they don't hurt me, so this is now what I do every night, but all I wish for is a LIGHT.

Sleep is a time for the body to heal, recover and process your memories. What is to happen to my soul and me if my body can't get any proper sleep? What fate is being created by the events I'm experiencing? What butterfly effect is all of this producing? What does this mean for my future, is my path mapped out, is it set in stone, or can we alter time and space and create our own destiny?

Halloween has finally arrived, and we are so excited. We have a wonderful tradition in our family. Instead of going trick or treating, we would get dressed up in a scary costume and take a pleasant spooky stroll with our dad to the shop at the bottom of the hill, where we buy lots of sweets. We have black witches hats that are purple and green with a spooky pattern. We also have capes, vampire fangs, fake blood and face paints. It's lots of fun getting dressed up. We really enjoy it, and Halloween always means quality time as a family because everyone has loads of fun.

My dad walks with us while my mum stays home. The walk is very spooky, especially around Keevil. Our route starts at our house, then we walk down our stone path and turn left. We then walk along the road past the creepy Church of The Holy Spirit that looks black and abandoned in the night. All you can see when you look upon it is the moonlight shining off the tops of the gravestones.

After the church, we come to the big, old gothic gates that stand tall with pride. They have a mysterious symbol in the centre where the gates connect, and this is the first place I have ever seen this symbol. I have no idea what it is, but I do know it's a bird of some kind. Only this bird's wings are on fire, and its feet are clutching a gothic Letter M. The letter M has blue roses and vines wrapped around it as though they are squeezing it tight. The gates have so much detail for a symbol made from metal. I can't help but wonder what's in there because these gates are always secured with the most enormous padlock.

Beyond the gates, all you can see is a long winding path with tall trees at each side in place of walls, you cannot see beyond one hundred metres, and no one has any idea who or what lies beyond these gates. There's never any news of what dwells beyond them, and no one has ever seen anyone entering or leaving. It really is a mystery. Once we pass the gates, we turn right and then walk down the hill to the sweet shop, which stays open later on Halloween. We pass by a few people along the way, and we make sure we say happy Halloween and sometimes admire other people's costumes. It's great fun.

On the way back, we begin talking about what we think is beyond those gates, but we make sure to have fun with it, coming up with ideas that are out of this world. When we arrive at home, we sit and talk, whilst eating our sweets of course. But before I knew it, bedtime had arrived. On Halloween, I'm allowed to stay up later than usual, so I get to go to bed at the same time as Talia. I thought to myself that maybe tonight might be different. Perhaps if I can get to sleep before Talia, I will be able to rest in peace tonight!

We brush our teeth and get into our beds, and my dad performs a spooky spectacular PIPPY at the door. After the show, my mum and dad tuck us in and say goodnight. I ask if we can keep the door open and the LIGHT ON in the hallway. My mum says yes, and this makes me smile. I feel a wave of RELIEF come over me, and because Talia's going to bed at the same time as me, they don't wind THAT music box or play my cassette tape. Talia and I talk for a little while about Halloween and some spooky cartoons from today. But my mum soon tells us to be quiet because they are about to watch a movie and they insist that we are not to make any more noise and go to sleep.

We tone it down to a whisper but quickly stop talking and close our eyes to go to sleep. I suddenly open my eyes with an unexpected feeling that I need to check for the pointing finger and the face in the curtains. The long pointing finger was present and still there just as it was every night, only it's perfectly still with no movement. It's not even swaying with the breeze of the wind. It's a clear night, and there's not really any wind or rain, and I can see the moon shining brightly through a crack in the curtains where they have not been closed correctly. The finger is entirely still, and to my DELIGHT, there is an absence of TAPPING. I realise that I don't feel uneasy tonight, and I feel like I can FINALLY get a good night's sleep.

....

Meanwhile....

Downstairs, my mum and dad are watching a scary movie. After all, it is Halloween. We have a big television, and it's the type that has a wooden back with a glass screen. A big circle ariel is attached to the top to get a signal for the few television channels that are available. The movie is playing on a VHS videotape and is about halfway through by this point. There are bright flashing LIGHTS coming from the television. But besides these LIGHTS and the upstairs hallway LIGHT, left on for me, there are no other LIGHTS on in the house.

As the movie plays, there is no need to look anywhere other than towards the television. But for some reason, my mum and dad look up at the exact same time and there in the corner of the room is a **BLACK** entity just hovering there, filling the corner of the ceiling and polluting the room with a terrible feeling, a feeling of pure **DREAD**. It was there, and then just as fast, it was gone. A definite evil presence swept over my mum and dad, and they are not entirely sure they know what they have just seen. For comfort, they decide to write it off, convincing themselves that they imagined it because they are in the middle of watching a scary movie.

My dad knows it was something more. He believes in ghosts because he has seen them before and has experienced many strange things. My dad knows it was something, but he did not want to worry or scare my mum because she has never voiced that she believes in ghosts.

Had I known this was happening as I tried to sleep, I may have learned more about the UNSEEN, but I would not hear of this until many years later from conversations with my parents. My mum and dad had no idea what they had seen, what it was or what it wanted.

I suddenly wake up, and I hear footsteps on the stairs. I can hear my mum and dad coming up to get ready for bed. They brush their teeth, but then I hear their footsteps getting closer, they come to our door, so I pretend to be asleep, thinking in my head, please leave my door open, please do not turn out that LIGHT. They both say goodnight to us from the door and that they love us, and then to my delight, they leave the LIGHT ON. I wonder why they are so ok with it tonight.

I had no idea that I would not find out the answer to my question or their reason until I was much older.

They leave our door open a crack, and they also leave the LIGHT ON. I immediately feel very happy about this. Then I hear our mum and dad go into their room and close their door. Even though the LIGHT'S left ON, I still feel a yearning to stare towards the window at THAT finger. I also still bend my legs at my knees. To keep my feet away from the edge of my bed and away from that THING.

THAT finger is still frozen and locked in time with no movement at all, I'm happy about this, but I can't get rid of this feeling that something is wrong and that the UNSEEN will still show up.

I quickly fell asleep, and to my amazement, the UNSEEN did not show up. I was FINALLY SAFE FOR NOW!

Chapter Seven

Migraine

Today I woke up feeling great for the first time in as long as I could remember. I finally got a good night's sleep. The LIGHT was my FREEDOM. Last night there was no sign of the UNSEEN. Is this my solution, my escape? There is only one huge problem I will not be allowed the LIGHT on every night. For now, though, I am going to enjoy my day.

Halloween means time off school, so we still have a few more days left to enjoy. Talia and I have planned to play with our toys today in our usual location, the stairs. I ask her if she has seen BEEBLEDOSH recently. Talia responds positively at first, explaining to me that he visits often and is coming today. I wonder if I will ever see him, so I bring it up to her. But the answer I immediately got is a **NO**, then Talia promptly changes the subject. She certainly does not like to talk about him much, and it's clear she only likes to talk to him on her own.

My dad left to go to work, and my mum began doing some housework. She opened all the windows and put music on to fill the house with happiness and positivity. She does this to make cleaning the house more fun. Before I go to play, I check with her to see if she wants any help, and she responds, letting me know that I can dust her Hedgehogs if I want to. My mum has a whole collection of them. She keeps them in a shelving unit, and they look really good because they are beautifully displayed. I enjoy helping my mum and learning about her likes and interests. I said to myself that one day, I'm going to get my mum a gift, a very special hedgehog that she can enjoy and keep for all time.

Now that I have finished helping my mum, I walk over to our stairs to set up my area to play a game with Talia. We start by talking about what we want to get for Christmas because it's getting close. The LIGHT goes **OUT** and then immediately comes back ON. We both turn and look at each other. We both thought out loud and said how that was weird. Just as we go back to our game, we hear our mum shout up the stairs that it's all fine and we have nothing to worry about, so with that, we continue our game. We soon got bored of playing with our toys, so we went downstairs to the living room.

We have books, movies on VHS and cassette tapes in the living room to choose from, but we decide to get Talia's cassettes out. She's been collecting them for a while now. They are called The happily ever after cassette collection, and they are kept in a red case that the company sent to her. The cassettes are **BLACK** tapes with YELLOW writing on the front of them that reads the title of each story. Talia enjoys them, and so do I. We sit on the carpet, looking at them, trying to decide which one we want to listen to on the stereo. Talia picks one, places it in the stereo, pressed play, and then closes the case. Somehow whilst she was closing the case, she hurt her arm and screamed out in pain! I didn't see what she did, and I can't understand how closing a case could have hurt her so badly.

Our mum came rushing in demanding to know what happened. We explain that all Talia did was close the case of cassettes. So we don't know how she hurt herself, but our mum was adamant we must have done something because Talia can't hurt her arm that badly just by closing a case. That truly was all Talia had done. It does not make any sense. My mum called my dad on the phone, and he quickly came home to take Talia to the hospital. My mum and I stayed home because there was no need for us all to go.

My dad and Talia are on their way to the hospital, so my mum lets me watch a movie to take my mind off things. As I get the movie ready, my mum goes into the kitchen to make me a cup of hot chocolate to help me feel better because she knows how worried I am about Talia. I honestly hope she is going to be ok.

As I sit here, I start to feel a bizarre feeling that I have no words to explain. I continued watching the television, only to find my right hand began to feel like it was swelling up. It felt like it grew three sizes larger, then it started to go numb. I could no longer feel my hand. I started prodding it and hitting it, but nothing. I had lost all feeling. I began to get worried. But when I called my mum, my words were all muddled up and jumbled. I could not make any sense. Nothing I meant to say would come out my mouth.

My hand then started to get pins and needles along with a tingling sensation that started at my fingertips and went all the way up my right arm. The feeling began to return in my hand, and my fingers felt as though they were returning to average size. All I can hear is silence. The movie is still on, but I blocked it out. What is happening to me? Is this what it's like to die? Am I dying?

The feeling has fully returned to my hand, but the pins and needles have moved to my tongue, running all the way down the right side. I could feel it becoming numb, just like my hand was. I did not try to speak. I thought I would just sit here and not move and try to watch the television. Right there on the screen was this odd circle. It's blurred with some sort of blurred squares pixilating all over the circle area. Part of the screen is missing, I could see the screen, but a circle of about five centimetres is missing from the picture. It's just so blurred, but the surrounding area was crystal clear. I swiftly moved my head to focus on the room in the hope it was the television. But to my horror, the circle followed anywhere and everywhere I looked.

I looked down at my body, and my arm appeared to be there. I could see it, but I can't comprehend that it's connected to me. It has become unattached. It's not mine anymore, and it feels like I have no control over it. It feels like I am looking at someone else's arm. The blurred area started to get bigger, and I desperately needed to close my eyes. I lay down on the sofa, and I close my eyes, thinking I can escape the surreal reality that this has become, because that LIGHT that I once begged for, now I wanted it to GO AWAY, it started to really hurt me. I suddenly got an awful feeling. The LIGHT has become painful, is this revenge because I escaped the UNSEEN last night or am I genuinely dying?

I became horrified, and I felt like my soul was trying to leave my body. Why is my arm no longer attached to me? Was I going blind? What was this blurred area? I could feel in the very pit of my stomach that it had started to turn. Sick came flying straight out of my mouth. There was nothing I could do to stop it. I began trying to hold my mouth shut, but it was forcing its way through. I could not hold it back. The vomit was landing all over the floor, and my tears came flooding down my face not long after. I was worrying that this was it, that my time was coming, was I to become one of the UNSEEN?

My mum came rushing in with a bucket and tried to sit me up. I yelled out in pain and fear because I just couldn't move. It hurt so much. My mum was confused about what was hurting me. I began to hold my head with both hands blocking out the LIGHT because now it's hurting worse than ever. It was like someone had a knife, and they were stabbing it into my skull repeatedly. My mum continued to hug me, but I could not hold back the vomit. She was doing her best to make me feel better.

The vomit has stopped for a moment allowing me to open my eyes, and I realise the blurred area has gone. My vision has returned, but an intense pounding inside my head has replaced it. It feels like something is squeezing my brain as hard as possible. Every other second, my brain pulsates. But with each pulse of my brain, the pain strikes through my head like lightning. I noticed my arm had returned to my body around the same time that the blurred circle disappeared. But now I'm left with excruciating pain in my head, and I still can't stop being sick. Pain medication has had no effect at all, so my mum suggests that I lay on the sofa, close my eyes and listen to the movie and try to sleep. I fear if I fall asleep, I may never wake up.

I open my eyes, and I see my mum. I quickly realise that she has stayed with me on the sofa all night. I can still feel a slight pain in my head, and it still hurts a little, but nowhere near as much as it did last night. I ask my mum if Talia's home and if she's ok, my mum explains to me that she is home and will be just fine. Talia has fractured her arm, and everyone is still not entirely sure what happened. The main thing is Talia's ok. My mum says that she's still worried about me and wants to make sure that I'm ok and check how I'm feeling.

I still feel a little bit weak, but I know one thing, I'm glad that I was able to get a whole night's sleep despite the way it came to be. I never want to go through that ever again. I honestly thought I was going to die, that this was the end. I always wanted to know what happens when we die, where we go, and what happens next? I'm just not ready to get these answers myself. I'm not finished with my life yet. I have barely begun. I'm starting to understand why these questions remain unanswered. It seems the only way to retrieve these answers is to embark on that journey YOURSELF.

Chapter Eight

Christmas

I'm so excited because December has finally arrived. It's my favourite time of year. I begin my day by writing my Christmas cards to send to all my friends at school. Each year they have a post box where everyone puts their cards, and then the teacher gives them out at the end of the day. It's always so exciting.

I decide to write a card to everyone in my class because I don't want to leave anyone out. I already ate today's chocolate from my advent calendar because I always do that as soon as I wake up. I always look forward to the first day in December because my mum always puts up the Christmas decorations, and it's Talia's birthday.

I already said happy birthday to her this

morning when she unwrapped her birthday gifts. She's extremely happy today, but we know we still have to get ready for school. Walking to school was never fun in the winter because of the cold and frosty mornings. Sometimes it rains too, but I do love the fact that the air smells of burning wood in these winter months. It floats through the air, spreading down our road and up to the sky. It's almost as if the burning of the wood is cleansing our village. Casting out that ominous mist that plagues our streets and fills the air with an eerie glow whilst the world sleeps in the deep dark of the night.

I run all the way to school because I'm so excited to put my cards into the mailbox. I meet up with my friends and go to class. Today everyone seems so excited for Christmas, and it's the best feeling in the world seeing everyone smiling and laughing. It brings a perfect warm fuzzy feeling to my stomach, and I feel like today will be a good day. As I sit at my desk looking out the window, I can see the remains of Jack Frost melting under a dull sun that sits out of sight, hidden behind the dark winter clouds doing the best it can to warm the temperature slightly.

Then out of nowhere, and I need to look twice to see it, a tiny snowflake falls from above. I sit and watch as it gently floats down from the sky, hitting the floor to melt instantly. Then just as I almost lose hope for Jack Frost this year, I notice more snowflakes are following it. More and more of them fall to the ground, and it begins to really come down out there, so I decide to shout out to let everyone know,

IT'S SNOWING!

We all run across the room to the window to get a closer look, including my teacher. It's like magic. We request to go outside, but of course, the answer is no, so we just pray that the snow will still be there after school. My teacher announces that we won't be having our traditional story at the end of the day because we have some time to go outside and play in the snow. Time quickly passes, so we all run with pure intent to get our coats, hats and scarves, and off we go out into the snow.

I can see my mum from the playground coming to collect me. Her hair and shoulders are covered in snow. My mum never did like the winter because she doesn't like to be cold. So I know we will need to walk home as fast as we can. When we arrive at our house, I plan to ask my mum if we can make a snowman. It's not very often that Jack Frost blesses us with this kind of snow. The kind that actually sticks around and settles on the ground, turning a dark world into one of pure light, creating a sheet of white dust as far as your eyes can see. Now it really does feel like Christmas.

Talia beat me to it because she asked our mum whilst we were walking home. I guess she took the opportunity to make sure we didn't waste any time. Once we arrive at our house, my mum lets us build a snowman, because her view on it is that it's Talia's birthday so we can do whatever we want until dinner time. I find myself standing outside the front of our house, and I suddenly become unable to move. I stand completely still, not moving a muscle, and I look up at my bedroom window. I find my eyes are pulled towards THAT long, thin tree branch. The very tree branch THAT torments me every night, THAT long, old, bony, pointing finger that in the darkness comes to life out of nowhere, accompanied or followed by the UNSEEN.

As I stand here, locked in this moment, staring up at THAT branch, I realise that it's scary in the nothingness of the night, but as I stand here gazing upon it in the LIGHT, I see it. But it is JUST a branch, part of a tree that has stood here longer than I can comprehend. Why is this branch such a threat at night? THAT tree is just a part of nature, and the extreme conditions of the weather affect this tree just as they affect us. Trees feel the cold just as we do.

I look upon THAT branch, and I notice that it's now become Jack Frost's prisoner. TRAPPED in a web of never-ending ice that has completely entangled itself around THAT branch, locking it in place. I can't help but think Jack is showing the tree, THAT branch, how IT makes me feel in the deep, dark, nothingness of the night. Has Jack reversed the tides by putting it into my shoes? Is THAT branch just a tree, or something far more sinister? Or is all this just in my head?

Talia's yelling my name repeatedly. She wants my attention so I can help her with the snowman. But I'm stuck in a trance, so hypnotised by THAT branch that her voice has faded out to silence. Her mouth is moving, but I don't hear any sound coming out of it. I just continue staring towards my window and **THAT** branch. I begin assessing if it can even reach my window. Then a thought suddenly comes into my mind. Why didn't I ever come out here and take a look at this before?

I realise that Talia is still calling my name. But just as I look over to her out the corner of my eyes. She slips on some ice and falls, instantly breaking the trance I have been stuck in. I immediately run over to help her. Talia's not impressed that she's been calling me for so long, and she now thinks I was ignoring her. I begin to explain that I'm not actually sure what happened. All I know is that I could hear her at first, but then her voice just disappeared. Talia's response startled me because she compares what just happened to me with the first time she ever spoke to **BEEBLEDOSH**. I decided not to pry for any more information because today is her birthday. She never likes it when people ask about **BEEBLEDOSH**, so we get on with building our snowman and having a few snowball fights along the way. We also make some snow angels on the ground to lighten up the mood.

My dad pulls into the driveway, and it's great

to see him arrive home from work. He gets out of the car to see us running up to give him a big hug. He begins telling us how amazing our snowman looks, but we need to make sure we don't get cold hands. He then goes inside to see my mum, and we finish building our snowman.

We finish Talia's birthday with a special dinner and a birthday cake. I know she's had a perfect day because she is so happy. But bedtime is creeping in fast. I just can't stop thinking about how Jack Frost has **THAT** branch locked in a cold, tangled web of ice. It's really helping to keep my fear away. I get myself ready for bed, but tonight, I climb onto Talia's because it's her birthday. Then we wait for my dad to perform tonight's special birthday PIPPY at the door. My dad is so good at making us laugh. He truly is the best and has the best ways to show us we are loved.

Once the story's over, Talia goes downstairs, and my dad says goodnight to me. I ask if I can have the door open and the hallway LIGHT ON. My dad tries to convince me that the dark will not hurt me and that I should focus my energy on falling asleep. My dad genuinely does believe that I'm safe. He reminds me that the dark is just the absence of LIGHT. He tells me that it's the same room with all the same things, and the only difference is that it's harder to see them in the dark. Then he promises me that he will never let anything hurt me.

My dad winds THAT music box, and as it begins to play THAT song, my dad closes my door but leaves the hallway LIGHT ON. I can see the glow of LIGHT highlighting the perimeter of the door, leaving me feeling slightly relieved. I hear him going downstairs, and with each step, he sounds further and further away.

I know my dad was trying to make me feel better because he didn't want me to be scared, but I don't think anyone can stop the UNSEEN! I realise that I may as well try and do what my dad has suggested. I plan to do my best to fall asleep, so I pull my legs up, bending them at my knees, and I move my feet away from the edge of my bed, just as I now do every night. I do my best to get comfy while maintaining my precautions against the UNSEEN. I cuddle PIPPY pulling him in tight, and then I just lie here listening to THAT song.

The old Keevil bridge will not stay up,

Will not stay up,
Will just not stay up,
The old Keevil bridge will not stay up,
Trapping us inside....

The old Keevil bridge will not stay up,
Will not stay up,
Will just not stay up,
The old Keevil bridge will not stay up,
Trapping us inside....

THAT song goes on and on, in what feels like a loop of infinite melody. I continue to listen whilst I lay here peacefully with my eyes closed. I feel hypnotised by the comforting feeling that I know some LIGHT is expelling from my door.

Goosebumps begin to spread all over me, and I start to feel my breath the same way it feels when you are outside in the snow, was Jack Frost revisiting us? Is he here to keep me safe?

Tap,

Tap,

Tap,

Tap,

TAP,

TAP,

TAP,

TAP,

I don't want to look. What does THAT long, bony, pointing finger want? Can it possibly be, Jack Frost is also powerless when it comes to the UNSEEN? I close my eyes even tighter in an attempt to convince myself not to look. Then out of nowhere, the thought suddenly dawns on me. Outside in the daylight, I saw THAT branch with my own eyes. It is JUST PART OF A TREE. It is not even long enough to reach my window. I tell myself, you imagine all of this, just STOP, none of this is real, just STOP and get a grip, open your eyes and take a look. You will see that nothing's there.

Nothing is there!

Open your eyes!

I slowly open my eyes and look towards the window. THAT shadow has never been more evident. THAT long, bony, pointing finger that finds pleasure in tormenting me is unmistakably present in my room. Only I find myself feeling confused instead of scared. THAT long, bony, pointing finger is different tonight. It's not pointing towards me, but it is pointing towards Talia's bed. But this makes no sense at all. I close my eyes with a quick snap and then open them again. Within a second, THAT shadow moved. It's now pointing firmly towards me. I begin to question myself, has it been pointing at me all along? Did I imagine it? Was it ever pointing to Talia's bed? Is it trying to mess with me? Is it going to harm Talia? Is this a sign, or am I truly just on a long, dark path to insanity?

The TAPPING stops abruptly in perfect

timing with THAT music box, and silence spreads throughout the room.

Thud,

Thud,

Thud,

THUD,

THUD,

THUD,

THUD,

THUD,

I can hear someone coming up the stairs, and I can tell it's Talia because I can now hear her in the bathroom brushing her teeth. I lie here feeling so confused. How can THAT branch move from one direction to another, and how can it tap on my window? **THAT** branch cannot even reach. It is impossible.

> **The old Keevil bridge will not stay up,**
> **Will not stay up,**
> **Will just not stay up,**
> **The old Keevil bridge will not stay up,**
> **Trapping us inside….**

> **The old Keevil bridge will not stay up,**
> **Will not stay up,**
> **Will just not stay up,**
> **The old Keevil bridge will not stay up,**
> **Trapping us inside….**

THAT song begins to play again, and I decide that I've had enough! I reach out to grab **THAT** box, and I realise it hasn't finished unwinding. That must be why it suddenly stopped. Maybe it has become jammed somehow. The **TAPPING** thankfully has not returned. I can feel my heart racing. Why is this happening? Is this the **UNSEEN** playing games? Or worse, is this actually in my head? Am I creating all of this? Is this my mind's dark path into despair, into actual depths of cruelty that are becoming tangled beyond any point of repair in my own twisted reality?

Talia comes into the room and gets into her bed, and it's clear she has assumed that I'm asleep because she remains silent. I move back into my previous position, and I watch THAT branch. I do not take my eyes off it.

THAT box finally finishes playing THAT song, and now silence plagued the room, but I tell myself that no matter what, I will not take my eyes off THAT branch. The more I stare at it, the more it makes me feel crazy. It is crystal clear that it remains still, not moving at all. As I watch, I hear nothing, and I keep my feet well away from the edge of my bed.

I feel a very heavy sensation come over me, and I start to think maybe I'M FINALLY FALLING ASLEEP. I try to move, but I quickly realise it's not possible, so I make the tough decision to abandon THAT branch and look down towards the floor next to my bed. All I can see is darkness pixilating because my eyes were so focused on THAT branch that now they were unfocused to the darkness. I begin to see what almost resembles the shape of someone's head, but

I can barely make it out.

I freeze….

As my eyes begin to adjust, this THING becomes clearer and more precise. The harder I stare, the more apparent it becomes, a body is crouched there sitting, squatting next to my bed, the UNSEEN. I suddenly begin to feel sick to my stomach. My mattress begins to gain pressure. Something is tugging on my covers. Then one bony finger followed by the next, IT'S coming for me. Walking ITS long bony fingers, one by one, across my sheet to find their final destination. Always my right ankle, wrapping each bony finger around my skin, entangled and locked into place.

I look at this THING intently. I try so hard to make out what it actually is, but it is far too pixilated in the dark. My eyes can't focus properly, and it's as if the nothingness keeps changing the depths of the darkness.

That THING is laughing silently at something. Then I see THAT face on the curtains from the corner of my eyes. I must look again, and just as I fear it remains there, I see pure black in the eye sockets, and I can only just make out a closed mouth with a sinister smile. The head is slightly moving like dust particles floating in the air. The face has become smothered in darkness, pixilating to hide its secrets. There is just no way to see it clearly. I was so focused on the face. Trying to see a clearer image, I didn't even notice the two children jumping on my bed. They jump up and down just as they always do. But why do they never touch my bed like that **THING**?

I look across the room to see if I can see Talia. From what I can make out, she appears to be sleeping soundly. I look to my wardrobe and see what I can only explain as floating vertical lines stretching from the ceiling to the floor. They keep fading in and out, sort of glowing in different shades of black while they glide across the room. There are loads of them moving in all different directions. They seem very disorientated, like people shopping in a big city going in different directions and walking through each other. I keep watching them. I can't help it because I just don't understand what this is. Why has this not happened before? I must be imagining this. Could I actually be dreaming? Have I made all of this up in my mind? I wish someone would give me answers?

THAT bad, awful, musty smell begins to fill the air once more, and it's so unfamiliar to me. It's such a terrible smell that it makes my stomach turn, and now all I can think about is how I want to be sick. Out of the corner of my eyes, I see a different type of darkness moving through the room. As it progresses, it plagues everywhere it slithers with a darkness more profound than any before. I see it land at the end of my bed. Simultaneously I noticed that all those glowing lines that seemed to be walking around just faded away like a rubber erasing pencil markings from a piece of paper. I close my eyes so tight, all I can hear is the deafening lack of noise, a silence so painfully loud that it would make anyone question their reality....

The awful smell is becoming so overpowering that I'm beginning to find it hard to breathe. I remember the last time this smell was here and how it vanished when I opened my eyes. Have I just figured out that the UNSEEN are using this as a method of control? I decided to test this theory and do as the UNSEEN seems to want and open my eyes. As I open them, I find myself looking at my wardrobe. I slowly move my eyes towards the end of my bed, realising that I'm still unable to move my body. Out of pure fear, I still make sure I keep my feet immaculately still, so I don't agitate that THING. I now find myself looking towards the end of my bed, past the two small children and right there standing motionless at the foot of my bed was THAT exact black figure. It took on more of a shape of a man this time. Whatever this is, it just stands there, watching. I can't see a face, but I feel a significant presence being expelled from it. It just stands there staring right through me with absolutely no movement whatsoever.

My all too familiar tears roll down my face. I'm still trapped and unable to move, yell or scream. What did this UNSEEN want with me? Is this my deep descent into madness? I have no option but to close my eyes and wish it all away, to hold on to some kind of HOPE and have FAITH that I will be ok. I think to myself that the sun will soon rise. Even the UNSEEN can't stop the sun from rising at dawn. I manage to use what little strength I have left to pull PIPPY in even tighter. I close my eyes, scrunching them shut until I can see nothing but that YELLOW, GOLDEN colour that brings with it a sort of peaceful, calming feeling. I begin to think with a POWERFUL, INFLUENTIAL voice in my mind as if I was speaking the words out loud....

The UNSEEN is not real!

None of this is real,

Not real,

Not real,

The UNSEEN is not real,

None of this is real,

Not real,

Not real,

NONE OF THIS IS

REAL....

I feel ready to open my eyes. I genuinely need to BELIEVE in myself. I know deep in my heart none of this is real. How could it be, it goes against everything we know to be true? I open my eyes in a quick swift movement, only to my horror and disbelief in what I'm seeing. Nothing has changed. The UNSEEN are still very much here. I feel so isolated and trapped, and I don't know what else I can do? I look over at Talia, hoping she will wake up, but she's still asleep, looking so peaceful. I notice an odd pixilated area next to her bed, but I cannot make anything out. Maybe it is just my eyes playing tricks on me or the darkness feeding on my fear and making me see things that are not really there. But there is unmistakably an area of different darkness next to her bed.

As I look back towards Talia to take a closer look at that abnormal dark area by her bed, she suddenly sits up. She just swiftly sat up and now remains sitting there with her arms held out in front of her. In the very same way, I would when joking around with her about BEEBLEDOSH. But She's perfectly motionless. I can see the white glow illuminating from her eyeballs, her eyes are open, but she does not alter. She remains entirely still, and she's never done anything like this before. I find myself wishing she was awake, but it's evident that she's in some kind of trance.

I begin to feel a different kind of fear sweep over me. The unsettling kind that Talia's now in danger or unwell. But no matter how hard I try, I just can't yell out to her. I need to know she's ok. What is wrong with her? I can't think of anything else to do but close my eyes and wish it true by thinking it over and over....

Dad, come up stairs!

Dad,

Dad,

Dad**,**

Dad**,**

Dad, come up stairs!

Come up stairs,

Please, come up the stairs,

Dad, you need to come upstairs, NOW!

AGHHHHHHHHHHHH HHHHHHHHHH!

Suddenly all I hear is Talia screaming out.

Someone FINALLY comes rushing through our bedroom door, so I open my eyes....

The LIGHT is ON, and the first thing I notice is that I'm FINALLY able to move freely. The UNSEEN are completely GONE, just like that, as if the LIGHT has immediately cast them out. I look over to Talia, and my dad is hugging her and making sure she's ok. The strange thing is she's saying that she has no idea why he's hugging her. She has no idea that she screamed out or how she became sat up in bed. My mum is standing in the doorway, and she looks over to me to make sure I'm ok. I make sure that she is fully aware of how scared I am, and I plead with her to leave the hallway LIGHT on and our door open.

My mum and dad calm Talia down, and now that they are happy she will be ok, they leave our room, making sure to leave our door open and the hallway LIGHT ON. I feel so relieved, but once again, I have so many unanswered questions. I hear their door click shut, and I know we are both very creeped out, so we talk for a while about our friends and school to take our minds off everything. But we avoided the elephant in the room because neither one of us wanted to relive the events that had just taken place. We quickly fall asleep, and before I know it, a beam of pure LIGHT comes streaming through the window because, just as I had told myself, the sun will always rise.

. . . .

A fair bit of time has passed since THAT night Talia got spooked, and my mum and dad have continued to let us have the hallway LIGHT ON, and I have never felt better. My sleep has been excellent, and I feel so refreshed. I've also forgotten all about my fears and the dread of the UNSEEN, for now anyway! Today is Christmas eve, and I'm so excited because Christmas is my favourite time of year and I get to stay up a bit later on special occasions. We always do fun things all day with our family and then go to bed at a good time because we want Christmas to arrive. Talia and I go up to bed for a special Christmas, PIPPY at the door, and after my mum and dad say goodnight, I begin to get so excited, and I just can't sleep.

Talia tells me she can hear Santa and we need to close our eyes, so I do this, and all I can hear is someone moving around in our room. I know it's not the UNSEEN because we have the LIGHT ON keeping us SAFE. Suddenly out of nowhere, Talia shouts for me to open my eyes, I move my feet in an attempt to get comfy, and I hear a rustling noise coming from the end of my bed. I jump up with such excitement, thinking this is my stocking from Santa, but it's just a plastic bag to my disappointment. Talia has pulled the ultimate prank on me, and she is sat there in her bed laughing so hard. I start to laugh as well. After all, I also find this funny, mostly because I can't believe I fell for it. I just really wanted Christmas. My eyes begin to feel heavy, and I can't hold them open much longer, so I pull PIPPY in closer. I can now see that familiar, soothing, GOLDEN colour, and I know I am almost asleep.

The morning soon arrives, and we wake up to find our stockings on the end of our beds, full of presents. We open them and play with the toys, and as we play, we get a big whiff of gingerbread and cookies. The smells are flowing through the whole house. We run downstairs to see where this sweet smell is coming from, and I turn to the dining table, and I see so many freshly baked treats. They all look so good, and the sweet smell flowing through the house is so irresistible. My mum has been up since the crack of dawn, especially, to bake them for us. They taste so good. Christmas day is the only day each year except easter that we can eat snacks first thing in the morning.

We all go into the living room and sit by the Christmas tree, my mum puts on some classic Christmas ballads, and we all begin to open our presents. My favourite gift is my new bike. Talia got one as well. Once all the gifts are open, we sit and play whilst my mum makes Christmas dinner. I wondered when our nan would arrive. I'm so excited to see her, and we get to spend the whole day with her because she's coming to spend Christmas day with us.

I can hear a knock at the door. Talia and I instantly drop our toys and run to the front door as fast as we can. My nan is just walking in and hanging up her coat. She only just gets it on the hook as we begin smothering her with hugs. She is so happy to see us, too. We exchange our gifts, and then we all sit down at the table to have a lovely Christmas dinner. Christmas day always passes extremely fast because it's so much fun. I can enjoy myself so much because my family is around me, and Christmas is about being with those you love.

With the way things have been lately, it's amazing that we are still allowed to have our bedroom door open and the hallway LIGHT ON. It certainly has added to the Christmas magic. I can fully enjoy my day knowing I don't have to worry or even think about the UNSEEN. Snow starts to fall from the sky and settle on the ground. So we all step outside to look at everyone's Christmas LIGHTS. We also show Jack Frost that we appreciate his presence by playing in the snow and having a big snowball fight, the perfect way to end a perfect white Christmas.

Chapter Nine

Two Years Later – 1996

Life has been incredible these last two years, and I have been sleeping incredibly well. I am totally free of the UNSEEN. I can't even remember what they look like, and their appearances are a distant memory. I'm doing far better at school, and I feel great about myself. All this has been possible because we continued to have our DOOR OPEN and the hallway LIGHT ON. But now that Talia is eleven, I have developed a significant concern that this will soon come to an end. Talia is growing up, and she continuously voices that having the LIGHT ON is a sign that she is still a baby, so she keeps asking my mum if we can turn the LIGHT OUT.

I am heartbroken about this, and I have

decided to voice it because I overheard Talia the
other day in conversation with her imaginary friend
BEEBLEDOSH. From what I heard Talia say, it
seems like BEEBLEDOSH is mocking her and
making her believe she is a coward to be sleeping
with the LIGHT ON. A thought suddenly dawned
on me, was BEEBLEDOSH working with the
UNSEEN, doing all he can to get the LIGHT
OUT?

I began to remind my mum about the events
from Christmas two years ago, the very
circumstances that led to the LIGHT being ON
and the DOOR remaining OPEN. My mum
explains in Talia's defence that a lot of time has
passed, she did put her own feeling aside for me,
and we are both two years older now, so things are
very different. Maybe if I offer a solution that can
keep us all happy, my mum and dad will agree. I
straight up ask if I can move into the spare room? I
knew this was a long shot because my dad uses this
room for his work. But it was worth trying because
then Talia can have the **DARKNESS** she desires,
and I can have the LIGHT that I yearn for to keep
the UNSEEN away.

It turns out I can't move into my dad's

workroom, and as much as I want to, I fully understand, my dad works extremely hard and is very good at what he does, and this room is where he gets his best ideas. I am very proud of my dad. We all are, and this room is where he creates his music. It's the music he thought up in this room that got him onto a record label. Now his songs are being played all over the radio around the world. He achieved it all in this room, so I know it's an exceptional location. Deep down, I know my dad needs this room more than I do, and I know that plan was not a good idea. I need to think of a new way to keep the UNSEEN away.

My dad sometimes lets us in his workroom to do some painting while he works on his music. My dad is very talented, and I always enjoy listening to his songs. Maybe one day I will sing in one. My dad has such passion for his work anyone who sees him while he's working can undoubtedly see how much he cares about what he is creating. He even has a song about my mum, which went live on the radio. But he made it out of love to show my mum just how much he loves her, it's so romantic, just like a fairy tale, but my mum does not need a song to see how much my dad loves her. He works hard on his music and works a full-time job to ensure we have everything we need. I'm lucky to have such great parents who have so much love in their hearts.

I know that my mum and dad will always keep us safe. But one thing does not sit right with me after talking with my mum. She explained how she would not let anyone hurt me, well the UNSEEN are not people, and they are very much present in the darkness. I can't understand why she can't believe me, or is that she DOES believe me, but she is trying to keep me from being scared. I guess my mum is lucky to have never been visited by the UNSEEN. But now I fear if Talia gets her way, they will undoubtedly return and perhaps this time with a vengeance because the LIGHT has banished them for all this time. My mum is the best in the world, and she always does everything she can for us, only she can't protect me from what she does not understand and can't be SEEN?

I plead with Talia to let us keep the LIGHT ON. But she just says how she must grow up and that BEEBLEDOSH tells her so. She begins to explain what he has been telling her, and I found this a step forward because she never likes to talk about him. He told her she needed to be in the dark and let go of all the childish nonsense. She went on to say that she has seen him a lot over the last two years, and now all he does is go on about how she needs to grow up and turn the LIGHT OUT.

Although I have never seen BEEBLEDOSH, I do entirely believe that he visits Talia. He is not like the UNSEEN that torment me because Talia sees him during the daytime, whereas the UNSEEN only come out at night. BEEBLEDOSH is very different, I always get a sinister vibe when Talia talks about him, but she portrays him as a good friend, most of the time. Talia has never mentioned him hurting her or scaring her. She talks about him the same way she speaks of her friends at school. We call him her imaginary FRIEND. I guess he was to everyone else, but I know she feels like he is very much there and very much REAL.

I know I will not be able to keep the LIGHT ON much longer. It may even get turned OUT tonight. I start searching the house because if I can find a TORCH, maybe that will keep the UNSEEN away. It is a form of LIGHT, after all. I searched everywhere, and I just couldn't find one, but then I thought, what about my dad's room? He must have one in there, so I head upstairs to his room and push the door open. It creaks as it swings towards the wall sending a whiff of paint past my nose. I love that paint smell. It always instantly reminds me of all the good times we have had in this room.

I proceed into the room, closing the door behind me because I do not want anyone to know I am in here. I creep along the floor, trying not to make any noise because the wooden floor creaks with every step I take. I notice the room has a sort of 3D wallpaper with vertical lines running down it. The lines are all different shades of beige and brown on a crème background creating a vintage look. Perhaps the paper is from years ago, and maybe it has even been there since before we moved in. I have never asked my dad if he decorated this room. What a strange thought to suddenly have? That's never crossed my mind until now. Being alone in this room makes me really look at it, paying close attention to everything I've never noticed before. With no distraction, I felt silence fall upon me.

I continue looking around, trying to find a

TORCH, but I don't want to move anything because I respect my dad, and this is his stuff and his area. My dad's desk and floors are clear and tidy, but I cannot see a TORCH anywhere to my disappointment. I then find myself looking towards one of my dad's paintings that sits on a wooden stand, and it's positioned prominently in front of the window. All I can think when I look at this painting is how fantastic it is. I have never seen anything so magical.

I walk closer to the painting. To get a better look, I focus on the deer stood there in the middle of the woods. The intense detail and the clarity of the moment my dad has captured draws me into the picture. I feel like I'm in the painting. I can smell the autumn leaves, I can feel the wind that blows those same leaves up into the air, and I can hear the pitter-patter of the deer's feet moving in the loose dirt on the ground. I feel the peace and tranquillity, and the magic is intensifying. I wish I could stay here forever because all my fears and worries just instantly melted away.

I suddenly come back to reality and find myself still looking at the picture. Out of nowhere, this overwhelming feeling rushes over me, making me feel like I **MUST** look down. This feeling is the same kind of feeling that sweeps over me when **THAT** long, bony, pointing finger begins **TAPPING** on my window. It's this total uncontrollable need to look, and it consumes your every thought. Keeping my wits about me due to this sudden ominous feeling, I slowly look down towards the floor....

A TORCH, a small, yellow TORCH, I immediately begin to think I'm going to be SAFE now. Any worries I have built up out of fear of **LOSING** the hallway LIGHT just immediately floated away. I know I will be able to put this under my pillow to keep me SAFE tonight.

I am positive that this TORCH was not here before. I began to feel very strange because I'm sure I checked this whole room and there was nothing on the floor, is it possible that I missed it the first time I looked. I decide I will not question this too much and just be thankful I have a TORCH. Now that I have found what I was looking for, I quickly leave because I know I am not meant to be in my dad's room. I run straight to my room and put the TORCH under my pillow, making sure it is out of sight, then I head downstairs to see what Talia is doing.

I start to worry about what will happen once the darkness returns. Will, the small amount of LIGHT projected from the TORCH be enough to repel and evict the UNSEEN? How much longer will the batteries inside the TORCH last? I have no idea how to replace them, and I wonder if my dad will even notice that the TORCH has gone. Does he even know he had one in his room in the first place? Something just doesn't feel right about how I found it because it just appeared, and I'm sure it wasn't there when I first went in.

My conscience began haunting me. I know I should not have taken the TORCH without asking. I need to fix what I have done wrong. I just keep thinking about going to my dad and asking him if he has a TORCH? Then explaining to him that I have borrowed his yellow one because even though I am eight, I know that lying is wrong and I will not do it. I decide I'm going to ask him at dinner. In the meantime, while we wait, Talia and I go outside to the garden to find our dad. He is out here doing some work on the pond at the bottom of our garden.

We sit down on our swings, so I thought

maybe I could take this opportunity to ask Talia what **BEEBLEDOSH** looks like and what he talks about when he comes around? I quickly change my mind, and I don't honestly know why I'm just getting a weird vibe from her. As if she read my mind and telepathically told me, do not ask about him today. This feeling is overwhelming, so I trust it, and I leave anything to do with **BEEBLEDOSH** alone. Instead, we have a jumping competition to see who can jump off the swing and land the furthest away.

Our mum soon calls us in for dinner, we rush inside to sit down at the table while my mum dishes up everyone's food. My mum has music playing on her stereo as she always does while she's cooking. She turns the music to a low volume so we can still talk. I wait for a chance to ask my dad about the TORCH, but I don't want to interrupt anyone, so I have to wait for a silent moment to cut in. Everyone went quiet as my mum walked over with the plates, so I took my chance. I ask my dad if we have a TORCH anywhere in the house? His response is just as I feared. He explains that we don't have any as far as he knows! He then adds that we have a LIGHT for the attic but that

LIGHT is big and chunky, so he does not class it as a TORCH. He went on to say how it is strangely powerful and more of a portable LIGHT than a TORCH, and he finishes by asking me, why am I asking?.

I began to explain to my dad that I found a small yellow TORCH on the floor next to his painting in his room today. I immediately apologised for going in there without getting permission, pleading with him and telling him why I went there. I continued to explain how I just needed a TORCH, and I looked all over the house first, but this was the last room I had left to check, so I thought if I made no mess and touched nothing, it would be ok. I then finished my apology to my dad by letting him know how incredible his painting is and how it caught my attention for the longest time.

My dad responds to me saying, exactly what I feared he would say. He unmistakably does not have a TORCH in his room. He explains how he always uses SUNLIGHT to paint and the main LIGHT in the evenings when he works on his music. He lets me know that I am not to go into his room without asking next time. But he does

115

appreciate my honesty, and he confirms that he's not mad. I'm so glad that he's not angry at me. He then insists he does not have a TORCH, but I can keep this YELLOW one because no one knows where it came from or how it got in the house. I feel so relieved to have corrected my mistake, and I am thrilled that my dad is not mad at me.

Chapter Ten

Pippy At The Door

I stood in the bathroom, squeezing the tube of toothpaste in the direction of my toothbrush, allowing the paste to ooze out in a perfectly straight line. I begin brushing my teeth, HOPING that Talia will be ok with it and let me keep the LIGHT on tonight. On second thought, NO, she will never allow it. She created such a fuss over this whole situation to Mum and Dad. Maybe if I think about it hard enough, the UNSEEN won't come!

I have unwelcome thoughts and so many questions running through my mind, back and forth, back and forth. I must figure out how to keep the UNSEEN away? How much LIGHT will I actually need? How long will the batteries in this TORCH last? Is tonight the night that the

UNSEEN finally get me once and for all? And what of BEEBLEDOSH? Is he involved, or is he, in fact, nothing to do with any of it? Did Talia really make him up? Or is he indeed simply a figment of her imagination? Has she completely convinced herself that he is a real friend, or is he something much more?

I finally finish in the bathroom, and I realise I got caught up in my thoughts for a bit too long, so I walk to my room. As I walk past Talia's bed, I see her getting comfy, and she had her small bear, Born with her. She's cuddling with him under her covers, so I walk over towards my bed and shout;

DAAAAAAAAD!

DAAAAAAAAAAD!

DAAAAAAAAAAAAD!

DAAAAAAAAAAAAAAD!

He comes running up the stairs and stands just inside the door to our room, wanting to know what is wrong. I simply ask him if he will perform a

PIPPY at the door for us. I take extra care to say please. He responds to me, insisting that next time I need to come downstairs and ask, not yell so erratically because he thought one of us was hurt. I just really want my dad to perform a PIPPY at the door, it's the best part of the night, and to my delight, my dad is more than happy to perform a show for us. I pass PIPPY to him, and then I get comfy under my covers, ensuring that I have the best view and I'm ready for the show to begin.

My dad began to explain that tonight's spectacular, this particular PIPPY at the door is for my benefit. My dad is going to make the story about how PIPPY Conquers his fear of the dark. Only it is not the dark I fear but the UNSEEN, for some unknown reason, they only come out in the dark of the night, which is very unsettling to me. Why can they not show themselves in the daylight? Why can they only manifest in the darkness? I push these thoughts to the back of my mind for now because my dad is about to begin. He collects some of our stuffed animals to participate in the show, making PIPPY the protagonist and starts the story....

My dad really has tried to help me overcome

my fear of the dark, but it's not the darkness that's the problem. I fear going to bed and having the LIGHT out, but my real fear comes from within the darkness. They are not a story. They are very much there, they are coming, and they are coming for me. I feel sad that PIPPY at the door has finished, and it's almost time for that dreaded moment when my dad hits that LIGHT switch into the OFF position, letting darkness flood through the room. How can I stall him? How can I buy some time to think of a better plan to block the UNSEEN to ensure they remain banished.

I decide to ask my dad for another PIPPY at the door, and I start to plead with him. To my amazement, Talia joins in with me. I begin to feel lucky because there is more of a chance that my dad will say yes if we both want another story. She yells out to my dad to persuade him with a loud and drawn out PLEEEEEEEEEEEEEEASE, and I knew in my heart that he would not say no to both of us. We are his pride and joy, he loves us very much, and he loves to spend time with us. Just as we love and adore our time with him. To my delight, my dad agrees to one more show, he truly is the best, and we both shout out to him,

We love you DAD.

I'm pleased that my dad will spend more time with us. My dad knows how to make me and Talia laugh, smile and bring us joy. I'm excited for the next edition of PIPPY at the door, but the closer it gets to the loss of LIGHT, the more I just can't shake this feeling of dread. It's there just as it always is, waiting in the back of my mind, constantly prodding at me, reminding me that I have been on borrowed time, the darkness and the UNSEEN are coming. The UNSEEN has been cast out by the LIGHT for so long, put on standby, harbouring in the dark, just sitting and waiting to pounce once IT gets the perfect opportunity.

I honestly believe that IT knows I can only stall my dad for so long. I know all too well what waits for me. My fate is already decided. I have no say in any of it, and I can only delay the inevitable. I wish it would go away and be gone with all my might, thinking about anything else, and I continue to do my best to ignore it. I lay back on my pillow and snuggle down into my covers to watch another one of my dad's inspirational stories about PIPPY.

I feel completely at peace, I manage to clear my mind, and for a moment, I feel normal, and I'm able to relax and enjoy the fun. Time certainly does pass too quickly when you're having a good time. My dad's story has once again come to an end. Out of nowhere, PIPPY comes flying towards me from above the door. I reach out and catch him because I know those dreaded words are about to follow. All I can do now is listen to those words come from my dad, letting us know it's now time to go to sleep! He goes over to Talia, gives her a kiss goodnight, and then he comes over to me and gives me a kiss goodnight too. Then in a hushed, gentle voice, almost a whisper, he explains that he doesn't want me to be scared. Nothing will hurt me, and if I always remember the phrase,

Don't forget who you are and hide in fear, face the fear and rise!

Then I will remind myself that I am safe and nothing can hurt me as long as I have,

HOPE, COURAGE AND STRENGTH

FROM WITHIN.

He begins to wind up **THAT** music box, twisting **THAT** dial turning **IT** around and around and around until it would not click any further. He then tells us that he loves us more than anything as he walks over to the door. As he stands in the doorway with his hand just resting on the LIGHT switch, I know what's about to happen, and my heart immediately sinks.

I feel severe bubbling in my stomach and an empty feeling in my mind. My heart beats so fast that I suddenly become boiling, and my breathing grows out of control. I take a long deep breath, followed by another and another, thinking this will help. I then accidentally find myself starting to hold my breath like I unknowingly forget to breathe. I become fixated and so focused on my dad that I can't move my eyes from my dad's hand resting on the LIGHT switch. Silence takes hold of the room, and I can't even hear **THAT** song coming out of **THAT** box. All I can hear is my mind repeating out loud amongst the loudest silence,

DON'T TURN IT OFF,

DON'T TURN IT OFF,

DO NOT TURN IT OFF,

PLEASE DO NOT TURN IT OFF!

The overwhelming silence fades away, and I start to hear THAT song coming from THAT box, then those dreaded words come from my dad. As quickly as I hear the words, goodnight and not to let the bed bugs bite....

CLICK, THE LIGHT WAS OUT.

Chapter Eleven

Don't Forget Who You Are And Hide In Fear

Darkness falls over me, and all I can hear is THAT song coming out of THAT box,

> The old Keevil bridge will not stay up,
> Will not stay up,
> Will just not stay up,
> The old Keevil bridge will not stay up,
> Trapping us inside....

It goes on and on in its cycle, and it will continue until it finishes unwinding. I'm doing my best to block it out, I look over to Talia, and she is somehow already asleep. A feeling of jealousy sweeps over me because I wish I could fall asleep that fast and sleep soundly in the dark. I hook the blanket under my feet whilst moving my legs away from the edge of the bed, bending them at my knees just as I always do when I'm alone in the dark. I make sure to face the edge of my bed, and I tell myself the UNSEEN will NOT get me tonight. I am sure of it. I get into a comfy position, and I wait, I stare out into the nothingness, and I look out at the room. I WILL BE READY for the UNSEEN. I know they are coming; I can feel it. I tell myself I will not lose focus, continue looking, and keep waiting.

As I lay here staring out into the room and the nothingness, all I can see is the outline of the furniture, and all I can hear is THAT song coming from THAT box. But it seems to be getting louder and louder with each verse that plays in desperation to be acknowledged.

The old Keevil bridge will not stay up,
Will not stay up,
Will just not stay up,
The old Keevil bridge will not stay up,

Trapping us inside....

The old Keevil bridge will not stay up,
Will not stay up,
Will just not stay up,
The old Keevil bridge will not stay up,
Trapping us inside....

The old Keevil bridge will not stay up,
Will not stay up,
Will just not stay up,
The old Keevil bridge will not stay up,
Trapping us inside....

The old Keevil bridge will not stay up,
Will not stay up,
Will just not stay up,
The old Keevil bridge will not stay up,
Trapping us inside....

Then nothing....

It just stops dead, complete silence falls over me, and I can't hear anything. I continue to look out into the room, scanning everywhere as I look from left to right. I can't help but think this is really strange. There are NO UNSEEN. Why are there no UNSEEN? Where is the TAPPING on the window? I quickly thought to myself, did I seriously imagine it all? I take the TORCH from under my pillow and turn it ON. I point the LIGHT towards Talia, and I can see she is still fast asleep. Then I scan the room with the LIGHT, but everything is normal and as it should be.

A critical memory begins to surface, and I start to remember that previously the UNSEEN did not arrive immediately. Sometimes they have taken a few hours to become SEEN. Maybe there's hope for me yet, and I'm not crazy after all. I know they are here hiding, and I know they are going to come OUT. I can't explain why but I suddenly need to wind THAT music box. I don't understand where this feeling is coming from, but I'm not able to stop myself. Then a strange, unfamiliar feeling comes over me. I almost feel SAFE IN the DARKNESS, safe to lie down and fall asleep. Is this a false feeling because the UNSEEN have not shown up? Was this feeling because I know I have a LIGHT? Whatever this feeling is, I FINALLY feel SAFE to sleep in the dark, so I decide that I'm going to take it.

I adjust myself to try and get comfy. I also move my pillow closer to the wall. To allow me to get as far away from the edge of the bed as physically possible. I make sure the covers remain under my feet and my legs stay pulled up away from the foot of the bed. I move my arm to pull PIPPY in closer while adjusting my covers at the same time.

....THUD

I hear a loud noise, and to my horror, I realise that the TORCH has rolled onto the floor, rolling way out into the middle of the room. I begin to get annoyed with myself. All I can think about is how I need that TORCH. What now? Maybe if I can quickly fall asleep, I'll still be SAFE. I stare out into the nothingness, and as I try to concentrate, all I can hear is THAT song coming from THAT box.

The old Keevil bridge will not stay up,
Will not stay up,
Will just not stay up,
The old Keevil bridge will not stay up,

Trapping us inside....

As I listen to **THAT** song, I continue to stare out into the nothingness. I glance up, looking towards the curtains. They seem normal, so I continue to watch the room as I wait to fall asleep. It seems the more I stare, the more I can see what appears to be a face, a dark outline of a male face. I remember seeing this before, but has it been here this whole time? Are my eyes playing tricks on me, or is this the **UNSEEN** manifesting in a more advanced way? Are they evolving? Have they become intelligent? I look away and close my eyes as tight as I can, then I snap them open and slowly move my eyes along the floor and up the wall. But as I get closer to the curtains, I find myself saying, please don't be there!

I look directly at the curtain, I can see the ruffles where they hang down, and I can see **THAT** face clear as day. The hair seems to be in a kind of mullet style, and it has a medium-sized nose with a mouth that appears to be closed. I see round black eyes that are gazing straight back at me. The deeper I stare at its face, the more I notice the expression of dread transforming into a long sinister smile. I know I've seen THAT face before. I can't take my eyes off IT, and I can no longer hear THAT song playing from THAT box, but I know that it's still playing underneath the deafening silence.

Once again, I begin to feel as though I'm unable to move, I look out the corner of my eyes to the other side of the curtain, and all I can see is a tall, dark, black figure. It's as tall as the window. IT has a long body with long arms, and they both glare at me. I can't do anything but look straight back, and I hold on to the HOPE that if I keep watching them, they won't move.

The old Keevil bridge will not stay up,
Will not stay up,
Will just not stay up,
The old Keevil bridge will not stay up,
Trapping us inside....

The old Keevil bridge will not stay up,
Will not stay up,
Will just not stay up,

The old Keevil bridge will not stay
up,
Trapping us inside....

The old Keevil bridge will not
stay up,
Will not stay up,
Will just not stay up,
The old Keevil bridge will not
stay up,
Trapping us inside....

The old Keevil bridge will
not stay up,
Will not stay up,
Will just not stay up,
The old Keevil bridge will
not stay up,
Trapping us inside....

The silence falls, and I can now hear THAT song loud and clear. As I stare at THAT face and THAT tall man, I truly start to question myself, is this real or not? What depth of my imagination has come out to play? Or is this happening in real-time? Do the UNSEEN have the ability to bide their time before they CHOOSE to strike? All I can do is stare and listen. Darkness holds many secrets, and darkness can make even the most innocent room appear to be something it's NOT. What if darkness is the truth? Does the darkness expose the actual reality that's shadowed by the LIGHT? Do we all live in a deceptive lie? Do we all live in a fraudulent reality, where only a select few can recognise it for what it is, understand the absolute truth, and recognise the UNSEEN?

THAT **song continues to play....**

The old Keevil bridge will not stay up,
Will not stay up,
Will just not stay up,
The old Keevil bridge will not stay up,
Trapping us inside....

The old Keevil bridge will not stay up,
Will not stay up,
Will just not stay up,
The old Keevil bridge will not stay up,
Trapping us inside....

The old Keevil bridge will not stay up,
Will not stay up,
Will just not stay up,
The old Keevil bridge will not stay up,
Trapping us inside....

The old Keevil bridge will not stay up,
Will not stay up,
Will just not stay up,
The old Keevil bridge will not stay up,
Trapping us inside....

Tap,

Tap,

Tap,

Tap,

No! It can't be!

No, No, No,

TAP,

TAP,

TAP,

TAP!

It's not real,

It's not real,

IT'S NOT REAL!

THIS IS NOT REAL!

TAP,

TAP,

TAP,

TAP!

All I can think is **NO**, I don't want them here. I automatically close my eyes, I squeeze them shut until I see that soothing GOLDEN colour. I do not want to look. Why can I no longer hear **THAT** song? Why did the TORCH have to drop onto the floor? I begin to panic. I can't feel PIPPY anywhere on my bed. I scramble to try and reach him whilst maintaining my effort to keep my legs away from the edge of my bed. I feel a shiver go straight down my spine. I suddenly sense that I need to stay absolutely still, is this it? Is this the UNSEEN? Are they back? I do my best not to breathe, but I can't help it.

I feel an intense cold air leave my mouth. I sense goosebumps appearing all over me, and I've become so cold. It came over me like the tide coming in over a sandy beach, but why? What is this? I was genuinely beginning to believe that all of this was in my head. But then, just as I start to accept my fate, the UNSEEN show up. Just to prove me wrong, it appears.

I remain focused on the GOLDEN colour as I remain here thinking to myself. Do I look? Where is PIPPY? What will I see when I open my eyes? I suddenly have a change of thought, and I begin to wish I still had the TORCH, but despite my situation, I decide that I need to see for myself. I require undeniable proof that the UNSEEN are back. I take a deep breath, and I count,

One,

Two,

Three,

Four!

I then squeeze my eyes as tight as I can, shifting that GOLDEN colour to **BLACK....**

I open my eyes with one quick movement, but they are out of focus, and all I can see is darkness. I scan the room as I wait for my sight to adjust, and as it slowly comes into focus, I see Talia's bed. I become startled by an ORANGE GLOW illuminating from the nothingness next to her bed. It alarms me because this is not any UNSEEN I've ever seen before. I slam my eyes shut, and all I can think is that something must be on fire. I try to yell out to my mum and dad, but nothing will come out and once again, I find myself unable to speak or move. All I have left is to open my eyes and look. I take another deep breath and count,

One,

Two,

Three,

Four!

I squeeze my eyes shut as much as possible, and then I immediately snap them open....

I slowly look towards the floor and move my eyes in the direction of Talia's bed. As I look over towards her, I begin to see THAT ORANGE GLOW. I stop, frozen in place because my eyes will not let me look any further, but I know I have no choice. I have no other option, so I slowly look up towards THAT ORANGE GLOW. It begins to turn to flames, visible at first, but it's fading in and out. It's like a lit fire, but a strong wind blows over it, turning its flame pure **WHITE**, then it suddenly burns ORANGE once again. I slam my eyes shut and hold them still. All I can hear is my breathing, my whole body feels numb, and I abruptly get an intense cold shiver all at once.

I know I need to open my eyes. I need to make sure this is an UNSEEN and not a real fire. I remember my dad telling me,

DON'T FORGET WHO YOU ARE AND HIDE IN FEAR!

I must FINALLY be brave. Once more, I take a

deep breath and count

One,

Two,

Three,

Four!

I open my eyes to **THAT** same **ORANGE GLOW**. So I slowly move my eyes up towards it. But **THAT GLOW** starts fading away, turning pure **WHITE** before disappearing into complete darkness.

All I see emerging out of the nothingness is a long, black cloak, but it's a different shade of black, more of a deep charcoal colour than black making it stand out against the darkness. I continue to look, moving my eyes up in a vertical direction, and a hat becomes clear. One of those old fashioned ones you see in old photos and movies, a sort of top hat, but it's sitting on top of nothing but darkness. It's as if it's floating. I can't stop looking at it. Why am I stuck staring at it when all I want to do is look away? But I can't look away. I must make sure THAT this UNSEEN does not harm Talia, so I stare, and I stare.

Out of nowhere, ITS head suddenly tilts, with an instant diagonal jerk. It snaps ITS eyes open, and there, watching and staring right back at me, are two intense, deep RED EYES. IT glares right through me. I feel like it's looking deep into my soul to watch all my memories, and there is nothing I can do to stop it. Before I can even comprehend or make sense of any of this, it snaps ITS head back into a straight position. It looks over towards Talia and instantly vanishes before my very eyes. I feel a shiver fly straight up my back, and I feel cold and numb. I dislike how this UNSEEN has left me feeling. It's different. It's not like any other before, and I sense IT has taken something from me, something important that I didn't even know I had. All I feel is emptiness. Maybe if I close my eyes and count, my feelings will return to normal....

One,

Two,

Three,

Four!

I take a deep breath, and just as I'm about to open my eyes, a tear gently rolls down my cheek.

The UNSEEN are here.

I feel THAT thing's hand wrap around my ankle and restrain me. There is nothing I can do. Once again, I'm trapped. All I can do is close my eyes harder than they already are, bypassing that soothing GOLDEN colour because all I see is **BLACK**.

This is not happening,

This is not happening,

This is not real!

It can't be!

Open your eyes,

Open your eyes!

Open them,

Now!

I continue to try and convince myself that all of this is in my head. But I can't move, I can't open my eyes, and the UNSEEN have me completely isolated.

I begin to feel a draft, and I'm sure someone keeps walking past my face. It's a gentle breeze blowing towards me every few seconds. I try to count the time between each draft in the hope that this would distract my mind from whatever it actually is.

I feel the breeze,

One step,

Two steps,

Three steps,

Four steps....

Then I feel another breeze, and this goes on and on. It just keeps going, and whatever this is, IT'S pacing up and down right next to my bed. As I lay here, I feel a rocking sensation. My bed is moving ever so slightly, but just enough that I can feel it, then it simply stops.

What's happening?

My bed starts to tremble. Then again, it just stops dead.

But then it starts to shake again.

What is going on?

I can't stop my thoughts, but I MUST open my eyes.

I NEED to open my eyes.

NO, I can't.

I have no idea what **UNSEEN** waits out there.

NO, I must be brave, because whatever this is, **IT** has me already, so I HAVE to open my eyes.

Don't forget who you are and hide in fear, face the fear and rise!

So once again, I take a deep breath and start to count,

One,

Two,

Three,

Four!

I take another deep breath, and I open my eyes!

As I look out into the darkness, I see a black

figure looking directly towards me while it paces up and down my room. I try to look towards my leg because I can still feel THAT thing's hand wrapped around my ankle, but I'm still powerless to move. I slowly move my eyes to the side of my bed, and I force myself to look down past my ruffled covers. All I can see are two deep black eyes in the centre of an outline of what resembles an old face. As THAT thing starts to lean over the side of my bed, IT notices that I'm watching IT. But IT continues leaning across my mattress, gazing at me, and it grows more and more intense because it's not moving. It's as though it froze, locking me and IT into an eternal moment of judgement.

I'm frozen and trapped within a moment filled with eternal pain. I have emotions that I've never felt before. Are these feelings coming from THAT thing? IT'S staring straight at me, and IT appears to be getting closer and closer but further and further away at the same time. Then IT starts to laugh silently and finally slides down the side of my bed, abruptly interrupting the stare, but THAT thing does not release my ankle. IT just holds on tighter.

I look to the end of my bed where the shaking

is coming from, but I see two black figures standing next to each other. They resemble the two UNSEEN children who jump on my bed looking like they have suffered terribly. Only these black figures that stand before me feel ominous and sinister. They don't move. They just stare, I start to get an overwhelming, intense feeling, and my entire body begins to shiver. I manage to whip my head back to my pillow and just stare up to my ceiling. I squeeze my eyes shut as hard as I can, and I clear my head and cling to one thought. All I think is,

I Need you, PIPPY.
Where are you? This is not real,

   I Need you, PIPPY.
  Where are you? This is not real,

      I Need you, PIPPY.
    Where are you? This is not real,

PIPPY, WHERE ARE YOU? NONE OF THIS IS REAL!

This is not real,

This is not real,

THIS IS NOT REAL,

THIS IS NOT REAL....

Chapter Twelve

Do You Believe In Ghosts?

The next morning

I look across the room, and I see the
TORCH. It did roll to the other side of the room.
It's now closer to Talia's bed than mine. I
immediately scramble to find PIPPY. I remember
how I did everything I could last night to locate
him, but he was nowhere to be found. How is it
possible that he's now sitting at the bottom of my
bed? I don't understand how he could have got
down there. I knew the UNSEEN would be back
as soon as the LIGHT was GONE.

This time was strange. The UNSEEN seemed
to have evolved and become far more intense. I
can't help but think they are back with a vengeance

because the LIGHT banished them for so long. I need a way to keep the LIGHT ON, but how? I decide I'm going to do whatever it takes at this point because I need the LIGHT ON. I do not wish the UNSEEN on anyone. But, if only my mum and dad could see the UNSEEN just for a moment, they would FINALLY understand how terrifying it truly is. They would see just how much power the LIGHT actually holds.

Today is a Saturday that means no school, but Talia has made plans to go over to her friend Rylie's house, and because my mum is also friends with her mum, we all get to go. I instantly became happy because Rylie is my best friend Paisley's, sister. I quickly get dressed and run downstairs to get my breakfast, Talia comes down to join me, but she looks exhausted. I don't understand why because she slept so soundly. As I look at her eyes, I notice that they seem heavy, like she's dying to close them. I ask Talia if she's alright because she did not see what I saw last night, but she responds, explaining that she is fine. What more can I do? She says she's ok, so she must be ok. We strangely just sat there in complete silence, which is not normal for us. We would always talk or giggle about something, but this time we just sat there. I feel as though we both just need the company.

I decide to bring my cassette player with me, so I run up to my room to grab it. I start to look for it, but I quickly realise that I'm struggling to find it, I can't find it anywhere. I suddenly thought maybe Talia borrowed it and forgot to tell me. I walk over to her bed and start to check all the places I would have placed it. I pull back her pillow....

What is this? I pick up the wrinkled piece of paper that lay there and in the centre, looking right back at me is a drawing. The drawing is of a tall, dark, **BLACK** figure wearing a top hat with big RED EYES that glow bright, and the bottom half of IT appears to be on FIRE. I quickly shove the picture back under her pillow and shuffle myself backwards, all the way back towards my bed. I stumble and fall onto my pillows, and I can feel every single beat of my heart. What is this? Why is there a picture of THAT FIGURE that stood over Talia's bed, under her pillow? I decide to stop and hold my breath for a few seconds.

One,

Two,

Three,

Four!

I tell myself out loud, you have merely imagined IT, so calm down. It's not there. Just go back over and move the pillow, and you will see it's just a blank piece of paper.

I take a deep breath and slowly stand up. Once I get to my feet, I take one step, then another followed by another, and suddenly I find myself looking down at Talia's pillow. I reach out and grab the corner in my hand, crumpling it inside my tight grip. I pull it up towards me, but I continue to stare at the ceiling. I tell myself to LOOK DOWN, and as quickly as I say it, I start to roll my head down towards the bed, but my eyes are squeezed completely shut. I can only see black, but I feel my head become low enough to look. I take a deep breath, and I start to open my eyes slowly....

Out of nowhere, I hear the words, WHAT DO YOU THINK YOU'RE DOING? As Talia simultaneously shoves me out of the way. I fell to the floor and simply responded to her, explaining that I was looking for my cassette player. She quickly corrects me, letting me know it's called a Walkman as she pulls it out of her draw and hands it to me. I decide it's now or never. I need to ask her about the drawing. After all, she knows I saw it. I immediately ask her about it, and I get an unwelcome response. She snaps at me, confirming what I'm already thinking, that it's a drawing of BEEBLEDOSH. She then abruptly informs me that I am not to ask her about him ever again.

I just sit here not knowing why I have no motivation to move. I just remain sitting here on the floor thinking about everything. What is this? Can Talia see the UNSEEN? I know BEEBLEDOSH is her imaginary friend, but I saw HIM, I know I saw him, he was standing over her. Is BEEBLEDOSH not so fictional after all? She used to say he's always there eating beside us, in the car among us and playing games, including us. Was he actually there, or is he genuinely imaginary? Does Talia's belief in him allow him to channel her energy to find a path into our reality? Or is it worse has BEEBLEDOSH drawn us into HIS reality? Is he the one who is real, and Talia is, in fact, **HIS** imaginary friend?

Our mum shouts for us to come downstairs to leave, and Talia just looks at me with a silent look that says so much. We walk to Rylie and Paisley's house because they only live down the road from us. On the walk over there, I decide to stay quiet because I'm just not in the mood to talk. I look around this village and find myself looking towards Big Foot Farm because the fields are empty. I guess the cows are in another area at the moment. My attention then turns to The Church of the Holy Spirit because I notice an eerie, ominous mist creeping through the graveyard. But I can't help but stare at those big gates at the end of our road the most. You really can't see anything beyond them except a path. I can't help but wonder, what if it's all fake? What if I'm just in one big, massive dream.

I begin thinking that maybe I should do something to show myself that I'm genuinely awake. I will think of something and then see if it happens. Like when you have one of those dreams where everything is going well, then suddenly, out of nowhere, something terrible happens, but you can change it. You have complete control over the story, so you make the dream return to a good place. But some dreams are nightmares or just horrible dreams, and no matter what you do, you can't change them. You have no control. I began to think of one that I get a lot, where I'm in a race, or I need to run somewhere, so I start trying to run, I'm running with all my might, but I just can't move. Then I began to think of another one, the type of dream where I'm completely aware it's a dream. I'm aware of what is happening, but I just can't open my eyes. I try everything I can, but they just won't open.

I then start to think of the scariest ones of all, the dreams that feel completely real, the ones that are so intense that I don't even try to wake up or change them because I believe it's actually happening. Then I suddenly wake up shaking and confused, not understanding why I'm in my bed. At first, I thought it was part of a dream when I saw the UNSEEN, but I never woke up from it, it happens in real-time, so I know they are NOT a dream. I can't help but wonder how dreams have the power to make me question what is real and what is a dream? What if dreams are, in fact, reality, and what if when we think we are awake, that is actually the dream? I can't stop thinking about all of this. The more I think about it, the more I want to know about **BEEBLEDOSH**, but most of all, I want to know why no one knows what is beyond those gates!

We arrive at Rylie and Paisley's house, and they are delighted to see us. My mum went into the kitchen and sat down with Lydia, their mum. I just realised I never knew her name until I just heard my mum say hi to her. They began to play rock music at quite a high volume because they are both huge fans, and it's one of many things they have in common. We go into the living room, where their little brother Henry is sitting and watching a dinosaur movie on the television. Even though I've seen it before, I'm enjoying it because I can clear my mind and not worry about anything as I sit here.

Watching television starts to get boring, so we decide to go upstairs to Rylie and Paisley's room. Henry stayed downstairs watching the movie. We start trying to decide what to do, but then Talia and Rylie randomly leave the room. I look at Paisley, but she just stares towards me blankly, wondering where they went. But before we have a chance to shout them to ask, they come back into the room. Talia is holding some paper and a pen, and Rylie has hold of a plastic arrow and a candle. I have no idea what this stuff is for, so I ask them to explain. Rylie then tells us that we are going to contact spirits and speak to them from beyond the grave.

Rylie starts to explain, but I don't pay attention because I have an awful feeling about this, and I know it's a bad idea. I don't want to make them mad or seem like a coward, but I don't want to do this. I became very concerned about who or what we would contact. I look towards Talia and give her a look to show her that I don't want to be involved. Talia then suggests to Rylie that it's not a good idea and we don't know what we would be messing with, so she recommends doing something else. I felt so relieved that Talia's protecting me just when I needed her help. Deep down in my heart, I know that she will always keep me safe in times of need, just as I will always do the same for her. I suddenly feel a stronger connection towards Talia. I know I have the best sister because we may fight and fall out, but I know that when it matters most, we will ALWAYS be there for each other.

Suddenly I hear Paisley speak out and ask

everyone a question. She asks, who believes in ghosts? Talia, Rylie and I all respond by saying that we believe. But, Paisley clarifies that she doesn't know if she believes in ghosts or not. I decide to ask a question to see if any of them have the same thoughts that I do, so I ask, what do you think ghosts are? They all have mixed responses, but they all have one similarity, they all think ghosts are the spirits of the dead who can't move on. Their responses start a more extensive conversation between them about their opinions.

I don't respond out loud. I simply sit here listening and thinking to myself because I used to think the same until the UNSEEN became SEEN. I now question everything because the UNSEEN appear to be much more than a remaining spirit of someone who has passed away. They act like they have an agenda, some kind of mission, or is it actually their world, and we are the ones imposing on their privacy, and it's us who can't move on?

Time is passing quickly today. My mum comes upstairs to get us because it's already getting dark outside, it's never fun leaving friends, but I'm sure we will be back soon. On the walk home, it comes flooding back to me that I now need to find a way to keep the LIGHT ON tonight. I feel disappointed because I was hoping to go over to Paisleys and forget about the UNSEEN. But instead, all we did was talk about creepy stuff. Why can't I ever get away from all of this?

We walk past those big gates, but this evening they have a different eerie feel. Is it because I have been thinking about the UNSEEN for most of the day, or is it something to do with the considerable amount of fog drifting up to the dark and cloudy sky? I see a glint of moonlight beaming down and reflecting off the mist as it floats just above the ground. As I look up, I see the moon sitting just beyond the gates like it's been perfectly placed there in some sort of illusion. I just want to get home and hide under my covers....

No, wait, that's not safe either. I can't escape. I'm trapped. I just want my mum and dad to sit down with me and explain all of this. What is this? What is happening to me?

Chapter Thirteen

They Are In My Room

As I walk along the path towards our front door, I notice how dark the house looks, and this means my dad's not home yet because there are no LIGHTS ON. As my mum swings the door open, it starts to creak. I begin to think about how I have never noticed how loud this door is before. I remain just outside, looking straight down the dark hallway. I just stand here, unable to step into the house, because I honestly feel like the UNSEEN are already waiting in the darkness. I don't want to go all the way in, so I move my head in close to try and stare harder because I strangely feel safe outside. Then out of nowhere, the LIGHT beams on because Talia hit the switch. As I walk into the house, I feel a raindrop land on my hand. We arrived home just in time because it's just started to rain.

After only five minutes, the rain becomes extremely heavy outside. Our mum starts cooking dinner, so Talia and I plan to go and play while we wait for our dad to come home from work. We collect our toys and discuss where to set them up. I suggest the stairs because we both have a section to play in, separated by the turn of the stairs. It's my favourite place to set up and play, but for some reason, today, Talia is absolutely set against the stairs. She explains in a firm tone that we will play in the lounge area.

I ask Talia why she doesn't want to play on the stairs? We always play there, and it's an excellent location for our game. She simply responds, letting me know that it's where BEEBLEDOSH likes to play and that she doesn't want to see him anymore. I ask her why? She angrily instructs me to LEAVE IT ALONE, so I respect that and don't push it. I just can't understand why she is saying such things. If she really did create him in her mind, then how can something that comforted her, something she created to feel safe and less alone, suddenly become feared by her? The very thing that made her feel safe is now the thing making her feel scared. I just can't figure out one worrying fact, if she made him up then how come she can't just make him vanish?

As we began to play, the room filled with amazing smells of food from the kitchen. They were flowing all through the house. While we play, I decide to take the opportunity to ask Talia if she gets scared when it's dark and if she will help me tonight by keeping the LIGHT ON? She responds, telling me that she can't sleep if there is any LIGHT in the room. I thought to myself, there is a way to get what I want, but it's far to mean. I could have said to Talia that BEEBLEDOSH wants the LIGHT OUT, not you. But I know this would upset her, so I take extra care to make sure I DO NOT say it. It's not right to make her suffer to get what I want, and I care about her way too much to do that to her. However, I know that I need to do something drastic to keep the LIGHT ON. I then thought shall I tell her about the UNSEEN? Would she even believe me or just think I'm crazy. I asked her if we had an opportunity to have rooms of our own would she be ok with that, or would she become scared if she had to sleep alone. She basically said she would love to have a room of her own, but it won't happen, so there is no point thinking about it.

Our dad finally walks through the door, and the first thing he does is come over and give us a big cuddle because he's so happy to be home. He's a little wet from the rain because he's just walked up to our house from the car, but we don't care because it's good to have him home. He goes into the kitchen to give our mum a kiss and a cuddle whilst talking to her. Dinner is ready, so we all sit down to eat. As we eat, all I can think about is how close it's getting to my bedtime, and the UNSEEN are definitely going to get me tonight. I just know it. I finally decide that it's time to explain to them what has been going on and tell them that I need the LIGHT ON. Once we all finished eating, Talia and my dad went to watch television. So I take this opportunity to try and talk to my mum whilst she does the washing up.

I walk over to my mum, and with firmness, in my voice, I just blurt out the words, Mum, I need the LIGHT ON tonight. She responds to me, explaining that she feels completely stuck in the middle, Talia can't sleep with it ON, and I can't sleep with it **OFF**. I know she loves us both, but whatever she decides, one of us will be unhappy. My mum tries her best to get me to understand that we switch LIGHTS **OFF** at night. It's just what people do, and I should try and get past my fear because nothing will hurt me. My mum has just made me realise that the **UNSEEN** are scary at the time. But, my mum is right. They have never actually physically harmed me. I mean, **THAT** thing grabs my ankle and traps me, flooding me with fear. But, it's never left any marks or done any physical damage. I still can't accept this though, so I continue to plead with my mum because I need the LIGHT ON. I even resort to refusing to go to bed unless I can have it ON.

I realise that all hope is lost because the **UNSEEN** will never show themselves to my mum. She goes up to my room and spends half an hour looking everywhere for me. She looks in my closet, under the beds, checks the curtains and outside the window. She then explains to me that there is nothing in this room, that I am safe and that she and dad won't ever let anything happen to me, not now, not ever. I decide to accept that dealing with the **UNSEEN** is my battle, and there is nothing my parents can do because they can't fix what isn't there. I cuddle my mum, tell her I love her and thank her for at least looking even though I knew she would not see them.

I'm stood here in the bathroom, ready to brush my teeth. But as I look in the mirror, I see something behind me, so I turn around to look. Only I see nothing, just the door. I start to look deeper into the mirror, but the more I stare at my reflection, the more I begin to see it change. My features are appearing more evident, crisper, and the harder I stare, the more my features start to alter. I almost can't recognise myself. I feel like I've fallen into some kind of trance. I faintly hear my mum shout out to me, and simultaneously I close my eyes tight to break the magic spell that's somehow cast over me. I opened my eyes to look at my face, and thankfully it's returned to normal. I begin to feel fearful because this has never happened before. Is this the UNSEEN, or is my mind slipping in and out of what we know as reality? What was that? I decided to tell myself that it was an optical illusion and nothing more.

I climb into my bed and cuddle PIPPY tight. I check to make sure the TORCH is still under my pillow, and then as I always do, I bend my legs up under my covers, making sure I hook them under my feet. I move as close to the wall as I can get to make sure I'm nowhere near the edge of the bed. I notice my mum leave the door open, so the LIGHT in the hallway is still visible. She brings a chair to the side of my bed, and then she sits down facing me. She begins to explain to me that she understands I'm scared, so she will sit here until I'm asleep. She reassures me that she will remain here until she's sure that I'm sleeping soundly. My mum wound THAT music box as I lay there watching her. But I did not care to listen to THAT song. All I care about is that she is sitting here with me, and I will finally be able to sleep.

As I lay here watching my mum, just to make sure she doesn't leave, I hear her begin to sing along to THAT song coming out of THAT box.

The old Keevil bridge will not stay up,
Will not stay up,
Will just not stay up,
The old Keevil bridge will not stay up,
Trapping us inside....

The old Keevil bridge is no longer up,
Is no longer up,
Is just no longer up,
The old Keevil bridge is no longer up,
Without them inside....

The moment my mum began a new verse, I suddenly thought to myself, I didn't know there were more words to THAT song. I whisper towards my mum, hoping she hears me ask if she's singing the official words or making it up as she goes along? My mum stops singing and explains that there are many versions, and no one knows the song's true origin. I close my eyes again, hoping that she will continue to sing. When she sang to THAT song, all the negative energy attached to it disappeared, and it somehow became SOOTHING and PEACEFUL. To my delight, she begins to sing another new verse. But I know I will have to ask her about the whole song another time because I can feel my eyes becoming extremely heavy.

The people of Keevil build it back up,

Build it back up,
Just build it back up,
The people of Keevil build it back up,
Trapping them inside....

....

TAP,

TAP,

TAP,

TAP,

I suddenly wake up, and all I can hear is
THAT tapping, THAT music box is now
SILENT, but the TAPPING seems to be getting
louder and louder. I keep my eyes shut, I don't dare
look, I just lay here, and I know the LIGHT is
OUT because my eyelids are dead **BLACK** I know
when a LIGHT is ON because I can see that
GOLDEN colour that brings peace, but all I can
see is pure darkness.

TAP,

TAP,

TAP,

TAP,

It grows louder with each tap, so I pull PIPPY in tight and do my best to pull my legs up as far as possible while ensuring they are still close to the wall. I feel pressure on my blanket because, once again, something is crawling over it. The tugging moves towards me and is now very near my legs. I can feel the blanket that's around my feet close in around my ankle, butterfly's form in the pit of my stomach and a tingling sensation makes its way up my back. I need to open my eyes, I need to make sure Talia is ok, and I need to see for myself if THAT thing is back. The blanket keeps moving, and I know deep in my heart that this is it....

Just as I decide to open my eyes, the darkness on my eyelids turns GOLDEN....

A LIGHT **is** ON....

I open my eyes to see my dad coming towards my bed, and I don't even care why. I just immediately become happy and filled with HOPE. I look to my feet, and I see Speckles sitting there. My dad starts to explain that he's been looking for him everywhere. We both began wondering what Speckles was doing in my room because he rarely came in here. My dad picks him up and hugs him. I look at Speckles because I'm so relieved that it was him sitting on my bed and not the UNSEEN. As I look at him, suddenly, out of nowhere, he turns his ears sideways and then flat to his head as he arches his back. He squeals, and his fur spikes up, making him look as though he just got electrocuted. As he leaps from my dad's arms, he runs up the curtain, reaches the top pole, and he begins meowing and hissing. We see him clinging on for his life with his claws. Something has undoubtedly spooked him. Can he see the UNSEEN?

I watch as my dad reaches up to hold Speckles

despite the danger of getting scratched, to release his claws and get him down. My dad frees him from the curtain and pets him until he begins to purr. He managed to help Speckles calm down, but what scared him in the first place? Was it the UNSEEN or maybe even BEEBLEDOSH? Whatever it was, this has not happened before, and the TAPPING has been interrupted, so perhaps this means they can't return. My dad is a firm believer that cats can sense things, and because something scared Speckles in my room, my dad lets me know that I can keep the hallway LIGHT ON. I give my dad the biggest hug and make sure I tell him that I love him millions, and then he walks to the bathroom to get ready for bed himself. I didn't realise it was so late.

I lay back down, and because I'm so happy the LIGHT is ON, I just lay here for a while, thinking about what just happened, and I realise I have so many unanswered questions. Does my dad believe me? Does he sense the UNSEEN? Has he SEEN them before in this house or maybe when he was younger? As I lay here, I look over to Talia to make sure she's ok, and I see that she's sound asleep. I suddenly get an urge to look over to the doorway. I thought I saw someone standing there, but nothing was there, so I lay back down. I see something again in my peripheral vision, so I sit up to look again, but nothing is there. I put my head back down to my pillow and snuggle into PIPPY, but I can't budge this overwhelming feeling that someone is there. I can't settle, so once again, I sit up and look to the doorway....

As I look to the hallway, I see a black figure walk just out of sight. I slam my eyes shut, but I immediately open them to take another look. Right there, before my very eyes, I see a black face. IT'S leaning its head around the door and staring straight at me. Once IT noticed that I was looking directly at it, IT moved completely out of sight. I can't help but feel like it's mocking me because now IT'S been SEEN with the LIGHT ON, the one thing that kept me safe, but this UNSEEN has somehow found a way to be here, despite the fact IT'S just playing games. I could only see a black silhouette of a face, but was this the UNSEEN or BEEBLEDOSH? I slam my head to my pillow and close my eyes.

I reach for my TORCH and turn it on. I point it to the hallway, but nothing's there this time. I keep it shining there for a while, thinking to myself, don't come back. While I look towards the hallway, I notice that our bedroom door creates a shadow, reflecting onto the floor in a diagonal position across the carpet. I decide to tell myself I imagined the black silhouette because I want and need to believe the LIGHT keeps the UNSEEN away. It's all I have. I suddenly get a chilling thought, if LIGHT keeps the UNSEEN away, then it must have been BEEBLEDOSH. After all, he did visit Talia many times during daylight hours. I turn my TORCH off and place it back under my pillow, and I lay back down. I keep my eyes on the door and its shadow, watching as they remain still because something just isn't right.

TAP,

TAP,

TAP,

TAP!

I hear the **TAPPING** on the window, but I choose to ignore it because the LIGHT is ON this time. I hold on to the HOPE that if I don't think about the **UNSEEN**, they won't have an opportunity to be, **SEEN**. Then as I lay here watching, I see the shadow of the door move slightly. I immediately sit up and stare at the door. It seems to be swaying, the same way that a tree branch sways in the wind. It's barely noticeable, and I only noticed it because I was watching the door's shadow.

TAP,

TAP,

TAP,

TAP!

The **TAPPING** continues to get louder in some desperation to be acknowledged. The door also continues to sway as if it stands in the wind. Suddenly, I see **THAT** long, bony pointing finger on the curtain out the corner of my eyes. How is **IT** here in the LIGHT? **IT'S** putting up a good fight, though, and there's no denying that. It's just I don't get the same sinister feeling from **IT** in the LIGHT. Does the **UNSEEN** need the darkness to function? Could the LIGHT truly be the solution because the LIGHT indeed banishes them? Is **DARKNESS** the key to their power, or do they feed off my fear and if I refuse to give it, would it render them HELPLESS?

TAP,

TAP,

TAP,

TAP,

SILENCE fell upon the room, the door and

its shadow became still, so I look over towards the window, and THAT pointing finger has gone. I instantly feel uneasy and begin to breathe extremely fast. I start feeling sick to my stomach, but this time I can move, and I can speak, so I yell out to Talia,

TALIA,

TALIA,

TALIA WAKE UP,

TALIA WAKE UP,

WAKE UP!

TALIA finally wakes up and asks me to explain what's wrong. I just simply request to sleep in her bed because I don't want to be over here alone. She responds to me, saying, of course, so I gather my courage, grab PIPPY, and run over to her bed. I ask if I can sleep by the wall, and I'm happy she says yes. I cuddle into PIPPY, only this time I'm staring over towards my bed. It's surreal seeing it from over here. I wonder what would happen if the LIGHT was **OUT**, but I was over here instead of over there. Would the **UNSEEN** still target my bed, or would they come over to Talia's? Or would they not show up at all? Do they actually have the ability to think? Would they even know I'm over here and not over there? They are as real as you and me but are they intelligent like you and me?

Chapter Fourteen

Dad Believes

The following day I wake up and immediately thank Talia for letting me sleep in her bed. Thanks to her, I finally got some sleep last night, but this can't go on and needs to stop. But how? I know the LIGHT keeps the UNSEEN away, but I'm not so sure about BEEBLEDOSH. I need to find out if it's even him that I'm seeing, and I know one way to find out. I need to find a way to convince Talia to talk about him without becoming defensive. I felt a powerful connection with my dad last night, which has made me realise what I need to do. I know he BELIEVES because I felt it in my heart, I must talk to him as soon as possible to finally explain everything.

I leave my room to go and find my dad,

hoping that he's not left for work yet. As I get to the bottom of the stairs, I see him sitting at the table. I walk over to him and politely ask if we can talk. My dad responds, letting me know that talking will be fine because he has some time before leaving for work. I pull out a chair and slowly sit down because I know this won't be easy.

I begin to explain to my dad that I need the LIGHT ON at night because I seriously can't sleep without it. I have tried and tried but fail every time because I see things in the darkness, in the night. They are hiding amongst the nothingness, and they know I see them. It all begins with a TAPPING on the window that's persistent, and the more it's ignored, the louder it gets. Then it makes me look over to it with a powerful, overwhelming feeling that I can't avoid. Then there it is, I see it, THAT long pointing finger. I become frozen where I lie, and I'm unable to move. It's as though I'm locked in time with no choice or control over my actions.

After the deadly warning from THAT long pointing finger, I begin to feel something. A HAND creeping along my bed, and once it gets far enough, it moves my covers and grabs my foot. It begins wrapping its hand tight around my right ankle. It locks its entangled long fingers into place. Then once it has me trapped, it develops this uncomfortable, sinister look on its face. I refer to it as THAT thing because I have no words to describe the horror it brings with it.

Once THAT thing has me trapped, I see two small children dressed in clothes that I've never seen before. They jump continuously on the end of my bed, but they don't make contact in the same way as THAT thing. The small children have this disturbing look of dread and fear on their faces. They didn't feel ominous initially, but so much time has passed whilst the LIGHT has banished them. It's almost as if they have evolved, soaking up the energy provided by the LIGHT to come back stronger.

Now all they do is stand there at the end of my bed. The children have become more intelligent, powerful and intense because they no longer appear to be transparent. Now they look solid, just like THAT thing. Before, they seemed as though they were not entirely here. But now they stand before me motionless, looking as alive as you and me. It's almost as if they are being given commands by the tall black figure who stands between them. But recently, that look of pure dread has left their faces. They look seriously tormented and tortured, expelling a powerful feeling. I also get an overwhelming sense that they want people to know they are being controlled or punished.

The figure I see standing over Talia is tall and dressed in a black cloak with a top hat and burning from the waist down. I feel like it's BEEBLEDOSH, but because she is very withdrawn and hesitant to talk about it, I don't know if it is him. I thought I found a drawing under her pillow that resembled what I had seen standing over her. But before I could get a proper chance to look, she came into our room, and she wouldn't say much to me about it. She asked me to leave it alone, so I respected her and backed off. I have many questions though, because BEEBLEDOSH appears to be quite different from the UNSEEN.

I call them the UNSEEN, who are now, SEEN. I know as time passes, the UNSEEN become more robust because they are evolving. They are more aware, and more of them are showing up. Lately, something has been pacing up and down next to my bed and blowing a draft towards me. They stare at me Dad, looking past my face and my body. They look deep down into my soul and my very being. It feels like they want something from me, and they won't stop until they get it. The more they come, the more intense they get, and the only thing that stops them is the LIGHT.

At least this is what I should have said, because now that I'm sitting here with him, I can't find the right words. Anything I think to say makes it seem far less scary than it is. I have no idea how to make him see what I'm going through. I finally decide to start telling him because I'm done thinking it over, and I know I can't tell him everything. So I begin with Dad, I need the LIGHT ON at night because I seriously can't sleep without it. I have tried and tried but fail every time because I see things in the darkness, in the night. They are hiding amongst the nothingness, and they know I can see them.

My dad interrupts me and tells me that I don't need to explain any of it. He says that when he saw Speckles last night, it became clear that there was, and is, SOMETHING in this house. He goes on to tell me about a night when he saw something.

He describes a night where he was in bed, but for some unknown reason, he suddenly woke up. So he looked forward, and to his horror, he saw a tall, dark figure with a top hat sitting on its head, standing at the foot of his bed. It gave him such a fright to the point that he jumped under the covers and stayed there for several minutes. He began getting too hot, so he pulled the covers down from his head, and to his relief, the figure was gone.

My dad then explains that he's telling me this because he has seen things too. Many of which he can't explain, just like me. He then tells me that strange things also happened in the house that they lived in with Talia before I was born. A big picture in a frame flew off the wall and crashed to the floor. My dad explains that there was no way it could have possibly fallen upwards over a big hook and then down to the floor.

My dad then informs me that we have a real human skull in our house, and it's been sitting in the glass cabinet all this time. He has a theory that it could have brought something into our home with it. It may have possibly opened a door for whatever it is to be able to enter. My dad looks towards me and notices that I'm becoming a little worried, so he walks over to the cabinet and grabs the skull. I began thinking to myself, how it's incredible that I had never noticed it before. My dad brings the skull over and lets me take a look at it to help me realise that it can't hurt me. I ask my dad an important question, while the skull itself can't hurt me, what about its spirit? Its soul?

My dad explains that because the skull sits in our house, its spirit may not be at peace. He asks me if I want him to move it somewhere else. I explain how I don't want to upset him, but I would prefer it if it weren't in our home. He explains that he will take it to nan's house on his way to work. He also reassures me that he believes me about the UNSEEN. He then tells me that I will never have to sleep in the dark again unless I choose to do so. I began to feel confused because I knew how Talia would get mad if she had to sleep with the LIGHT ON. I ask my dad what he means, but I barely get an answer. My dad responds, informing me that his time has run out, but I will get an explanation later, and it will all become clear. On his way out, he does promise me that I will be ok.

My dad walks out the door to make sure he gets to work on time. I remain sat here confused about what just happened. But I do feel a wave of relief because my dad answered my original question. Now I know, DAD DOES BELIEVE.

My mum soon lets me know that it's time to go to school. I have no idea how I will concentrate because all I can think about is the conversation I've just had with my dad. What does he mean? Will I finally be free of the UNSEEN? What about BEEBLEDOSH? Was it him who stood by Talia's bed? I think I will at least try and talk to her about him today, no matter what.

Today flew by, but I'm glad because all I want to do is get home and talk to Talia. I need to understand the difference between BEEBLEDOSH and the UNSEEN. On the way home, I notice the big gates that lead to the unknown are open. I've never seen this before. I become excited because I get to see these gates in this position for the first time in my life. I can't help but wonder why there open, and I'm still curious about what goes on in there. I will find out one day because I think about it all the time, especially when I walk down this road.

We arrive home, and as I walk towards our path, I notice my dad's car is here. I immediately want to know why he's home early. I run inside so fast, and I see him standing there smiling at me. He calmly asks me to come with him because he has something to show me. He walks upstairs, and I follow right behind him. We walk past the bathroom door and both bedroom doors. We stop right in front of his workroom door, where he paints and composes his music. He places his hand on the door handle and turns around to look at me.

As my dad looks directly into my eyes, he swings open the door. To my complete surprise, I see all my things, including my bed. I feel a wave of relief and happiness sweep over me. I don't even go into the room, but I do wrap my arms around my dad. I squeeze him tight and give him the biggest cuddle I possibly can whilst whispering thank you in his ear.

My dad began to explain that he could see how scared I was, and he knew at that moment exactly what he had to do. I make sure he knows how much I appreciate what he has done for me, and I thank him again as I walk into my new room. It makes me seriously happy to see so much LIGHT, and there's now a lamp sitting on the table next to my bed. There is also a bright LIGHT shining down from above me. I'm thrilled to see PIPPY sitting there in the middle of my pillow to greet me because no room is complete without him. My dad shows pure kindness and is the best dad in the world to sacrifice his space to help me.

Today is a good day because I began to look forward to going to sleep for the first time in a long time. I love my new room. It's so perfect, but I know I will miss the fact that Talia was right there. I wonder if she will miss me. I'll ask her when I get the chance because I still need to talk to her and see if she will tell me anything about BEEBLEDOSH. Even though from now on I can have my LIGHT ON every night, I am still very worried about the UNSEEN.

I walk into my old room to see if Talia is there, and I find her rearranging her stuff. So I ask her if she wants any help because this means we have a chance to talk. She responds with a yes, so I begin to help her, and as I move some of her things, I notice that she has so much more space now. But I suddenly began to think, will the UNSEEN follow me? What happens when they figure out that the LIGHT in my new room will now banish them forever? Will they go after Talia? They never have before, so I feel pretty confident that she will be ok. Then a very ominous question came into my mind, what about **BEEBLEDOSH**? The **UNSEEN** only seem to haunt me, so I don't think they will go after Talia. But that night, when I saw **BEEBLEDOSH** stood over her, he wanted something. Will she be safe in here alone?

Talia asks me to push the other end of her wardrobe because she wants to move it to the other side of the room. I decide to take this opportunity to ask her about **BEEBLEDOSH**. I ask her all the questions I have, one after the other, so she can't interrupt me because I need to get them all out.

I begin to ask her, Who is **BEEBLEDOSH**? How old were you when you started seeing him? Where was the first place you saw him? Can you describe his appearance? When was **BEEBLEDOSH** last at our house? Is he GOOD or **BAD**? Where does he go when he's not with you, and why do you never want to talk about him?

She suddenly stands still and stops trying to move the wardrobe. As she stands there, she glares straight at me. But to my surprise, she responds for once and tells me to listen very carefully.

Talia begins to explain that her memories of

BEEBLEDOSH go back way before her memories of me. She then describes how she has no idea what he is or where he comes from, and she explains that sometimes he's here and sometimes gone. She says that he didn't ever explain where he goes, and she didn't dare ask. Talia then says that he used to be her BEST FRIEND, and they had FUN together. But now he's turned BAD, and she has no idea why or what happened.

Talia also explains that she's told him she is no longer his BEST FRIEND and NEVER wants to see him again. Talia then tells me that she told him to GO AWAY and hasn't seen him since. I'm also made aware that she told him to go away the day before she found me stood at her pillow. Talia then whispers one last thing to me. She explains that the drawing I had found under her pillow is a drawing she had done of BEEBLEDOSH! Then she asks me to please, never bring HIM up ever again.

I am completely shocked that she spoke to me about BEEBLEDOSH. But now I'm worried because the day she tells HIM to go away is the same day he became SEEN by me. What was he doing stood over Talia if she had asked him to go away? Has he revealed himself now because she refuses to see him, so he has had no choice but to become part of the UNSEEN? I can only hope Talia will be ok. She also let me know that she will miss me despite enjoying the extra space. Talia has asked if we can still have PIPPY at the door in her room. I, of course, agree because we have always had PIPPY at the door in here, and it would not feel right to change that. I finished helping Talia sort out her room, and it's looking fantastic. We both begin to feel so grown up now that we have separate rooms. Our mum calls for us to come down for dinner, so we rush down the stairs.

Bedtime soon arrives, and as I'm getting ready for bed, I realise something. For the first time in so long, I'm excited to go to sleep. I sit in my new room, on the edge of my bed, with the door open, just looking around. I begin thinking about how this seems too good to be true. Knowing this room is now mine doesn't seem real because it's what I've wanted for so long, and it's my only escape from the UNSEEN. I can't help but think, I better not wake up to find out that this has just been a dream and find myself back in the darkness. I pinch my arm to make sure it hurts to convince myself that

I'm not asleep. To prove to myself once and for all that this is all happening, and I will finally be FREE.

Then that all too familiar feeling sweeps over me. I feel drawn to look down the hallway and straight ahead towards Talia's bedroom door. I can't stop myself from staring at it, so I decide to get up and go down there to end this once and for all. I stop myself at the entrance to her room, and I stand in the doorway. I know the UNSEEN are there, but they hide and bide their time. But today, it is different because I'm not their prisoner anymore, so I say aloud.

NO, YOU HAVE NO POWER OVER ME ANYMORE. I AM FREE.

I continue to stand there looking into her room towards the space where my bed used to be. But I oddly discover that I'm feeling nothing but emptiness. I find this strange because for once, I have nothing to fear. But that place where the fear once lived is now nothing but a hollow space. I have no idea what to replace it with because I've spent so long thinking that it's normal to feel that way. Now I don't know how I should feel or what I'm supposed to believe. I'm no longer trapped, but I'm empty.

Talia comes up the stairs because it's time for PIPPY at the door, so Talia and I climb onto her bed to wait for our dad. He quickly comes up the stairs and carries out a great show, then once it's finished, I say goodnight to Talia and tell her that I love her. After brushing my teeth, I run into my room and jump onto my bed. My mum and dad follow me to say goodnight. They ask me if I want THAT music box winding. But I respond by saying NO thanks, because I want to listen to a story on my cassette player and fall asleep.

They tuck me in, and they both give me a kiss and a cuddle and say goodnight. My dad asks me which LIGHT I want to keep ON. I respond with a big smile and explain that I would like both of them ON please. As they turn around to leave, I shout to them to say thanks and tell them that I love them both. As soon as they go, I snuggle down into my pillow and pull PIPPY in tight. For the first time in as long as I can remember, I look out at MY room, into MY NOTHINGNESS, and I smile.

It feels so HAPPY and LIGHT....

It's NOW the UNSEEN'S turn to be TRAPPED.

Part Two

Chapter Fifteen

Sense Of Belonging

Eleven years later, October 2007

I shout goodbye to my friends as I leave work and walk over to my car, its already packed and ready for my road trip across Europe. I'm so excited to get two weeks off work and finally see my family. It's been a long year over here in Germany serving with the Army. My mum and dad have asked me to come home to look after the house while they finally go on their dream holiday to Hawaii. So whilst they are gone, I get to have the place all to myself.

I put some music on, set up my satellite navigation system, and then off I go. As long as I stick to my plan, I will arrive home in time to see my mum and dad before they leave for the airport. This first part of my journey should take around 5 hours. I set off from Gütersloh, Germany and head towards Duisburg. Then Eindhoven, then Antwerp and then finally towards Calais, France. Then I'm able to sleep because I have a two-hour ferry ride to get to Dover. Once I arrive, I refuel my car and head across England. It will take me about three and a half hours until I arrive in Keevil.

....

It's been a long journey, but I finally pull up outside our house, and it feels so good to be home. It feels like forever since I was last here. My job keeps me away for long periods at a time. But when I do get to come home, I appreciate it so much more. I step out of my car to see my mum and dad coming outside to greet me. My dad runs over and gives me a big cuddle. My mum then shouts welcome home as I walk over to her and give her the biggest hug I possibly can. They both look so happy, and I'm pleased to see them both because I've missed them a lot. My dad lifts my suitcase out of my car boot for me, and we all walk into the house. As I step in and look around, I Suddenly get an all too familiar feeling of comfort sweep over me. The house is the same as it was before I left. It feels incredible to finally be HOME.

My mum and dad don't have long until they need to leave. They quickly explain that Talia's at her house in Bath with her children, Jackson and Coral. But if I need anything while I'm home, then I should contact her. My mum also gave me an update on my niece and nephew. She lets me know that Jackson now likes to be called Jack for short, and he turned three this year. My mum also tells me that Talia's new baby daughter, Coral is now eight months old. I'm so glad my mum gives me updates because work keeps me very busy. So sometimes, I need a little reminder about these things. I respond to my mum, explaining that I'm excited to meet Coral because I've not met her yet. It was just bad timing that Talia had her the day after I left to begin my training with the Army.

My dad begins to load their car with the suitcases, whilst my mum walks me into the kitchen. She lets me know that they have stocked up the fridge and freezer with food and left me some treats in the cupboard. I let her know that I appreciate it and want her and dad to have fun and enjoy themselves. They have deserved this holiday for many years. My dad walks into the kitchen with a big smile on his face. He explains that it's almost time for them to leave.

I ask my mum and dad if they will sit down for a moment because I want to let them know something. They agree, so I begin with my dad. I look directly at him and tell him that I'm so proud of him for getting his movie out this year. It's a fantastic achievement, and it's already selling out at the box office. I congratulate him, making sure he knows that he deserves happiness. I tell him how much of an amazing dad he is and that I'm thankful for everything he does for me. I also make sure he knows just how much his sacrifice saved my life. That day he let me have a room of my own. He helped me banish the UNSEEN because he gave me LIGHT. I'm still thankful for that to this very day, so I make sure he knows how much that meant to me and still means to me. I also tell him that I want him to go and enjoy his holiday. Have some time to relax and not worry about anything because he truly is fantastic.

I then look at my mum to let her know that

she means everything to me and deserves her holiday just as much as my dad. I make sure my mum knows that I appreciate everything she does for me and everything she has done for me over the years. All the nights, she sat with me until I was asleep because I was so afraid of the UNSEEN and the darkness. She would always drop what she had planned to sit with me all those days when I was suffering from migraines. We would watch so many movies together. I make sure she knows that she is an excellent mum, and I love her and my dad more than anything. Then I give them both a cuddle and tell them to go and have fun.

I walk my mum and dad out of the house and give them another cuddle and a kiss. I tell them that I'll see them both later, and then I wave to them as they drive away. They promise they will call me once they land in Hawaii. I take a moment and continue looking down the road, and I can't help but think this feels different somehow. Has this place changed, or is it me who's different? I turn towards the house, and I stand there, finding myself frozen. I begin to get an all too familiar feeling, one I haven't felt for years.

I get an instant flashback to when I was a

child, and I stood in this very spot. I was staring up at THAT tree, and I was thinking about how THAT branch can't even reach my window....

Why am I getting this memory? I haven't thought about the UNSEEN for years, but I suddenly find it consuming my mind. I find myself once again trapped within this moment, staring up at THAT tree. All I can think about is how it hasn't changed one bit. It is identical to its former self, and all the branches are even in the same places. Maybe it's because it's winter, and that's the reason why it's developing THAT same old sinister look.

RING, RING,

RING, RING,

RING, RING!

I suddenly hear the phone ringing inside the house, but I remain standing there for a moment. I blink my eyes and look up to Talia's window, and I see something? What is that? I look away, and then I look back again because I'm sure I just saw a shadow of a person standing there looking out at me. But when I look back, there is nothing there. I begin to think that it's probably the bad memories coming back to haunt me and nothing more. I head inside to see who was trying to call us. As I walk over to the phone, I'm delighted to see Talia's name on the screen, so I call her back.

Talia explains on the phone that she's here if I need anything, and she also asked me if I'm going to be ok in the house alone? I feel like she asked me this because I've never actually been here alone before. I never realised that until now. It's strange how that's never crossed my mind because there had always been someone else here. I respond to her by explaining that we are not children anymore, and becoming a soldier has made me grow up a lot. All that childish nonsense is in the past, and I'll be just fine. I do my best to get her to stop worrying about me. But she does say one concerning thing to me though, that she doesn't like being alone in this house. Talia explains that she always makes sure she is never in a situation requiring her to be here alone.

As I place the phone down and look around, I feel an overwhelming sense of loneliness fall over me. There is such a loud silence flooding through this house. So I decide I need some sound and atmosphere going on in here. I put the television on and turn the volume up. To fill the empty void and block out that loud silence to cast away that feeling of loneliness. I walk into the kitchen and put the kettle on to make a cup of tea. Then I sit at the table to try and figure out what I'm going to do for the rest of the day. As I sit here waiting for the kettle to boil, my mind wanders. I think to myself that it was great to talk with Talia. I can't wait to see her in the week, it's a shame I can't go today, but I understand that she's very busy with her children.

The kettle clicks, so I make my cup of tea, then I walk through the hallway and into the living room. I walk past the cabinet, and I see some stuff in there out the corner of my eyes. I slowly walk back towards it and stop. Then I lean in to get a better look. I start with the top ledge, and I see some of my dad's trophies. Then I look down at the shelf below, and I see my mum's hedgehogs. I look down at the next one, and I almost spill my cup of tea. There in the middle of the shelf, sitting all alone, there it is staring straight back at me.

THAT SKULL!

Chapter Sixteen

You Can Hide, But You Can't Run

I stare at THAT skull intently, and I begin to wonder who it belonged to and whose face this is that stares back at me? Is its soul at peace? Has it travelled back to this house, entangled with its former head? Is it stuck in the dark depths of purgatory? Or worse, is it desperately trying to escape a prison of eternal entrapment inside my reality? The more I look at it, the more I try and imagine this person's facial features. Is it, in fact, one of the UNSEEN that used to torment me every night? After all, they didn't return once my dad moved THAT skull to my nans' house. Then again, I also moved into a room of my own and had help from the LIGHT to banish them for good.

I begin to feel nervous, as if I'm not ALONE. The more I look into those deep dark eye sockets, the more I get that all too familiar feeling like it's judging me. I turn around and look into the living room. I notice this house becomes enormous when it is empty. I've never realised before how much space we have here. I walk out into the hallway, place my cup of tea down and stare towards the front door, remembering all the good times I've had. But then, for some reason, all the bad memories come flooding into my mind and begin to block out the good ones. I suddenly think about the times I begged to stay up all those nights because I didn't want to go to bed and become trapped and tortured by the UNSEEN.

A shiver tingles down my spine at the exact moment I decide to go upstairs. I realise it's time because I need to go and face the music once and for all. Years have passed, and I'm not a child with an overactive imagination anymore. I need to face the fact that NOTHING IS HERE. I place my foot on the first stair, and I look straight up towards the first bend. I remember all the times Talia and I would play here. Now, all that happiness is becoming replaced. I'm getting this hollow, empty feeling deep down in the pit of my stomach.

As I stare up the stairs, I do my best to block out these feelings, but I almost imagine HIM…. BEEBLEDOSH stood there on the first bend because this is where Talia said they would always play. Goosebumps plague my whole body at the very thought of him standing there. I continue to stare, hoping that he won't be there if I do this for long enough. I'll walk right past, and all will be as it is. I take a deep breath, and with a quick flick of the switch, I turn the LIGHT ON. I'm so glad that there are two switches for the upstairs hallway LIGHT, one at the bottom and one at the top of the stairs. Now that there's a LIGHT on up there, I decide to go up. I think I will go slowly and take one step at a time.

I begin to walk up the stairs. As I place my right foot on the third step, it dawns on me that my mum and dad have changed them. They did tell me about this last year when they got renovations done to the house, but I must have forgotten. The stairs are now entirely different, and they seem a lot more modern. They have no back on each step, and the carpet wraps right around each stair. There is also now a space joining each step where the wood once was.

One thought and one thought alone crosses my mind. Something is going to reach through and grab my foot while I'm walking up. I need to run, not go slow. I rush up the stairs, I run the whole way to the top, and I stop by the bathroom. I turn around, looking back down the stairs. I try and shake off this overwhelming feeling that someone was following right behind me. Why on earth would anyone want stairs like that? They look great but make you feel very vulnerable to the unknown.

I turn around and look towards Talia's bedroom door and what used to be my old room. I know that it was a sad day when I moved out of this room because I still feel it deep in my heart. It tore my heart in half, but I know that everything happens for a reason, and you can't change the past. Strangely I am thankful to the UNSEEN for one thing though. Because of them, I learnt long ago to appreciate what I have and what could be and not worry about what has happened.

I walk closer to Talia's door and swing it open. I immediately sense that someone or something is in there. I walk into her room and slowly walk over to the area where my bed used to be. As I stand here, I realise that at some point, this room has become so eerie and ominous. What happened? This room was once so comfortable and filled with love and laughter during daylight hours. But now, it's entirely consumed by the UNSEEN. Or so it would seem, because no one has been in here for so long, to banish them or show them that this is OUR HOME, NOT THEIRS.

As I stand here, I look towards the wall and see a SKY BLUE colour where our old wallpaper used to be. Talia must have picked this paper before she got a house of her own. I walk right up to my old wall and run my hand over the SKY BLUE paper, and begin to reminisce about our old room. I feel my hand run over the line where the pieces of paper meet. I notice that the corner of the paper has raised slightly, so I slip my finger underneath and slowly pull a small part of the paper upwards. I immediately acknowledge that my mum will not be happy that I've torn the paper off the wall. I will make sure I fix it before she gets home, so no harm is done. The area where I have torn the paper away begins to reveal one of the cuddly bears. Seeing this cute bear has made so many memories come flooding back. I have had so many good times in here, and I notice a few tears suddenly start rolling down my face. I find myself unable to stop them.

Time passes so fast, and I'm so full of regret. I wish I spent more time back then thinking about my family. Rather than constantly worrying about the UNSEEN. Then a thought came into my head, and the tears immediately stop. I realise this is another thing that the UNSEEN has stolen from me. They consumed my life and left little room for the things that matter. I'm so glad my dad saved me and returned me to the LIGHT so that I could live, not just survive. Thanks to my dad and the LIGHT, I was finally able to have memories that mean something. Outweighing the memories of all those nights, I led there terrified, thinking that it would never end.

I abruptly shout out loud for all the UNSEEN to hear,

I WIN,

I ESCAPED YOU,

I BANISHED YOU, AND NOW I HAVE MY LIFE BACK.

YOU FAILED BECAUSE YOU DID NOT DESTROY ME, AND NEVER AGAIN WILL YOU OVERPOWER WHAT TRULY MATTERS.

I felt a wave of relief wash over me because I finally stood up to the UNSEEN. I knew it was time to face my fears and confront them. It's easier now because I've not seen them for so long, and the darkness no longer suffocates me. The fact that it's LIGHT outside has given me the courage to stand here and say these things. Would I do the same in the darkness? Probably not, but I honestly don't know.

My eyes start to move across the floor, towards the area where THAT thing used to sit every night, creeping across my bed to trap me where I lay. I felt a strange feeling in my stomach, like something is forcing me to look. I don't want these thoughts, but THAT thing is becoming entangled deep inside my mind AGAIN. No matter what I do, I can't get it out of my head. I stand here staring, unable to stop. Maybe subconsciously, I want it to become SEEN. Then I can prove to myself that I'm not crazy after all. I continue to stare, expecting it to show itself.

I am no longer in control of my eyes or mind, and I find myself still staring whilst I wait for THAT thing to show up. Then it dawns on me, the darkness is gone, the UNSEEN are all gone, but I'm still here in this room. Once again, stuck in a trance, staring out into the nothingness, waiting for the UNSEEN to show up.

NO, YOU WON'T DO THIS TO ME AGAIN.

I force my eyes to look up to the window because I know there hiding amongst the shadows. But I immediately become horrified. I see THAT long, bony, old, pointing finger, it's right there, right in front of me. It didn't bide its time or hide in the darkness. It's the UNSEEN, are they here?

I stand here questioning everything I thought I

knew. About the UNSEEN, and everything I thought I knew about reality. I firmly tell myself that none of this is happening, and it's all in my head. The LIGHT banished the UNSEEN, and there is no way they could be here. I take a deep breath and count to four,

One,

Two,

Three,

Four!

Then I take a step towards the window, followed by another and another. Until I find myself face to face with THAT Long pointing finger. I reach out my hand, hovering it over the bottom corner of the curtain, and I freeze. I begin breathing faster and faster whilst feeling completely numb. Then out of nowhere, I grab the corner of the curtain and rip it back to reveal.

NOTHING!

I move my head closer to the window so I can get a better look outside. All I can see is a far off shadow cast by THAT tree, which continues to stand outside our house after all these years. Somehow THAT branch is still a perfect imitation of an arm and continues to point towards our house. It still survives after all this time.

Staring at THAT branch makes me remember the picture Talia drew of BEEBLEDOSH. I decide to look for it in a far off hope that she has not taken it with her. I start looking through her stuff, but then I remember it was under her pillow. I then begin to approach her bed with caution just in case HE wants to show HIMSELF. The coast is clear, so I move her pillow to the side, and I become instantly amazed. I see a piece of old crumpled paper. I think to myself, can it be, is this it? After all these years of wondering, will I finally see Talia's perception of him? I pick up the piece of paper, turn it over and there HE is staring back at me....

It's, BEEBLEDOSH.

I take note of the fact that the temperature has dropped significantly in this room. This ominous feeling has become completely overwhelming. I know I need to leave, but before I do, I put the picture of **BEEBLEDOSH** in my pocket. I then put Talia's pillow back to how I found it. Then I run as fast as I can back down the stairs. I place the picture on the table and take a moment to take this all in. What is going on? I feel like the **UNSEEN** are here and want me to know it, but they refuse to show themselves this time. I can't see them, but I sense them. Despite being banished by the LIGHT, they will always find a way to come back and be **SEEN**. Just because I can't see something doesn't mean it's not there.

I slowly walk over to the stairs and look up towards the bend. Then I run, all the way to the top. I walk past the bathroom and Talia's room, only this time I don't look inside. But I pull the door towards me and close it, thinking to myself, if I can't see it, then I won't think about it. I continue down the hallway towards my room. As I arrive at my door, I begin to feel strange, hoping it's not another migraine attack. I thought about how I still suffer from these a lot. I had to get this thought out of my mind because sometimes, the very idea of getting one would bring one on. I stand right outside my door, but I find myself hesitating, I want to go in so badly to see my old things, but I can't make myself go in. I hover my hand above the door handle, wondering if it will still feel the same in there because this room was my freedom. I always felt free, safe and happy in this room.

I get a rush of courage from somewhere. I pull down the handle and push the door open with enough force that it swings to the wall and hits it, resulting in a small bang. I look into my room and realise it's the same as I left it. Nothing has changed, but one thing is missing, PIPPY. He's not in here because he's been with me. But as I look in here, the happy feeling that I once had every time I would see my room was absent. It's gone and has now become replaced with a sense of dread. It feels like a hollow, empty shell of what it used to be. Has it changed, or have I just been gone for too long?

I tell myself these eerie, ominous feelings are probably because Talia's picture of BEEBLEDOSH has finally become revealed to me. I think it's also because of THAT tree outside. It decided to cast its shadow in perfect timing with all the overwhelming feelings of being home. I take a seat, and I notice THAT music box sitting at the end of my bed in the same way it always has. I see that IT'S glaring at me with a look that could kill. I realise it's probably not been wound or played for years because it's something I just grew out of as I grew up. I began wondering why it's on the end of my bed. I was sure I put this away in the wardrobe years ago.

I lean across my bed and grab THAT music box. I hold it in my hands and look at it. It feels strange, almost like it has a soul or something. THAT box played nearly every night of my childhood, and I suddenly realised that I don't even know the entire song. I then remembered one of the nights my mum sang it to me while she sat with me until I fell asleep. It came flooding back to me that there is more than one verse and I never did ask or look up how the rest of the song went.

As I held it in my hand, it jingled THAT last note. I immediately drop IT, and as it lands on my bed, it jingled THAT note again. Hearing this note from THAT song sent shivers down my spine, and I felt my heart skip a beat. Those all too familiar feelings are back. They came flooding over me like

the ocean coming in over the sand on a beach. The
UNSEEN can't be here, they are nowhere in sight,
and the LIGHT is prominent. Still, this house
somehow makes me feel exactly how I did eleven
years ago, trapped, alone and isolated.

Automatically out of habit or some long lost
fear, I jump to my feet and look under my pillow to
see if my TORCH is still there. This time instead
of placing it back under my pillow, I put the
TORCH in the back pocket of my jeans. I don't
even know why I did this, but I do know that it's
making me feel a bit calmer. I glance over at
THAT music box once more to make sure it's in
the middle of the bed. I think to myself, actually, on
second thought, I'm going to make sure the winder
is to the end so there will be no possible way it can
play any more of THAT song. I pull on the winder
to make sure it's entirely unwound, and then I run
from my room to the bottom of the stairs without
stopping.

I still can't shake this feeling that someone is
following right behind me. Despite knowing I'm
here alone, I can't get rid of this unexplainable
tension that someone else is in this house. I guess
all this time, I've just been hiding from the

UNSEEN. Will I ever escape them? Am I just running away? I sit down at the table and slide Talia's picture of BEEBLEDOSH over, placing it right in front of me. I can't help but stare at it, noticing that he is pulling me in and I become entranced, staring deep into his eyes.

Chapter Seventeen

The Dark Truth Of The Old Reavil

Bridge

I don't even remember falling asleep last night, but I wake up to find myself still lying on the sofa. I drag myself to my feet and walk to the kitchen, where I put the kettle on. Through the sound of the boiling water, I thought I heard THAT music box. I walk over to the bottom of the stairs and look towards the top. I try and listen to see if it will play again, but nothing happens. I begin to think about THAT song that plays out of THAT box, trying to remember how the words to the second verse went. I make my cup of tea, sit down at the table and open my laptop to look up THAT song.

I type **KEEVIL BRIDGE** into the internet search bar and press return on my keyboard. It offers so many links to choose from, but they were recent facts about the bridge. Nothing was showing up about its past or a song of any kind. I decide to click on the images tab to see if anything different comes up. I choose page ten of the search, in a last desperate hope to find something. To my amazement, I notice the song. I see one image and one alone with the title, The old Keevil bridge. It's a photo of what I can only describe as a dark brown page from an ancient book. I never realised it would have so many verses, so I proceed and read them one by one to try and find out what THAT song represents.

As I look at THAT song written down in words, I notice that all the verses are similar. However, the words on the lines are slightly different. But they are repeated and sang in the same way, with the same tune. Now I understand why I sang the same verse repeatedly. It's because each one has the same beat.

The words tell the story of the old Keevil bridge. The first verse explains that the bridge will not stay up because something keeps destroying it, while the second verse shows what is happening. I begin to feel like **THAT** song is taking me on a journey. The words to **THAT** song allow me to understand its deeper meaning whilst showing me how important it is to repair the bridge. To find a way to make it finally stay up. But then the forces of nature fight back, and the curse of the old Keevil bridge begins to reveal itself.

The rest of **THAT** song goes on in the same way, the bridge is repaired but will not stay up. Despite being fixed each time, no matter what happens, it just won't stay up. I now see a verse where the tone suddenly changes because the people of Keevil become stuck, but the bridge finally stays up. Could the presence of people stop the curse of the old Keevil bridge and eventually make it capable of staying up. **THAT** song reveals the shocking fact that as soon as the people fall asleep, once again, the old Keevil bridge will not stay up.

The last verse of **THAT** song is almost identical to the first. But the final lines stand out. They are different instead of saying,

Trapping us inside, it says, Without them inside.

Is the last line different to confirm that the old Keevil bridge is cursed to never stay up? I feel like some of this song is missing, or it's a smaller version because it seems like there is more to this. I'm left wondering how does it stand there today? They must have somehow found a solution. I found myself getting caught up in the words of THAT song. I mean, of course, it's not accurate because the bridge is still stood there, at the very edge of Keevil.

Now that I think about it, I drove over the bridge to get home, even though there are other ways to enter and exit Keevil. But I do know that long ago, the old Keevil bridge was the only way of getting in and out of the village. I wonder, could THAT song have some fact to it? Did this bridge indeed have a history of continuously breaking in the past?

I can't help but receive an eerie message from THAT song, could the presence of the people stop the curse of the old Keevil bridge? Or are the people, or some other mortal soul, the very reason for the curse? I began to feel a little sad that I never knew the words to THAT song after hearing it play all those nights when I was a child. I used to sing the same part of the song, over and over in my head. I was completely oblivious that it has so many more words and a far more complex story going on behind the scenes. But what does all of this mean? Where did THAT song even come from, and more importantly, who wrote it?

I now have an unexplainable need to search for the person who wrote THAT song. I type my question into the search engine, but I don't have high hopes because it was hard enough to find THAT song in the first place. I see a lot of different information, but the problem is it's all recent. After a few hours of reading and clicking, I finally find two versions of events that could have inspired THAT song. I have continuously hit complete dead ends, but I have found out that the author of THAT song is unknown. None of this helps me put my overactive mind to rest because this shows that the origin is a total mystery.

I'm going to write both versions down to refer back to them. First, I move Talia's picture of BEEBLEDOSH up to the top left-hand side of the table, then I sit down, pick up my pen and begin.

The history that I could find on the old Keevil bridge

The first version I found was regarding an apparent attack on Keevil, back when it was known as 'Eivele' in 1666. A Viking named Erik led this attack and controlled the war. However, this version seems incorrect because no document exists recording this as fact. This theory has never been talked about again. The main problem with this theory is that it only accounts for one attack on the old Keevil bridge.

The second version I found was a dark truth hiding in a hidden message for all these years, desperately yearning for someone to hear it. Some people say that The old Keevil bridge has taken many lives. The only way it could stay up is if it always bears a human life within its walls. If that human were to die, the bridge would perish along with that mortal soul and come crashing down.

The first verse of THAT song is very common, even though the rest of THAT song is *almost impossible to find. But I have also found a child's game that I personally never knew about and never played. But apparently, it's popular all over the world. There seem to be many versions of THAT song, but the game is always the same in every culture. Two people make an arch and the rest run under and around them. Then when a specific word in the song is said, the two people suddenly bring their arms down and trap whoever is in the middle.*

I place my pen down.

I place my note next to me in the bottom left-hand corner of the table and stand up to take a step back. I think to myself that this is a serious mess. I feel like it's almost impossible to figure out the true origin of THAT song. The game these children are playing worldwide seems way too sinister to be a game, for a song, about a broken bridge. I begin feeling amazed at how much mystery there is around THAT song that plays out of THAT box. One thought does not sit right with me, Why is there so much mystery surrounding THAT song? Why is there no solid evidence? Everything I have found out is apparent and not factual. A place such as the old Keevil bridge, that's an icon of Keevil and a pillar in the advancement of civilisation, should have a documented account of its history. Was **THAT** song genuinely inspired by an attack on Keevil carried out by a Viking named Erik? Or worse, was it a product to expose a closely guarded secret of human sacrifice?

I close my laptop and decide to drive out to the old Keevil bridge. I don't know why this is bothering me so much. I feel like it's something I need to do. **THAT** music box has something to do with the **UNSEEN**, I just know it, I feel it in my soul, but I can't explain it.

Chapter Eighteen

One Man's Story

I drive to a small area and park in a space facing the old Keevil bridge. I sit here for a while, looking towards it, and I can't help but side with the version of events involving human sacrifice. Whilst I look at this bridge, I begin to visualise where they possibly trapped all their mortal souls. It's ironic how I've lived in this village all these years, and I have never really looked around at the very things that make it, Keevil.

The old Keevil bridge as it stands today is flat at the top, so vehicles have a passage in and out of the village. There are also two solid square ends like pillars built up high, and arches stand tall with pride at the entrance and exit. It seems like they have been put in position carefully to mark where the bridge connects the land on either side. On the underside of the bridge, a rounded arch shape sits parallel to the water. I can see how they say the people of Keevil were trapped inside. I can see how they would feel like there was no way out if this bridge perished. But why are some of the bricks a different colour? The ones nearest to the ground are a deep red and look like they don't belong there.

I step out of my car and head towards the bridge, I can see a signpost up ahead, so I walk in that direction to see what it says. As I approach it, I see a map of Keevil. But, there Is no factual information regarding the history of the bridge. I get flooded with disappointment and feel like it's just a dead-end and a wasted journey. I notice a bench on my left, and the weather is nice today, so I may as well take a seat and enjoy it for a while. It's better than being alone back at the house.

I look towards the bridge and take a deep breath. Then I let out a sigh of frustration. I realise that I don't even know what I'm looking for, but I can feel that something is here. Am I chasing an empty obsession? Am I trying to compensate for my lack of knowledge about the UNSEEN by trying to find a connection between THEM and this long lost urban legend? Or maybe there is a link, and there is something more to this?

I drop my face into my hands, and I try my hardest to block it all out, but I hear someone approaching. I didn't see anyone around here when I arrived, so I lift my head to check who it is. I see a tall man walking towards the bench. It strikes me immediately that he's dressed entirely in black. He is wearing a black suit with a black tie, and he also has a black fedora hat on his head, but I'm not getting a bad vibe from him. So I look towards him and watch to see what he's going to do.

He asks me if he may sit next to me. His voice does not sound how I had expected. He spoke so softly but deep at the same time. I feel like he is harmless, and I've always trusted my instinct when it comes to stuff like this. So I let him know that he's more than welcome to sit on the bench next to me. He left quite a big gap between us, which is nice to see because many people lack respect these days. It's nice to know there are still some out there who have respect for other people. We sit here in silence, and I feel like he just left a funeral or something, so I don't know what to say. I look back out to the bridge, then I drop my face into my hands once again to shut it all out, and I remain as I am. Then I suddenly hear the man speak.

He starts to explain to me that this bridge has a horrifying dark past. One that no one living is aware of, but today he's going to tell, ME. By revealing their story, he will finally fulfil his purpose because there will now be at least one living soul who knows this terrible truth. He warns me that nobody has ever spoken of this until this very day. I start to sense that he's looking right towards me. I hear him say one last thing before he begins. He says that it will be up to me what I do with this story once I know.

I hear him go on to say,

There was a village full of people long ago, and not one of them had ever left. There was no way for them to get across the massive body of water that lies at the edge of the village. They began planning to build a bridge to get across. They spent so much time trying to make it perfect, but it only stood tall with pride for the night. By morning, unfortunately, they all woke up to find their beloved bridge crumbled in the river.

The village people built the bridge again using better materials, but the same thing happened. The second bridge perished, but nothing would stop them. They were determined to fight fate and rebuild it, hoping they would get lucky by using even stronger materials on the third attempt. They were unsuccessful, and once more, they woke up to find their beloved bridge torn down and broken in the river. What was doing this? How could three bridges break in the same way? The bridge will not stay up, and they demand to know why. So the Elders of the village decide to hold a meeting in the church. Everyone who lives in Eivele, children included, were to attend, and if you didn't show up, the punishment was death.

The meeting commenced, and one of the Elders conducted a name call to check that everyone showed up. A man, his wife, and his two children were missing. The fact that this family was absent began causing a massive distraction. The meeting became fixated on where they were instead of focusing on the bridge. After confirming that this family is officially missing, they are given a punishment of death in their absence. Then the meeting immediately went back to discussing the bridge, but no conclusion was agreed.

Once again, they get better materials and begin to rebuild their bridge. However, as the final bricks are about to be placed, the construction abruptly pauses because the Elders have a plan. Everyone in the Village has been looking for the man and his family. The leading elder orders that anyone who finds him or his family must immediately turn him in. The Elders are excited to hear that a member of Eivele has finally tracked down the man and his family.

An old lady, one of the most senior members of Eivele, saw the man through his window. She knew every person in the village because she was born and lived here her whole life. She could have turned away and left the man alone. She didn't need to say anything to the Elders. She could have minded her own business, but this lady went as fast as she could to report him. No one knows her reason for handing him over. Some say the Elders took peoples children and will only return them if they make a trade. They must hand over the man and his family to take the place of the children of Keevil.

The leader and his Elders went straight to his home and broke through the door for the fourth time. He had not been there the last three times they broke in. This time, unexpectedly, they find him, and they drag him across the village, along with his two children. The Elders lock them up in the town hall until the next day. Once morning arrives, the Elders gather the whole village and instruct them to go and wait in front of the old Keevil bridge. The people receive orders to remain there until further notice.

Then at dusk, the Elders once again drag the man and his two children across the village. The Elders carry the two children over to the bridge. At the same time, the man gets ordered to stand in this exact spot where we are sitting right now. Despite hearing the screams of his children, the leader of the Elders tells him that he is not allowed to move, and he is to continue looking at the bridge no matter what.

Then the Elders surround the man and force him to follow their orders, to remain watching the bridge at all times. What he saw next **NEVER** left his mind. The Elders move one of his children into the left pillar of the bridge, despite the child kicking and screaming. They finish building the bricks to the top, locking his child in with no air, no windows, no LIGHT and no way out.

The Elders disappear out of sight. Then suddenly, out of nowhere, they reveal themselves at the pillar on the other side of the bridge. They do the same to his other child. They build the bricks up, leaving both of his children locked in tombs to be buried alive. There was no escape and no way out. The leader of the Elders then stands next to the man. To instruct him to stay there all night and watch his children. But most important of all, he is to make sure the bridge stays UP.

The man begs and pleads with the leader of the Elders, but it quickly becomes apparent that his children will never be free. They inform the man that he can go home when the sun rises as long as their bridge still stands. The man stands there for eight days and eight nights. He does not alter, he does not move, and he NEVER once takes his eyes off his children. The Elders check on him whilst they come to check on their beloved bridge. They offer the man food and water, but he always refuses! He only ever responds saying, please let my children out, take me instead, and if my children go without, then I go without, and the man remains there with his children. He continues to stand there staring, watching and waiting for his children until that ninth morning when he perished.

As the man's mortal soul parted with his vessel, their beloved bridge began to crumble once more. The Elders came rushing to the bridge and went straight to the tombs they created to find the children dead. The Elders put two and two together and made ten. The leader then announces that the bridge must have a guard until they fall asleep. The Elders shout at the top of their voices. **YOU WILL VOLUNTEER, OR WE WILL CHOOSE FOR YOU. NO MATTER THE COST, THE OLD KEEVIL BRIDGE MUST STAY UP.**

I remain sat with my face in my hands, and I can't help but feel for that man in the story. He endured such suffering and pain, but he showed complete FORTITUDE to stand by his children and not run back to the village to get revenge. He knew what truly mattered, and that is his children because no amount of anger or vengeance would bring them back. The leader of the Elders and his followers of this village did a terrible thing in this story. Some people crave power, they want it, and they need it, but at what cost.

I must know more. I decide to lift my head and ask the mysterious man sat next to me if this story is real? Did these events take place? Why did the man and his family not attend that meeting? I need to know more about this story. But as soon as I lift my head, the man is gone. None of this makes sense, and I didn't even hear him get up or walk away. Who is this man that has just been talking to me? Where did he come from, and where did he go? I remain sat here looking towards the bridge. Only this time, all I can picture is the man stood where I sit, and the children being forced into those pillars, forced into their tombs, never to be SEEN again.

I slowly walk back to my car, but just before I pull away to head home, I look ahead into the distance. I look at the bridge one last time, and I get a sudden wave of emptiness, and a terrible thought washes over me. The UNSEEN, it just dawned on me that in the story, the man and the two children were from centuries ago and seemed very familiar to the ones I would SEE in the darkness. Is this too close for comfort that the UNSEEN includes two children who had looks of dread and torture on their faces? Is it simply coincidental that there was a tall man who would stand at the end of my bed watching them? But then the UNSEEN evolved, and the man now stands between them. Is he controlling them or simply protecting them?

Have these children visited me? They died and were the price to pay for the sake of a power-hungry man's selfish sacrifice for a bridge. Do they want to tell their story? Do they want to be remembered? Or are they the UNSEEN seeking revenge from beyond the grave? Are they trying to make others feel trapped in the same way that they once were? Or maybe they are just trapped in purgatory, desperately trying to escape. Or worse, could they be sinister and trying to inflict their pain onto others? This mysterious man's story was too close for comfort, I can feel my body trembling, and the last thing I want to do is go home where THAT music box is waiting.

Chapter Nineteen

The Neurologist

Whilst I drive home, I can't help but think about THAT song that plays out of THAT music box. The lyrics now seem so sinister after hearing that story. When I think of the words to THAT song, I can't help but find myself thinking it's purely about sacrifice because all the innocence has faded away. It's a well-hidden memory disguised in a so-called innocent song, created by someone unknown with one purpose and one alone, to expose a long lost, horrendous crime.

The darkness is closing in fast. I don't particularly enjoy driving at night, so it's a good job that I'm almost home. As I drive through the village, I notice those big legendary gates. So I pull over to get a better look. Whilst I walk up to the gates, I run my hand over the metalwork because I still can't believe how much detail they have included. They are fantastic, and to this day, I've never seen anything like them. I know that I could stare at them for hours, but instead, I take a picture. Once I get a good shot, I look through the gaps between the metal, but I can only see a long bending path and nothing more. The fog is drifting in thick tonight, and I can barely see anything, making it almost pointless to continue trying. I tell myself once again that one day I will find out what is hiding beyond these gates.

....

I arrive at home, and as I walk through the door, I go straight over to the table to print out the picture of the gates. I place the photo on the left-hand side of the table. It now sits in between the image of **BEEBLEDOSH** and my notes about the bridge. I then write down a brief description of the mysterious man who I met today. I include every detail from his epic but tragic story. I suddenly start to feel strange, I can see my arm, but I can't sense it. It appears to be there, but it seems like it's not mine, but I know this feeling all too well. So I place the notes about the man at the bridge next to Talia's drawing of **BEEBLEDOSH**. Then I immediately go and take a seat on the sofa. There it is, I see it, that circular, pixilated blind spot, its beginning, and I know the migraine attack is imminent.

Whilst I'm still able to, I grab PIPPY and lay down on the sofa. I try and fall asleep before the rest of the symptoms start. I learnt long ago that the only way to get through these attacks is to sleep as soon as possible. If the symptoms get too far, I will become extremely sick and unable to sleep it off. I must get to sleep because when these attacks occur, they wipe me out, and I become unable to function.

I decide that I'll call the doctors surgery tomorrow morning to make an appointment because I've lived with this my whole life and now I need answers. I've seen so many doctors and neurologists in the past and got no real solution. None of it helps because they always come up empty, leaving me with no explanation other than to suffer through it. I've even had my brain checked thoroughly to make sure everything is as it should be. I've had MRI and CT scans, but the results always say no significant problems. Surely they can do something with all the technology that has become available and all this advanced research.

....

I've achieved a lot already this morning, which is good because I'm usually still a little drained after a migraine attack. But I have my appointment with the neurologist today, so I forced myself to get things done. I got referred to the hospital straight away because they are already aware of my problem. I must be there promptly at noon, but until then, I plan to relax for once. So I turn the television on and start flicking through the channels to find something to watch while I wait.

It's incredible how fast time flies when you're watching television. It's already almost noon, so I run out to my car and set off to the hospital. I arrive just in time, and I'm only waiting for five minutes before Dr Wyatt calls me into his office. He begins by asking me to explain all the symptoms that I experience. I start describing my whole journey from beginning to end.

I explain that I've suffered from these weird symptoms ever since I was a child. I also let him know how I find something quite strange. I've never spoken to anyone else who's ever experienced the same thing. I don't think anyone will ever fully understand what I'm going through. Many doctors I've seen in the past have told me that they cannot comprehend how hard this must be for me. I explain each symptom to him in great detail and the stages that they occur, trying to get him to see how this affects my life. Then I explain the migraine and how it only begins once the symptoms have stopped. I then start to vomit, and the only way it can end is by going to sleep.

I also explain to him that I have no idea what the trigger is. I've done food diaries, stress diaries, and even recently, I've completed sleep diaries. I'm completely at a dead end with this. A long time ago, I accepted that this has taken over my life because they happen randomly. There is no pattern, and whatever I'm doing at the time of an attack or any plans I may have had must be cancelled because once the symptoms set in, that's it. I become unable to carry on, and the only thing I can do is sleep.

Dr Wyatt pauses and looks at me for a moment. I look back at him, noticing his grey hair as he moves his fringe out of his eyes and pushes it to the side of his wrinkled face. Dr Wyatt looks a lot older than me, and this fills me with the hope that he's got a lot of experience to offer. He slowly removes his glasses and sets them down in front of him and says, you can call me Sebastian. Dr Wyatt stands up, walks around the desk, pulls up a chair, and sits next to me. I hear him say that while he can't offer me a cure, he can shed some LIGHT on what is happening to me.

He asks me to pay close attention to what he has to say because we have a lot in common. Dr Wyatt informs me that he also suffers from the problems that I have endured my whole life. He explains that the horrifying symptoms that I've been experiencing right before the onset of the migraine are medically known as an aura. He states that only fifteen to twenty per cent of people experience this, hence why I have never met another who also suffers from them until now.

He goes on to say.

Aura is caused by, Oligemia, which is where the blood flow decreases. It begins at the back of the brain and then moves forward towards the front. It causes electrical and chemical waves to spread across the brain. Depending on which part of the brain receives the waves will determine which symptoms occur.

Dr Wyatt begins to explain that there are many different types of aura. But, some of the symptoms I've mentioned come under a few specific ones, cognitive, aphasia receptive, and expressive aphasia, which causes the inability to talk or understand what people are saying. Dr Wyatt then informs me, the numbness that I feel in my hands and fingers, which travels up my arm and stops at my elbow, is a symptom of Hemiplegic migraine. He also tells me that Hemiplegic migraine typically only affects a few people who suffer from migraines with aura. This numbness then jumps to the ipsilateral side of my mouth, and as I described, the tingling down the side of my tongue begins. Dr Wyatt confirms that the symptoms I'm suffering from are, in fact, a sensory aura. It truly is the scariest thing ever to experience.

Dr Wyatt informs me that the disconnect I feel

with my arm has recently become known as the false perception syndrome. This disconnect is unlike any other symptom of aura because I lose the ability to perceive things correctly. This false perception syndrome is where the eyes can see something, but there's a problem with what I see compared with what I feel. This disconnect in the brain, called perceptual displacement, makes things seem bigger or smaller than reality. He explains that this is what I'm experiencing when I feel this disconnect with my arm. Creating the horrifying effect that it's no longer connected to me even though I can see it.

Some people refer to migraine with aura as being a guest at a strange but scary event taking place in the dark depths of hell. Dr Wyatt says this is because people like us, who will suffer from aura for the rest of our lives, are known as the damned. Were known in this way because we experience these things and have no control over them whatsoever. They can happen at any time, day or night. Once the aura passes, it leaves us with not only an excruciating headache but we also get dragged into a seriously frightening situation with no way out.

He summarises our conversation by explaining that there could be several triggers and not just one culprit. He gives me a couple of examples to watch out for in the future, but I'm already aware of some of them. I know to watch out for Stress, LIGHTS, different foods, medications and too much or not enough sleep. But I did not realise that worrying about getting an attack could end up causing one. I tell Dr Wyatt that I will watch out for this one in the future.

I thank Dr Wyatt, I mean Sebastian, for his help and all the information he's given me. At least now I have a medical explanation and a name for what happens to me. Maybe being more aware of what's going on inside my head might make it a bit less overwhelming next time I get a migraine with aura. It felt different meeting someone who knew what I was talking about and who also suffers from this same problem. His personal experience and point of view allowed me to be understood finally.

As I leave the hospital to head home, I realise that I'm in a fantastic mood because I feel like some of the weight on my shoulders has gone. Now that I understand more about migraines with aura, I feel like I can put this problem in the back of my mind for a while. I will make sure that I save the knowledge Dr Wyatt has shared with me for the next time one occurs.

As I look through my windscreen, I see a big sign outside the old Keevil church. It says there will be a medium guest speaker for one night only. It also says in big letters, **EVERYONE IS WELCOME**. I begin thinking that I've never met a medium before, let alone ever spoken to one. Maybe they will know something about the UNSEEN, and I could get some answers. I decide there's no harm in going. I think it might be interesting, the sign says it's tomorrow evening, I will make sure I come back, but I'll head home for now.

Chapter Twenty

A Broken Aura

I call Talia on the phone to see if she wants to come with me this evening to see the medium speak, but she can't get a babysitter at such short notice. I decide that I'm still going to attend because I've never been afraid to go somewhere alone. Besides, it's taking place at the church, so what could go wrong?

I spend some time cleaning the house because I've been sleeping on the sofa. I don't know why I've been doing this, but I feel like I can't go upstairs once it's past nine o'clock at night. I don't understand why I think this way, but I can't make myself go up there no matter how hard I try. I even say to myself out loud, get a grip. How can you be afraid of a couple of rooms, you're an adult now, and the **UNSEEN** have not been **SEEN** for over eleven years. Nothing seems to work, and I remain unable to convince myself to go up there to sleep. As a result, I always fall asleep on the sofa.

I walk past the glass cabinet where **THAT** skull lives, and I can't help but look inside to ensure it's still there. I get a different vibe from it this time. I can't explain why, but I find myself thinking back to the mysterious man's story I recently heard at the old Keevil bridge. I can't help but wonder who did **THAT** skull belong to and what happened to them? I wonder if I would be able to find out whose skull this once was if I take it to a science lab somewhere and they test it.

I walk to the table, and Talia's picture of **BEEBLEDOSH** catches my eye. Maybe I'm losing it, but I'm sure **BEEBLEDOSH** has moved because his arms were down by his side before, and now one of them is sticking out. Could I have seen it wrong, or am I just going crazy? I think it will do me some good to be around some actual people this evening.

I decide to get ready for church, so I go upstairs to take a shower.

Taking a shower was a good idea because it's helping me feel more positive about going alone to the event this evening. This shower is so refreshing and it has helped me wake up. I turn the water off and step out, whilst grabbing my towel,

The old Keevil bridge will not stay up,
Will not stay up,
Will just not stay up,
The old Keevil bridge will not stay up,
Trapping us inside....

I hear THAT song coming out of THAT box. I mutter, NO, NO, NO, under my breath as I pull my dressing gown over me. I immediately push the bathroom door open, and I run down the hall and straight into my room. I go right over to THAT music box and....

NOTHING, THAT music box is silent.

I push the winder to make sure it's still unwound and won't move any further. But it's entirely to the end. What is going on? I swear I heard THAT song, and I know I'm not going this crazy. There's just no way. I know what I heard.

I walk back to the bathroom to finish getting ready for church. I play some music on my phone this time to ensure I won't hear anything coming from outside of this room. Just in case THAT music box decides to play THAT song AGAIN. The fact that it's not even dark makes my mind focus on this more than it probably should. Are the UNSEEN becoming more powerful? Will they start to be SEEN in the DAYTIME? Are they this desperate to come for me, that they must find a way to manifest themselves, despite being exposed to the LIGHT?

I've become seriously spooked in this house, and I don't want to be here alone for a second longer. So I lock the house and head towards my car to go and get some food before I go to church.

. . . .

Finally, the time has come. So I finish my food and head over to the church. I can't explain why, but I have become oddly excited. I walk along the road towards the church of the Holy Spirit, and I find myself drawn towards the gravestones in the churchyard. I can't help but notice them and immediately wonder if the children and the man from the old Keevil bridge are resting here. I think to myself that maybe the church has some old documents I can look through. It's a long shot, but I might be able to find something. I'm also hopeful that if I can see their graves, I can prove the mysterious man's story is factual.

I'm surprised how many people from the village and further afield have shown up. Every seat has someone sitting in it. Luckily I arrived a little early to make sure I could sit down. I would not like to stand up for three hours. As I sit here watching, I try my best to take this all in. I see many people taking small pieces of paper up to the front of the church. They place them into a box made of oak sitting on the alter. I wonder why they are doing that and what's on the paper. Should I be taking one up? I hope I'm not making a disrespectful mistake because I have no idea what they are doing. I feel like I'm suddenly hit in the face with reality because I'm not prepared for this at all, and it suddenly dawns on me that I have no idea what to expect.

Everyone finally takes their seats, and the service begins. First, we hear a prayer about how our eyes limit what we can see, but that does not mean it's all there is because the human soul continues after death. Then we sing a hymn about immortality and how everyone begins their journey pure. However, the life people choose to lead and their choices will dictate and decide the eternal judgment upon their immortal soul, which survives the body after death.

The hymn finishes, and a basket makes its way around the church for people to give donations. I put fifty pounds into the basket to show my appreciation for allowing me to come into their church. Everyone is making me feel very welcome despite having never attended one of these events before. The basket arrives at the front, which means that a guest speaker will talk to us about the afterlife any minute now. I'm completely shocked to see one of my old school teachers walk in and stand before us at the front of the church. It was Mr Maximus Marah, and he immediately began to read a passage he wrote regarding life after death. I had no idea he attended these kinds of events.

As I sit here listening to him talk about life

after death, all I can think about is the UNSEEN and BEEBLEDOSH. Are they just the immortal souls of people who once walked this earth? Are they life after death? Were they good people, or were they, bad people? If someone is a terrible person in life, is their soul condemned to remain evil in the afterlife? If an immortal soul lives on, then where is the man who showed immense FORTITUDE from that story I heard at the bridge. He suffered terribly, and no one should ever have to go through the pain and torture he endured. He did not deserve that punishment. **NO ONE DESERVES THAT**.

I'm finding myself unable to stop my thoughts. I have no idea why but my mind has become plagued with thoughts of that Elder. He does not deserve to be an immortal soul because he committed the ultimate crime. He took innocent lives. So where is he? How was his life taken? Did he suffer, or does the universe have a bigger plan for him? Maybe being immortal is a curse, not a gift, and perhaps if someone avoids facing their crimes in life, they suffer after death.

I became so lost in my thoughts that I almost overlooked Mr Marah finishing his speech and the medium coming out to take over. The medium introduces himself as Zavier and describes his background, including what he's achieved so far in his career. He then explains what led him down this path and inspired him to become a medium. Zavier then began his reading, and to my surprise, I'm finding his speech fascinating. He's speaking about what happens when we die and where he believes we go. He completes his presentation by talking about those who are stuck in purgatory. Of course, I am aware that this is his opinion, but what he's saying is very interesting.

Now that his speech is complete, I can't help but wonder what happens next. I hear everyone begin to talk and whisper amongst themselves. I remain sat here quietly, waiting for the next part of the evening to begin. Then all of a sudden, I hear Zavier speak out through a hidden speaker. He's no longer stood at the front of the church, but I can hear him loud and clear.

I hear him say....

Is there anyone here with us?

If you are here, show yourselves?

Come and talk to us let us be your energy,

Let us help you to pass on.

Is anyone there?

Then I hear some ominous music begin to play, and it sounds like it's coming from the organ. This suspense is an excellent thing to experience. I'm glad I took this opportunity to be a part of it. I've never experienced anything like this before. The music becomes more intense, and everyone in this room is silent, facing forward and looking towards the alter. I find it interesting that they all seem like they won't dare move. I know why they feel this way because I'm experiencing the same thing as I sit here frozen in awe at what is happening around me. We all remain seated, waiting for something to happen.

The LIGHTS go OUT….

The organ fell silent,

We all remain sat here in complete silence and total darkness. I almost freak out, but then I realise I'm not alone this time. There are so many other people sitting with me, and there is no way the UNSEEN would show up now.

We wait and wait!

There is so much tension, no one is moving, and no one speaks a word. If I didn't know any better id have thought that I was alone in this room. But while it feels that way, I know that I'm in a room full of people, even though it seems like they've all vanished.

Simultaneously,

The LIGHT beams ON, and I hear Zavier shout out in a loud booming voice,

WELCOME....

I suddenly see Zavier appear out of nowhere and stand in front of the altar. He looks different somehow, but I can't quite put my finger on it. He's smiling and enjoying himself, which is good because he's creating such a great vibe. Zavier begins to point people out from the audience and tells them things about themselves that no one could know. It's impressive, and everyone is shocked at the stuff he's producing. It does seem like this man knows what he's doing. But, Is this real? Is it possible that Zavier can talk to the dead and learn things about these people in such a short space of time?

I look towards Zavier and watch as he approaches my row. I can't help but think about what he's going to say to me? He begins to amaze each person sat in my row with his talent one by one. But then he looks towards me....

He gasps with fear....

His face changes instantly, his big smile turns into an empty blank stare, and he pauses. He does not move at all, and it seems like he's holding his breath. I feel like he's looking right through me. I'm giving him eye contact, but his eyes are not meeting up with mine. It's almost as though it's all happening in slow motion, but the blank stare on his face has begun forming into a look of pure dread. I notice a tear rolling out of his left eye, and it's sliding down his face.

What is he seeing?

Zavier abruptly breaks the trance he appears to be stuck in. He wipes his face and turns away from us. Then just seconds later, he turns around with a big cheerful smile back on his face. He does not speak to me like he did the others. He just continues to the next person whilst making sure to avoid me. What is going on? Why did he not speak to me, is there something wrong with me? Has he seen the UNSEEN? Would they follow me here, to a church?

Zavier finishes speaking to the people in the final row. He then walks to the front and stands at the altar. He turns to face everyone as he picks up the solid oak box that now contains everyone's mysterious pieces of paper.

He begins to speak out in a loud and confidant voice.

I hear him say....

Now the time has come for us to channel the power of the holy spirit. The spirit of this very church, to heal our wounded in both body and mind.

I invite you to close your eyes, bow your heads and think positive thoughts to provide a full recovery to all of our family and friends.

Russel Nyx

John Ozian

Achlys Armaros

Diana Baiza

Carol Miyeon

David Aadhila

Xander Mika

Shannon Conlan

James Amarantha

Rue Than

William Ludari

Annie Aeneas

The Amista Family

The church is now silent to allow everyone to send their thoughts and channel their energy to help heal these people. I have become very invested in this because helping someone heal is a fantastic thing to be involved in and support.

Zavier then began to read out a poem in memory of loved ones who have passed, to let them know that they will always live on and that we're thinking of them.

I feel a wave of sorrow sweep over me because it saddens me to hear him say....

That's all from me and to conclude the evening, I want to say a personal thank you to everyone for attending, and I hope to see you all again soon.

I remain seated because I decide that I will try and speak to him once everyone has gone. I must know why he froze in front of me, and I need to know what exactly it was that he saw?

It didn't take long for everyone to leave, so I walk up to the altar where Zavier stands completing some paperwork. I ask him if he wouldn't mind speaking with me for a moment. I explain to him that I'm not looking for anything and that I just have a question I would like to ask. He responds to me with that same blank look on his face, and he doesn't say anything. I lean in towards him to catch his attention. He steps back and just stares at me. This time to my surprise, I hear him begin to speak....

I should not be speaking to you.

YOUR MARKED!

They stand behind you!

They rarely leave you!

Protector or haunter, I do not know?

Your aura and soul are not as they should be.

They seem broken.

This damage extends beyond any simple repair.

A BROKEN AURA

How has this come to be?

You have many colours when most people only have one.

How is this possible?

Let me try and open your eyes....

Part of your aura is pink. From this, I know you follow your heart, you are kind, caring, and you are open, but at the same time, you understand that there are boundaries. I also see that part of your aura is blue. Meaning you have a powerful mind, but you are not yet using it to its full potential. I see so much purple mixed between the colours. Telling me, you have strong instincts and sensitivity along with great mental depths. But I must make you aware that a purple aura is known to hold the power of the third eye. I see you have psychic, empathic and intuitive abilities. These purple areas of your aura could be the very reason they have chosen you and the same reason they have **MARKED** you.

But your aura is also full of white, and you

have much more white than any other colour. I must tell you, this is unusual and it's extremely rare. I've never seen or met anyone in my life who has a white aura until **YOU**. They say that there has only ever been one other person known to have had a white aura. No one living knows their name, only that they were also from this village and one of the earliest settlers. Having white in your aura means that you have a connection with something much bigger than yourself. I also see one area of your aura that is pure black. The absence of colour shows me that you are very worn down, exhausted, and fatigued. You must level your energy if you ever want to be free. But I must ask....

Have you ever seen or felt anything strange in your life?

The colour of your aura is not as it should be, there should not be this many colours, and as I said before, your aura seems broken. You have a gap where there should not be one. This hole is terrible because you're providing them with a way in, without any way to stop them. You're sending out a frequency equivalent to you sending a permanent invitation to any entities or lost souls that are out there. Then they use that to drain your energy and use it for themselves, for good or bad.

You are letting out a rare frequency with no knowledge of how to control it!

You are unknowingly INVITING them in!

I can see you suffer greatly, spiritually and physically. I see you suffer from horrifying symptoms before a wave of pain comes pounding on your head. But somehow, you broke your aura at some point during your life, and it's out of my reach to tell you how to fix it. I don't know what's happened to you, but I feel you are a haunted soul and not at peace.

Being blessed with this gift is a great thing, but in turn, it is also a deep burning curse.

I FEAR for YOU!

Chapter Twenty One

What Lies Beyond Those Gates?

I decided to look at today differently because I was left terrified last night after the church event. How did Zavier do what he did? It was insane, the stuff he was saying, and although he was not specific, he described my migraine with aura. But how could he possibly know I suffer with them. It's very odd because I didn't tell him about that, so he must be psychic to some extent.

I also find it very strange how I've discovered, that I have and suffer from an aura from two different people with knowledge in various fields. The neurologist tells me the symptoms I suffer with are known as a medical aura. Then Zavier says my soul has an aura full of different colours, and it's letting out rare frequencies. I decided to look this up last night. I needed answers. How can these two situations have the same name but be different? Maybe they are the same or possibly connected somehow. Do I suffer from the medical aura because I have a broken aura surrounding my soul? Is this the real reason why there is no medical cure? I did find out that they are both known as auras, just of different types. If he knew the stuff about my migraines, then maybe everything else he said is true as well. Have I been unintentionally inviting the UNSEEN in all this time?

All I know is I'm going to have a day where I don't think about any of this, so I will count to four and then clear it all out of my mind and go out for the day and do something productive. Here goes....

One,

Two,

Three,

Four!

RING, RING,

RING, RING,

RING, RING,

I hear the phone ringing, but all I can think is, of course, it would choose now to ring at the worst possible time, but it's just how my life seems to go. I walk over to answer just in case it's my mum and dad or Talia. To my surprise, it's none of them, but it is the neurologist, Dr Sebastian Wyatt. I ask him if everything is ok, but he immediately explains to me that he's managed to get me an appointment to see a specialist at,

The Immortal Institute of Neuropsychology.

I respond to him, saying thank you, and I let him know that this sounds very impressive. I then ask him, what exactly is it that they do there? He explains to me that they study many different fields. But, they invite me to attend their institute to participate in a study of the brain to investigate my brain waves and frequencies. He also lets me know that he feels this will help me understand what goes on inside my head when I have an aura attack. Plus, he believes I could be an asset to their studies because they will find my brain activity extremely interesting.

He then gives me the postcode, but I immediately respond because the postcode he gives me is only one letter different from my house. But he assures me that it's correct and that I should arrive ten minutes early for my scheduled appointment at 1600, four o'clock this afternoon.

As soon as I finish talking to Dr Wyatt, I run to find my mobile phone to enter the postcode into the satellite navigation system. I need to check that this is correct and find out where this place is. I've never seen any institute anywhere in Keevil. I grab my phone from the arm of the sofa and input the postcode. It shows that it's just down the road. I still can't comprehend how there is an institute right here. So I grab my keys, lock the house and walk down the road following the map. I must see this for myself....

As I'm walking along the road, I think to myself, I'm getting closer and closer to those big mysterious gates, but I don't see any institute. Then just as I arrive at the gates, I turn and look down that bending path that I so desperately want to walk down, and my map stops moving. According to the map, I'm at the postcode Dr Wyatt provided me, and I'm standing precisely in the correct place. It's showing me that this is the location.

I become instantly speechless!

Could it be? After all these years, I'm finally going to see what lies beyond these gates? Or has Dr Wyatt made a mistake, and this postcode is, in fact, very wrong? Am I going to find myself disappointed at four o clock? Is today the day that I finally get an answer to something that has plagued my mind for so long? I honestly would have never guessed that it's an institute that lies, hiding beyond these gates. Not only will I get to step beyond this point, but the Dr's and scientists who work and study there may be able to help me.

I look at my phone to check the time, but it's only noon, so I guess I will head home to wait. But I'm so excited, and I feel like a child at Christmas because I can't get over the fact that I might finally get an answer to this mystery that's been a part of my life for so long. Then I suddenly thought about how I can't wait to tell my dad he's always wondering just as much as me, what's down that long winding road?

I approach the house, but I see something strange in the window as I look towards it. I stop still in my tracks to take a better look, but all I see is a face staring back at me. It's glowing in a white, golden sort of colour. I also notice that its hand is pointing directly at me, and it's the same colour as the face. I immediately panic because it looks like someone's in the house, but the more I stare at it, the more it seems less human. It moves its head a bit, but I find myself just standing here, thinking, what is this? Do I shout for a neighbour or call the police? Is someone in the house? Whilst I'm stuck in my thoughts, I see it fade away before my very eyes. Have I accidentally just **SEEN** the **UNSEEN**? Have they now conquered the LIGHT?

I decide I need to go and make sure the house is empty. After all, the reason I'm here is to keep our home safe. I walk towards the front door, and I notice the window's clear. I slowly push my key into the lock and turn it, trying my hardest not to make a noise. The locking mechanism clicks, and a noise I usually don't even notice echoed louder than thunder. I push the door away from me, and as it creeks open, it reveals an empty hallway. I proceed to walk towards the kitchen, making sure the coast is clear. I then go into the living room, and that room is empty as well. The house is making me feel intimidated. I've never felt this frightened in the middle of the day, but I know I saw something in the window.

I find nothing in any of the rooms on the ground floor. Now I must gather the courage to walk up those long bending stairs. As I approach the first stair, I hear a bang come from somewhere above me. What was that? Is someone upstairs? I lift my foot into the air and freeze. I begin to second guess whether or not I should go up. What if someone is up there? I tell myself that I found the door locked, I had to unlock it myself, and there is no sign of forced entry. I remind myself that I'm a soldier. I must get a grip and check the rest of the rooms. I immediately switch from frozen to fast, and I run up the stairs as fast as I can. I jump onto the landing, thinking I could catch them by surprise, but there is no one here but me.

I push open the bathroom door, and I don't

see anyone. It's empty, so I walk over to the shower curtain. Before I pull it back, I begin to feel floods of goosebumps spreading all over me. I close my eyes, count to four....

One,

Two,

Three,

Four!

I pull back the shower curtain in one swift movement revealing, nothing but an empty bathtub. But then, just as I turn around to leave, the mirror catches my eye. I stare hard into the mirror. I don't know how or why, but as I look deep into my reflection, I see my image overlap with a younger version of myself. It merges into one as though the years went in a super-fast forward motion from who I was to who I am. I stare harder, remembering all the good times I've had in this house and how lucky Talia and I are to have such great parents.

I begin to remember the mysterious man from the bridge. Who was this man who told me that story? I also want to know who the man in the story was? I suddenly felt so empty inside, thinking of him and what he must have gone through. I can't even comprehend such pain and sorrow. I must tell his story to others, because he deserves to have people remember him and what he went through. I know that man at the bridge told me all this for a reason, and I must do something. THAT Elder who made THAT decision MUST PAY.

What is this? How can I see so much within a simple mirror? Simultaneously with this thought, I see a black shadow standing behind me. It appears and then immediately disappears, but it was far too quick to figure out what it was or know for sure if I saw it or not. Could this have been my imagination playing tricks on me because I saw something in the mirror? Or worse, is this something else? Is this the UNSEEN?

I proceed to Talia's room. As I walk in and stand here, in this quiet, empty house, my heart begins to feel sad because I feel robbed of my childhood to a degree. I spent too long laid awake at night in this room out of fear. I'm just thankful I got to spend time with my dad and Talia whilst we enjoyed PIPPY at the door, and all those nights, my mum stayed with me so I could finally get some sleep. I'm sad because this was supposed to be our home, but the UNSEEN tried to claim it for themselves. It's a pitiful shame they never stopped to ask us if there was enough room here for all of us? All they had to do was ask.

It began to rain outside. All I can hear is a powerful pounding on the window from the water hitting the glass. So I slowly walk over and remain standing here, just watching the dark sky and the water pouring down. I begin to think of the good times I've had here with my family, in OUR house. I suddenly become drawn to look down at THAT tree, the very thing that feeds my fear. I can't help but notice how it stands out there in the rain under the dark clouds all alone. I almost feel sadness towards it. It stands there looking completely powerless. It's almost as if it's accepted defeat or somehow surrendered all of its former glory because it has no one left to torment.

I hear a bang come from downstairs, but I become stuck where I stand as I try to move to go and see what's going on. I'm unable to move, so I stare deeper out the window. I see a black figure wearing a tall hat peeping out from behind **THAT** tree. The rain is pouring down onto it, but it's not getting wet. It just stands there staring through me with its round, deep **RED** eyes. Out of nowhere, its eyes suddenly become brighter. Then with no warning, it rushed away behind **THAT** tree, leaving a trail of fire burning away on our front lawn. I suddenly felt like I can move and immediately ran out there to assist the rain in extinguishing the fire before it spreads.

As I stand here in the rain with water running down my face and dripping from my chin, I don't move even though I'm becoming soaking wet. I place my hand on the trunk of **THAT** tree, and I take deep breaths, in and out whilst trying to feel something, anything else other than fear.

Was he here? Was **THAT BEEBLEDOSH**? How could soaking wet ground catch on fire so quickly? Is that even possible? What does this mean? I suddenly begin to feel worried, like something terrible is about to happen. He was staring right through me, right through my soul, and he looked so **EVIL**. But he also seemed like a troubled soul at the same time. He gave the impression that he was very vulnerable at that moment, yet still intently creepy. Maybe they also feel things. Was he here looking for Talia? Can he not find his long lost friend? Does he not understand she no longer lives here? Or is this something more? Is he biding his time before he comes back with a vengeance? I can't help but wonder what he's planning?

I remove my hand from **THAT** tree and walk back into the house, and I grab a towel from the top of the tumble dryer to dry off my face. I stand by the dryer, which is situated close to the table. Hence, I pull the towel down from my eyes, and something I can't explain draws me in, making me look at Talia's drawing. To my complete horror, **BEEBLEDOSH'S** arm is back down by his side. I began staring deeper into it, hoping that it does not move right in front of me. Am I going crazy? How does a drawing move? I tell myself that I seriously need to get more sleep. I'm going to take a picture on my phone. Then if it moves again, I can compare and prove that I'm not going mad. Then I place my ticket from the Church event next to the picture of **BEEBLEDOSH** because I'm getting an overwhelming feeling that I need to keep it.

The kettle suddenly begins to boil, and I know I've not touched it, so this makes no sense at all....

The old Keevil bridge will not stay up,
Will not stay up,
Will just not stay up,
The old Keevil bridge will not stay up,
Trapping us inside....

The old Keevil bridge is no longer up,
Is no longer up,
Is just no longer up,
The old Keevil bridge is no longer up,
Without them inside....

Out of nowhere, THAT song began to play out of THAT box. It stops me where I stand, and I find myself unable to move. Where is THAT song coming from, and why does it seem so loud? It sounds too loud to be coming from upstairs, which is where I left THAT box. As I remain stood here TRAPPED in the LIGHT! I think to myself that I must get out of here. Something is just not right with this house lately. I wish Mum and Dad were here, or even Talia. I need HELP.

Silence falls upon the house, and I suddenly become able to move. So I immediately run into the living room where I see IT, sitting there staring at me from the middle of the sofa....

THAT music box!

I have no idea how it's in here, and I don't intend to stick around to find out why. An awful white noise began drowning out the dead silence in this room. I turn around, and I discover that the television has turned on. No channel is showing, just that black and white fuzz accompanied by that dreadful white noise. I notice that the remote control remains sat on the top of the television. But this isn't possible because televisions don't just turn themselves on. As I drop my face into my hands out of pure torment, it suddenly turns off. Once again, leaving an empty silence, this time expelling from its black screen. Covered with goosebumps, I struggle to catch my breath. I don't dare move, but I do make a drastic decision.

I open the glass cabinet door, and I grab THAT skull. I put it in my backpack, and I run to the front door, lock it and run down the street and

I keep running until I can no longer see the house. I stop at a bench outside the church of the holy spirit, and I just take a seat and stare back down the road towards the house. I don't think, and I don't move. All I do is just sit here and remain as still as I possibly can.

After about ten minutes, I feel calm, so I take my backpack off my back and open the zip to look inside at THAT skull. I only say four words to it, out loud....

WHY ARE YOU HERE?

I then close the zip and ensure that I remain calm. I decide that I need to find out who THAT skull belongs to, what IT wants and why IT has chosen me to torture. There are so many people in this world.

SO WHY ME?

I turn my head and look towards the church. I then suddenly remember that I want to look in the archives. Maybe if I go in, I can make an appointment and finally clarify all of this. I walk up to the big oak doors and push one open. As it swings inwards to reveal the alter up ahead, Pastor Indigo welcomes me. After some small talk about how he's not seen me since I was a little girl, he has allowed me to come back tomorrow. I have a four-hour window to come here and freely look through the public archives, with no limitation, and nothing will be off-limits. It's the perfect opportunity to finally get some answers. Or will I be left very disappointed?

Chapter Twenty Two

like A Phoenix

I stand before these legendary gates, impatiently anticipating my entry. There are four minutes left until it's four o clock. I can't help but feel so excited. Something is telling me that this will be an evening I will never, ever forget. I stare at the phoenix and the letter M that's carved into the metal. Now I understand why it's a letter M if they study migraines here. Maybe the phoenix represents the name of the institute. After all, it is named....

The Immortal Institute of Neuropsychology.

Creeeeeeeeeeeeeeaaak,

The gates swing open. I remain standing here

in awe, staring at them until they come to a complete stop. I then hear a voice boom from a speaker hiding away, possibly in the trees.

I hear the voice say....

Would you please proceed to walk down the path until you reach the door?

I think to myself, ok, well here goes, but before I set off down the path, I take a moment to compose myself.

One,

Two,

Three,

Four!

Then I say out loud for all to hear in pure excitement.

Let's go, let my adventure begin....

As I walk down the path, I can't help but notice the trees on either side. They seem to be getting closer and closer, and I feel like they are rapidly closing in on me. I quickly start to feel like someone or something is going to jump out in front of me. Ten minutes must have passed by now. They have gone to extreme lengths to hide this place. I've been walking for ages, and I see nothing but this path, and the tall trees that are so close together that there creating a solid wall and showing me the way. As I seem to get closer, I'm finally greeted by four pillars straight up ahead. Two of them are on the left, and two are on the right. One pillar is positioned right in front of the other on the left, and they are the same on the right-hand side.

One of the pillars on the left-hand side is sculpted beautifully with a big wave, and it almost looks like a tsunami. Whatever it represents, it's an awe-inspiring wave coming from such a calm ocean. It has captured the calmness, peace and tranquillity that water can show. But then it's colliding with such a rush of fury within a wave of pure destruction. The pillar on the right-hand side is entirely identical. I walk around them both with total amazement. Who could have carved such great details into such big rocks?

The other two pillars, one on the left-hand side and one on the right, are situated up ahead and are even more impressive. They also look identical to one another. All I can see is a big bird that looks so lifelike it's scary. Its positioned as if it's about to land, with both feet pushed out in front of its body. The flames burn bright with power and are so prominent within the stone that you instantly know this is a PHOENIX. But all I can think to myself is, wow, this is so magical. As I stand here before such a magnificent creature, I can't help but think, why have they hidden this fantastic art? Why stop people from seeing it? From admiring it?

I finally tear myself away from the pillars and proceed along the path. I walk a little further and then right there before my very eyes, I see it....

THE IMMORTAL INSTITUTE OF NEUROPSYCHOLOGY.

Wow, this building is impressive, it was definitely worth the wait all these years to finally see it, and it does not disappoint. It's massive, and this has to be the largest building I've ever seen. It's bigger than any hospital, school, college or university that I've ever been to, and I can tell this building has a V design. Could this represent the institute's name further because birds are known to fly in this same V formation?

The building stretches as far as my eyes can see. If I were to look at the institute from a bird's eye view, the entrance would sit in the centre, at the base of the V. I see the main entrance right in front of me. However, I remain still because all I can do is think about how they have hidden this place so well. Maybe this is the reason why they used this design. Condensing it backwards instead of outwards allows the building to remain this large, but it's much easier to hide.

I still can't believe this is happening. Am I here, or is this another cruel trick my mind is playing on me. Am I going to wake up on the sofa or in my room? I close my eyes and see that GOLDEN colour, then I squeeze them shut, surpassing this calming colour until I see nothing but **DARKNESS**. I keep pressing my eyes closed with as much pressure as I can create until I see nothing at all, then I snap them open....

I'm powerless to move from where I stand as I look towards this monumental building and realise that this **IS ACTUALLY** happening. As I remain stood here, a voice shouts out,

I hear the mysterious voice say....

Howdy,
You finally made it.
We have been expecting you.
What took you so long?

I look over my right-hand shoulder, and I see a short man in a suit wearing a bow tie. I notice that he has a long grey beard and a white top hat sitting on his head. It appears as though he came out of nowhere. I did not even hear him coming. He proceeds onward towards the institute, and I do nothing but stand here as I watch him pass right by me. But then I suddenly hear him shout....

Are you coming in or what?

Of course, I proceed to follow him. But I find

myself immediately running to catch up.

I then hear him say....

Once we reach the main entrance, I will introduce myself, and we will begin this evening with a tour of the institute. Please don't interrupt, and we will answer any questions you may have in due course. Would you please wait here for one moment?

I'm left entirely speechless. This gothic architecture is totally out of this world. No one has built anything like this since the 1600s. I have seriously never seen anything so spectacular in my life. I stand here waiting and wondering what to expect next because I don't know how anything can top this. I feel like I've walked into another reality or another world. Now I think I finally understand why they want to hide this place and don't want people here.

The man returns, so I pay very close attention to him as he begins to speak....

Good afternoon. My name is Dr Clay Durante, but please call me Clay. I want you to feel relaxed and at home whilst you are here, so if you are ready to begin, please follow me?

As I follow him, he continues to talk to me.

We will begin with a bit of background about the building because I can tell you are impressed. The founders of this institute knew that it would end up being a massive place once it was complete. The work to be carried out here was top secret, and the staff must never be disturbed, so we needed to hide it at all costs. The original plan was far too big regarding the length, which would have made it very hard to hide. Then one very valued member of staff, Dr Alfred Zavier, mentioned how the birds fly through the sky. There are so many of them, but they don't take up much space at all. Thus the V shape design came to be, and there was no questioning it because it made so much sense. Therefore today stands this epic architecture that I am blessed to be a part of, and it's a great honour that I'm able to be so involved in the work we do here.

I continue to follow Dr Clay Durante whilst I pay attention, but I can't help but wonder if this is the same Zavier from the church event. No, that is not possible. This building has stood here for many centuries, and I just saw that medium the other night. I know that Zavier is not a famous name. It's just I've never met anyone with such a name before. I hope that more people have this name and that this is just a strange coincidence. Or maybe I have begun to lose my perception of what's real and what's not.

Dr Durante continues....

Here at The Immortal Institute of Neuropsychology, we do intense research into the human psyche and psychic abilities, as you will soon see with your own eyes. From my experience, many people can't comprehend these things until they see them for themselves. We also recently set up a department to research psychic phenomena, which has already had a few breakthroughs as far as I understand.

Bringing me onto the reason, we invited you

here. When this building was finished back in 1666, it was initially named, The Immortal Institute of The Mind. This whole place dedicated everything to researching disorders of the nervous system. Especially migraine auras, but it soon became apparent that neuroscience is very similar to a big tree. Many branches are needed to find answers, and it's not as simple as everything fitting neatly into one scientific field. It also soon became clear that these fields of study would completely overlap with other sectors, making our tree grow many more branches. These additional branches representing fields such as psychology made way for us to rename this institute and re-evaluate how we look at scientific research.

Combining these fields of study has led to a better understanding of how we work in both body and mind. It is genuinely unique once you see the neurological connections between your body and your soul. I must let you in on a secret, one that you must never repeat to anyone no matter what. The first-ever documented neuroscience department was not officially founded until the 1900s. But these branches of science go way back into history. However, because we have been extremely successful in keeping our research a secret, we have been able to study these sciences since 1668. By this time, we had become completely set up, and we had an entire team. We had to spend two full years carrying out detailed testing on our staff. We needed to ensure they could carry out their work whilst maintaining complete loyalty and integrity at all times. To make sure all of our work remains a secret.

Here at The Immortal Institute of Neuropsychology, we are very proud of what we have achieved. We have only become successful because we are left alone to do what we need to do to help those like you who suffer every day. Most people just don't get it because they don't feel pain in the same way. We reward ourselves by focusing on our goals and helping people like you, more than caring about what the world out there thinks. We know and understand what matters most.

We arrive at a café, and just as I pull out a chair to sit down, I became surprised to see a member of staff placing a cup of tea in front of me. I think this is because Dr Durante just informed me that he needs to make a phone call. I'm glad I'm able to take a moment to take this all in. That was some intense history, but I've suddenly found myself realising this place may be able to help me after all. I can't help but wonder, Why was I allowed in here? Who decided I'm trustworthy? Why do I deserve to know all of this and possibly finally understand what is wrong with me? I decided that I'm going to embrace this and see where this journey takes me.

....

Dr Durante walks towards me, asking if I'm ready to continue the tour. I jump off my seat in excitement to follow him. We walk down a long corridor with walls made entirely of glass. The further into the corridor we go, the lower the lighting becomes. Then I see them swimming within the walls! So many jellyfish swimming around. It's so beautiful and intense that I'm rendered speechless. They all float about, highlighted by their bioluminescence, to show us the way down this almost dark passage. All we have to guide us is the LIGHT produced from their ghostly glow. I feel like I've stepped into an alternate reality. I'm genuinely stunned by this. They are so unique and completely magical.

At the end of this spectacular corridor sat a big hall containing many tanks. I notice that each one is home to a different type of jellyfish. In the very centre of this big room, I see a huge tank that stands alone. It's full of tiny jellyfish. I instantly become confused. Why are there so many jellyfish here at this MEDICAL institute?

Out of nowhere, Dr Clay Durante speaks....

I bet you are wondering why we have jellyfish here at the institute, allow me to explain....

These jellyfish are the key to one-day curing **MIGRAINE AURA** for good. It's uncommonly known that there is something profound inside their DNA. We need to extract this and do more experiments and research before using it on any human being. However, we still have a lot of work to do in this area of study.

Let me show you what I mean by showing you some of the work we have been doing here. Allow me to introduce you to the Turritopsis dohrnii, known by most people as the immortal jellyfish. This name is accurate because they are indeed biologically immortal. Immortality is a remarkable ability and one we are intently studying to one day implement into humans. However, we are in fact, closer to this scientific breakthrough than the world believes. But as I said, this is top secret information. If any government knew we had this knowledge, they would confiscate it and possibly use it themselves. However, it's not ready for the world just yet.

The aura you have suffered from your whole life has a heavy link to these tiny creatures. Studies have shown us this, and I would like you to see this for yourself when we reach the laboratory. Here at this institute, we set our goals high. We intend to combine the brain's power whilst in the aura stages with the jellyfish's extraordinary abilities to create a solid permanent cure. We also hope to unlock more areas within the brain that humans are not yet capable of using at this stage in our evolution.

Whilst we walk to the laboratory, Dr Durante oddly remains silent, as do I, because this is a lot to digest mentally. I suddenly remember THAT skull has been sat in my backpack this whole time. I then spontaneously decide to take this opportunity to ask him about it. In a normal tone of voice, I say, I have a SKULL in my bag. It's been sitting in our home for as long as I can remember. I know I'm asking a lot, but would you be willing to take a look at it for me? Would you be able to let me know who it once belonged to? To my amazement, he explains that they have the technology to get me an answer. He also says that he will personally make sure it's studied for me. I'm thrilled because I now feel confident that this place will save my life. I certainly owe Dr Sebastian Wyatt a lot for getting me this appointment.

We finally arrive at the lab, and Dr Durante asks me to sit in the chair in the centre of the room. He then hands me some paperwork and asks me to read and sign it, as long as I agree with the content. As I read through the pages, it quickly becomes apparent that all it's asking is if I give my permission to have some tests done, and then I must declare any health problems. So I sign them and hand them back because I'm eager to see how this place can help me.

First, they ask me to close my eyes and remain

as still as I possibly can. As I proceed to do this, they explain that they will monitor and measure any frequencies I'm emitting from my body. Then they put me into a big machine to do an MRI scan. I hear them explain that this is short for magnetic resonance imaging. They also explain that this uses radio waves and strong magnetic fields to produce pictures of my brain and its activity. Once this was complete, they carried out a CT scan and explained that this is short for a computed tomography scan. They also make me aware that this scan uses radiology to produce cross-sectional images of my brain.

Once the scans were complete, they move me to a different room for an EEG test. They explain that this is an electroencephalogram. During this test, they ask me to think of random things and do various activities simultaneously whilst recording my brain activity. I become increasingly impatient to see the results from these tests, mainly to see if any results differ from those I've had in the past. I wonder if Dr Sebastian Wyatt works here as well. He gave me the same trusting vibe that I'm getting from Dr Clay Durante.

Now that all the tests are complete, I must

wait for the results. I get escorted back to the café
to have some food while I wait. I don't know how I
feel right now, but I am very thankful to all the
doctors at this institute. So much has just happened
to me in such little time. I do feel privileged to have
had this opportunity. Just as I finished eating, I
noticed Dr Durante running towards me!

All I can hear is him yelling out....

COME ON,

IT WOULD BE BEST IF YOU CAME WITH
ME.

WE HAVE THE RESULTS, AND THEY
ARE POSITIVELY INTERESTING,

LET'S GO,

HURRY!

I jump up to follow him immediately, and I
find myself practically running. What on earth is he
so excited about, but then it suddenly dawns on

me, did the UNSEEN show up on the scans? No, that would be impossible. He abruptly halts in front of a door. I almost bump into him, but I'm able to stop myself just in time. He pushes the door open, revealing some comfy sofas and a big screen. He then asks me to take a seat.

As I sit down on this large and comfy sofa, Dr Sebastian Wyatt suddenly appears at the front of the room. Once I get past my shock, I think to myself, I knew it. Dr Wyatt begins by apologising to me for not telling me that he works here. I let him know I fully understand because I know why he can't talk about the institute to anyone outside. He then explains how this place has helped him, but my results are unique.

Dr Durante then joins Dr Wyatt at the front of the room, and I hear him say....

Let's begin....

You have somehow unlocked far more of your brain than anyone I've ever seen. You produce frequencies that no human being should be capable of, and no one has ever done before. If you use these frequencies in a certain way, you could channel your chakra and open doors to many other realities. Or dare I say it, universes. Many people worldwide have the same memories, but all the evidence has ceased to exist. This phenomenon is known by many. What happens is they all remember things in the same way. But, somehow at some point our reality merged with another, and things changed. Some say this is nonsense, while others live by this and believe it to be true.

Your frequencies, together with your overactive brain, could give you the ability to cross realities and cause this sort of phenomenon to occur. You also have everything you need to unlock rare psychic skills. You are using more of your brain than any other human ever has, and this is why you are having such a painful aura before a migraine attack. Your body can't keep up with it. Your brain is also overworking every other system within your body because it's sending out signals that the rest of your system can't recognise.

Could you please look towards the screen?

I will show you my brain scans positioned next to

yours for comparison….

I watch as he puts his scans on the left, and then he proceeds to place mine on the right, and I immediately notice that my scans have way more areas lit up with colour than Dr Durante. I can't help but feel like I'm a tiny piece of a much bigger puzzle.

He then continues to say….

You can now see my scans sitting next to yours. I carried out my tests this morning because it's only fair that they are from the same day. After all, we study science here, so all the evidence must be accurate and obtained under the same circumstances. I did everything the same as you, but as you can see, there are extreme differences between them. You use far more of your brain than I do. You can also see your frequencies compared with mine, and we see the same result occurring.

You have far superior results!

Let us look at the results from your brain's

activity. We can see that you're using a much higher percentage of your brain than we have ever seen before. We have also tested a third person today to further enlighten you on how impressive your results are. But again their results were inferior compared to yours.

I will give you a moment to take this all in….

Never in my life have I been so shocked. I should feel special and lucky right now, but all I can think about is how I'm cursed. Is this quite possibly the very reason why and how the **UNSEEN** become **SEEN**? Aura, migraine, immortality and frequencies, I don't know what I'm supposed to do with any of this. Wait, that medium Zavier mentioned frequencies to me when he was talking about my aura. Is this what he meant?

Out of nowhere, Dr Durante speaks, but this time in such a soft but firm tone….

I must tell you….

You hold great power.

You should unlock it and use it because it's a rare gift. I have never seen anything like your brain's abilities and what it could be capable of before today. I've seen people with migraines, and I've seen people with aura. I've seen people with telekinesis, and I've met plenty of mediums in my time, but you are **ONE** of a kind.

You have the key to it all.

But, I must ask, not only for the institute but for my curiosity, have you ever had anything unusual occur?

I decide now is my chance to let him know absolutely all of it because if anywhere is the right place it's here. So I tell him everything from the **UNSEEN** to **BEEBLEDOSH**. I then let him know how much I began to question myself and my reality. I then explain how I always second guess myself because I think I see things that are not there. I feel like I'm slipping into the deep darkness of insanity. I also firmly explain how I led there awake night after night during my childhood.

I had my precious sleep stolen because of an infectious fear that contaminated my mind for so long.

He then says....

When you leave here and get home, please do something, go back to that room. Instead of fearing it, embrace it, invite these entities in, ask them to show themselves, stop hiding, and show you exactly what they want. But whatever you do, **STOP** running from yourself and face it with FORTITUDE.

Don't hold back. Let everything out, confront the darkness, see and feel the difference. You must control it instead of feeding it with your fear, and when you face it, YOU must take away its power. The immortal jellyfish immediately defend themselves if you put your hand into their territory and forcefully try to grab them. They will self-destruct and revert to an earlier stage of their development to start over. Then they will grow back even more robust than before. Despite being real-life creatures that you see right before your eyes, these jellyfish have the same abilities as the legendary phoenix. Stories of such myths and legends claim that immortality IS possible, and these jellyfish prove that. So I know you can find the FORTITUDE you need to face this once and for all.

What if our souls are our immortality? What if one day we can control ourselves without a vessel? What if these **UNSEEN** you speak of are human beings but in a state of immortality?

You have been scared for many years, and your dark path to insanity has been your self-destruction. You must now act like the immortal jellyfish and invite them in to get the answers you so desperately need. Then you will be able to come back far stronger, but most importantly, you will finally be FREE!

There is a way to change it all and deviate from the path you have found yourself travelling down. Now that you know what you are, you have a choice to make. Do you continue along this given path to darkness, or will you change it all and do what is right? Life is precious, and you're the chosen one. You have the ability to be someone, make a difference, do what matters, and one day you will make dreams come true.

Let me prove this to you: I will slowly put my hand into this tank with care and confidence, and you will see what happens!

As I watch in awe, the jellyfish welcomes him, and he's able to touch it and follow it through the water. It's so beautiful to watch, and I can't help but feel calming happiness as I think to myself, ok, MR, you have made your point.

I became lost in a trance, watching the jellyfish elegantly floating in the water, and then I suddenly heard him say….

Now, do you see?

You are the LIGHT in the dark!

You are THE FIRE IN FORTITUDE….

I can see it in your eyes, now go and get your answers, be reborn LIKE A PHOENIX, with all your strength, the same you, only this time YOU hold the power. No more fear, no more loneliness and no more darkness. You are you, and you are FREE.

Chapter Twenty Three

Who Are You?

I wake up to find myself immediately thinking about how strange last night was. I jumped up from the sofa to check if it was real and not some twisted dream because I don't remember coming home or sleeping last night. I look on my phone, and there they are, the pictures of the immortal jellyfish. Dr Durante told me to take some pictures to look at every time I feel like this is all in my head. I'm glad I did because it has helped me prove that this is all real. They will be helpful in the future, especially for times like this.

I still can't comprehend everything they told me. But now everything that the medium who called himself Zavier, has said makes sense. I need to find him and talk to him again because I know this all directly links together somehow. I wonder if Zavier also suffers from migraine with aura. Maybe that's how he has psychic abilities, and that is how he could see my aura. I now have so many questions to ask him.

As I walk out of the living room, I stop and stare at the empty space where THAT skull would have sat. I can't help but wonder when the results will be available. Hopefully, they reveal who THAT skull belonged to, and I also notice THAT music box is still sitting in the living room. I never tried to find out how it got in here yesterday because I don't even want to know, deep down in my heart. I decide to put THAT music box inside the glass cabinet where THAT skull usually sits. I then close the door and think that nothing has ever moved from here, so let's see if you will stay put.

I decided to track down Zavier, but as I walked out the door, I thought to myself, where would be the best place to start? Then a thought comes out of nowhere, but it made perfect sense. The church! After all, I have my appointment today to check out the documents in the church archives. I can't waste any of that time because I want to get the most out of the four-hour slot they have kindly provided me. So I decided to quickly pop over to the church to ask for Zavier's phone number or contact details.

As I walk along the church path and past part of the graveyard, I see Pastor Indigo standing outside. He's tending to some flowers at one of the graves. I approach him and calmly ask if there is any chance I could get Zavier's contact details. I have a few questions that I would like to ask him about his event the other night. But Pastor Indigo just looks towards me with a blank look on his face. He has no idea what I'm talking about, which makes no sense to me. Suddenly I hear him abruptly explain that the church does not give out peoples details and that there was no event here the other night. He goes on to clarify that this church has not held any events for four years now. He also tells me this church is simply a place for people to respect and visit their lost loved ones.

I thank Pastor Indigo for his time, and then I immediately rush home to find my ticket because this now seems to be my only proof that this event took place. Once again, I feel like I'm going crazy and making this stuff up, but I know I'm not. I know this event happened. I need to find this medium because he saw something that night when he looked at me. I must know what it was that he saw. He must too suffer from aura because he knew way too much about it. I just don't understand why he is nowhere to be found and why is Pastor Indigo saying that he does not know of any event? Maybe it just slipped his mind, but now that I think about it, I didn't recognise anyone else who attended.

I run into the house and go straight to the table. Right next to Talia's drawing of BEEBLEDOSH is my ticket. I still have it, so how has it come to be that I have a ticket for an event that the church claims never happened. I rush back to the church, and as I arrive, Pastor Indigo is still tending to a few of the graves. I approach him to show him my ticket, but he still just denies any knowledge of it. He explains to me that the church was empty that evening. The only thing going on was the standard procedure where people could come in for private prayer. The last thing he says to me is that he apologises for not giving me the answers I desire. But the truth is the truth, and there was no event here the other night, and no one called Zavier has been in contact with this church since the 1600s.

I return home, utterly shocked because none of this is making any sense. I thought I was connecting the dots, but then I hit a total dead end. Two people have gone missing on me without a trace and just vanished into thin air. I stand at the table, open my laptop, and type his name into a search engine, but this was also just a complete dead end because I only know his first name.

Wait, Pastor Indigo said that no one called Zavier had contacted the church since the 1600s. But Dr Durante said that Dr Alfred Zavier mentioned how the birds fly through the sky, and his idea ended up being the actual design of the building **IN THE 1600s**. So there **WAS** a man called Dr Alfred Zavier, but I wonder if he's the same Zavier that contacted the church of the holy spirit back in the 1600s. But then, who is this medium called Zavier? How can a man just vanish? How can a whole night just disappear?

Then suddenly, a scary thought sinks in. The results from the institute prove that I hold the power and the ability to cross realities. Is this what happened? Did I cause actual time to overlap or rewind? Are Dr Alfred Zavier and the Zavier who took the event the same man? I get a strong feeling of dread wash over me. Am I experiencing these things that I've recently learnt about and have the ability to control? Have I somehow, by accident, caused this alternate reality to occur? Did I unintentionally do this to extract the information I desired because I had to find out more about myself to move forward? Or is this bigger than me? Is this something to do with Dr Alfred Zavier needing to complete his work? Is this why the church has no idea this event even took place? Is this why there is only one Zavier that anyone physically knew?

I look down at the table to put my ticket back. As I place it next to Talia's picture of **BEEBLEDOSH**, I notice that now his head is tilted as if he's trying to see something. I pull my phone out of my pocket to look at the picture I previously took of this drawing, and I feel instantly sick to my stomach. His head has moved, and my photo confirms it. I don't understand how this could have happened. How can a drawing move? Does this ultimately prove that everything Dr Durante has told me is real? I try my best to ignore the fact that Talia's picture continues to change, but

I can't stop thinking about how much it's bothering me. I decided to focus my mind on something else so I write myself a small note....

Knowledge from the Medium Zavier - There is one other known to have a white aura!

I then placed this in the top right-hand corner of the table. I've written this down because Zavier said this to me at the church, and I just know this is essential. If he truly is the same person as Dr Alfred Zavier, this could help me figure out who this other person with a white aura is. Zavier led an event that never technically took place, so if he does have a white aura, this may have enabled him to have the ability to do this?

DING DONG, DING DONG,

DING DONG, DING DONG,

I abruptly jump out of my skin,

The doorbell rang, this came by complete surprise, and it instantly frightened me because I'd not heard the doorbell in so long. Who could it possibly be? It can't be Talia because she said when she's next free that she would call me before she comes over. I walk over to the door and pull it open. I see a small man who I've never seen before, standing there. All he says to me is that he has a delivery, and it requires my signature. So I put my signature on his piece of paper and watch in confusion as he immediately runs off to his car.

I bring the box inside and place it on the table. I remain standing here staring at it for a moment, realising the only thing it could be, is THAT skull. I open the box to look inside, and I see THAT skull wrapped up in some protective paper. I pull it out of the box and sit it on the table, but then I see something else. An envelope is sitting at the bottom of the box, so I lift this out to open it. It's a letter, written in hand, which I find very unusual these days because most people use a computer. I do think it feels more personal when something is written by hand, though. I feel like it gives it more meaning.

I decide to read the letter out loud because it's far too quiet around here!

Dear our Legendary Phoenix.

Have you found what you are looking for yet?
Have you found your answers?

I do apologise for not personally delivering this to you. Some critical data has come up that I must tend to. Thank you for allowing us to study you. We only hope the knowledge we were able to provide you with can assist you in finding peace and turning your curse into the gift it should be. You are extraordinary, don't let anyone else tell you otherwise.

Now on to the information you seek,

This skull you asked us to look into has turned out to be very interesting. We have gained some fantastic data from this study, so once again, we thank you.
I must tell you that all the evidence we have

found points to the fact that this man is possibly one of the founders of **KEEVIL***. He has been the missing link for us in our DNA register. I can confirm that he was one of the Elders who once ran this entire village. His* **DNA** *is the only one of its kind, and according to the records, there was only one man back then who had no children, and he was the leader. From this, we know that this skull belongs to the leader and first Elder of* **KEEVIL***.*

I hope this helps you on your journey, and we welcome you to The Immortal Institute of Neuropsychology any time. We have put an identification pass inside the box for you that will never expire. We now see you as a trusted member of our organisation, and you have been proven worthy.

We look forward to seeing you soon,
Dr Clay Durante

I take a seat on one of the chairs at the table, and my mind is completely blank. I have no thoughts or words, but this makes no sense because I should be flooded with opinions right now. All I feel is fear because **THAT** skull has something to do with the **UNSEEN**, and if it belongs to the Elders' leader, then I'm dealing with pure **EVIL**. I immediately thought back to the mysterious man's story. It suddenly dawned on me that sitting on our dining table is that very Elder's head, the Elder who punished that man and his children. What does this mean for me? Am I actually in danger? Is that what this is all leading up to, my destruction?

Chapter Twenty Four

Rotten To The Core

Or Completely Misunderstood?

I compose myself and place THAT skull back into the glass cabinet, which leaves me with the problem of where should I put THAT music box? It's almost time for my appointment at the church, so for now, I will leave THAT music box on the sofa, which seems to be where it wanted to be before.

As I arrived at the church, I noticed that I didn't bump into anyone along the way. I decide not to read too much into this and proceed to knock on the door, but the big wooden door swings open as I raise my hand. I then see Pastor Indigo standing there waiting for me. I'm invited in

and directed to the basement because that is where
the old documents are stored. Before I go down,
Pastor Indigo advises me that no one has been
down there in years and the documents are most
likely not in any constructive order.

Pastor Indigo leaves me at the door to the
basement. It's an old, small oak door and covered
with cobwebs too. No one would even realise it's
here unless someone was to point it out. Pastor
Indigo also informs me that there is no LIGHT on
the stairs because this is an ancient building.
Therefore, he has given me a lantern. I tell myself
out loud, let's do this, so I push the door, and just
as I thought, it creaks as it opens….

I only take one step into the darkness and
immediately turn the lantern on to provide a beam
of LIGHT. I decide to take each step slowly
because I know that no one's been down here in
years, and I'm unaware of any broken stairs. The
steps go down in a straight line which is very
helpful. I reach the bottom, and the only word I
can find is, **WOW**. I see mountains of paperwork
down here. The boxes are stacked higher than me.
How will I find what I'm looking for in only four
hours? There is so much paper. Where do I start?

Where are my answers?

I see a red box in the corner underneath many other packages, and I don't know why but I feel like I need to look in that particular box. I trust my instinct, walk over to it, and brush off the cobwebs, utterly petrified of any spiders. But luckily, I haven't seen any so far. I tug on the box, pulling it towards me a little more each time, and I begin to feel it coming loose. It finally slides out, and the other boxes fall behind it.

I quickly remove the lid in anticipation to reveal many pieces of brown paper. I can still read the writing, so I clear a space on the floor and start to go through it page by page. At first, I have no luck, all I'm getting is paperwork about this church, but then I catch a glimpse of a page with the title, Members of the church of the Holy Spirit. I skim down the list looking for anything I recognise, and there, I see his name!

Dr Alfred Zavier.

Next to his name, it says his profession, and to my amazement, it clearly states he works as a doctor at The Immortal Institute Of The Mind.

The most exciting thing is that it says in his character profile that he is a trusted counsellor to the church. It also states that he has proven psychic abilities that they use to talk to the holy spirit.

Have I just actually found proof that the two Zavier's are the same person? Is this the missing link to prove that Dr Alfred Zavier is also a medium and in touch with this church? They have to be the same person, but this means it was me or Dr Zavier who crossed and overlapped our realities. It has to be one of us who opened the door, allowing us to meet.

I must keep looking. I continue to scroll down the list, and then I see another important name....

Elder Achlys Mallory Armaros!

Next to his name, it states his profession, and it says that he **IS THE LEADER OF THE ELDERS**. However, his character profile says he dedicated his entire life to his bridge and the church.

A burning thought takes over my mind telling me that there has to be more information here somewhere about Elder Achlys Mallory Armaros and his bridge. But for now, I keep looking down the list of church members. I try to see if I can find anything about a man with two children. But, unfortunately, this list does not hold that sort of information.

So I need to move on.

I continue searching through the box, and as I reach the bottom, I see a big heavy book. I manage to drag it out and dust it off. The title is written on the front in big gold letters saying, Births and Deaths of Eivele. Could this be the first book of its kind containing records of the first-ever residents of this village? I opened the book to reveal many names with dates to accompany them, providing essential historical details. The list is extensive for such a small village, but this book has dates from the 1600s to the early 1900s. I guess it must have been around the 1900s when this book got placed down here. There are so many families with two children that I will never find that man from the story this way.

I flick forward to the deaths section, and I skim through the pages, looking for a day when a

man and two children died. I immediately let go of
the book, and it falls to the floor as I shuffle
backwards....

I gather the courage to move back over to the
book, pick it up and proceed to read what it says
and I think I found him. Could it possibly be that
the mysterious man who told me that story was
repeating actual history? Are my eyes deceiving me?
According to this, the man and his two children are
REAL. I have found a man named Seth Amista,
and according to this book, he died of starvation
caused by a broken heart. But on the lines
underneath him are his two children, a girl named
Zuri Amista and a boy named Keefe Amista.
According to this, they both also die of starvation.

I feel sick to my stomach and empty inside
because if these people are genuine, it can only
mean one thing. This horrific event actually took
place, and this family was tortured in the worst
possible way. What they had to endure must have
been terrifying, and this only happened because of
THAT Elder's decisions. He killed them and what
makes this worse is that this village has hidden this
dark truth for all these years. They probably tried to
hide their devilish past, to stay high within society. I

begin to wonder if Pastor Indigo is aware of these hidden secrets. Did he hope there was enough paperwork down here to prevent me from stumbling into the truth? But one way or another, this man's story needs to be remembered, and that Elder needs to be exposed.

I think to myself, Amista, why is this name familiar to me? Then it dawns on me how I also saw this name a couple of pages back, I flick backwards in the book, and there it is....

Raylene Amista, according to this book she died eight days before the rest of her family. It says next to her name that she died of unknown causes.

I feel a tear roll down my face. My fears for this family have come true. They missed that meeting and suffered death in return at the hands of **AN EVIL MONSTER**. Seth, Zuri and Keefe must have been with Raylene at the time of the meeting. They were absent from a discussion about a bridge to spend time with Raylene in her last moments on this earth. Anyone would have done the same. A meeting can occur at any time, but they would never get back those precious moments with Raylene. They chose to experience those special moments with her because that's what mattered

most to them. It truly is a colossal tragedy because
they should never have had to choose. To punish
them for doing the right thing makes **THAT** Elder
utterly rotten to the core. It's despicable what
happened to Seth, Zuri and Keefe. **THAT** Elder is
nothing but pure **EVIL**.

I take a moment to calm myself because my
sadness for the Amista family quickly turns into
pure hatred towards Elder Armaros. I decided to
look around to carefully select the next box because
I'm aware that I'm on a time limit, so I must
choose wisely. I see an old, torn box, and I can tell
it was once white, but it's changed colour over the
years. I pull this one down to the floor and remove
the lid. I see blueprints for the old Keevil bridge,
and I get an instant fuzzy feeling in my mind telling
me that I've selected the correct box. I move the
blueprints to the side, and underneath them are
some letters. They appear to be from Elder
Armaros and addressed to someone called Xander
Mika.

There is no mention of who Xander Mika is,
but the content of these letters is terrifying. The
first letter commands Elder Armaros to build a
bridge so the people of Eivele can be free to travel

to other areas, towns, or wherever they wish.

The second letter is a response acknowledging that a fatality has occurred whilst building the bridge. Xander Mika says to Elder Armaros that he must get this bridge built no matter what because he owes this to the people of Eivele. They are trapped here, and it's been this way for far too long. There is a whole world out there waiting for them. Xander Mika also says if he doesn't build the bridge, the price will be dyer.

The third letter is another reply to Elder Armaros. This time, Xander Mika says he is sorry to hear about the builders' inability to keep the bridge up. But he has cursed himself and his bridge by letting a man die during the original build. Now the bridge demands living souls in payment for killing an innocent man. It's now the only way that the bridge will stay up. Xander Mika commands Elder Armaros to put living souls into the bridge and make sure they stay in there. **BUT NO MATTER WHAT, KEEP THAT BRIDGE UP**.

The fourth letter is the final response. Xander Mika punishes Elder Armaros because he refuses to supply more souls and fails to keep the bridge up.

Xander Mika curses him to walk the earth, trapped for all eternity. He will be unable to stop forming strong connections to any new souls who arrive on this planet. But only the ones who enter his house and are pure of heart.

Xander Mika firmly tells Elder Armaros he must heed this warning because he will be trapped forever in purgatory once his life ends. He will be nothing more than a watchman making sure those he will have no choice but to care for are always safe. He will become attached to any new souls that come into his house, and he must keep the ones he cares for alive. All this will continue to occur whilst he's doomed to walk the earth forever in eternal pain.

He will be made to forever watch....

One last thing is said before this letter ends. Xander Mika says there are only two ways Elder Achlys Mallory Armaros can end his own suffering and finally be free. The first is to leave the one he cares about to perish, and then they will both cease to exist, finally freeing him from his curse. But he will have condemned the one he cares for to death.

The only other way Elder Armaros can be free is if the one he cares for knows what **HE TRULY IS** and can completely forgive him. But this forgiveness must come from the heart and be offered freely.

I suddenly felt a cold chill as my LIGHT began to flicker, but it quickly returned to normal. I choose to believe this is because I'm sitting here in a cold basement with an old lantern and nothing more. I can't help but feel like all of this just got way more complicated. I continue to search in the box to see if there is any more information regarding Xander Mika, but I find nothing about him. There is no address on any of these letters either. I can't help but wonder if the letters are real, or have the Elders faked it all out of some desperation to justify their evil crimes?

I searched this box to the bottom, trying my hardest to find something about the identity of the fatality that took place during the construction of the bridge. Who is this man who suffered at the cost of Elder Armaros and his bridge? I can't find anything, not even in the book of births and deaths. There is no mention of anyone who died during the construction of THAT bridge. I'm getting a **BAD** feeling about this. It seems to be just more secrets or lies.

I jump to my feet, grab any box, and pull the lid off because I'm running out of time. This time I immediately see that name again, Amista. It's about the Amista family, but this time I can see an address. As I read it, I begin to get goosebumps all over my body, and I feel them spreading, bringing with them an intense cold shiver....

I immediately freeze where I am, and I make sure not to move.

The LIGHT **went OUT!**

I try to stay calm, but I'm very aware that I'm in a pitch-black basement. I slowly reach out to grab the lantern, hoping that nothing touches me first. I try to get the LIGHT back on, but I instantly find myself unable to move....

TAP,

TAP,

TAP,

TAP,

TAP,

TAP,

TAP,

TAP....

Out of nowhere, I get a complete fright when I hear an unexpected voice explain that they have brought me a new LIGHT because the one they gave me is temperamental.

A storm has begun outside, so thankfully, whoever this is has figured out that I would need a new LIGHT soon.

I felt so much relief come over me. I said thank you and went straight back to the box. However, I immediately get that same feeling of

dread because as I look at the address of the
Amista family from the bridge, I see my family's
address. To my disbelief, I see my house. The
house that I grew up in, and the house that my
family has made memories in. How do they have
the same address? Was my home, once their home?
I find myself confused. If this was their home, then
are they the UNSEEN? But if they went through
such pain, I don't understand why they would want
to harm anyone else? Why would they torment and
torture me?

I thought they were good and had suffered
terribly this whole time, but I can't understand why
they would want to harm someone else. Or maybe
I have just been looking at the UNSEEN all
wrong. Have I been scared of a family wanting to
be at peace in their home for all these years? After
all, if they are the UNSEEN, the man and his two
children have never hurt me. They have scared me
right to my core, but I guess I didn't understand
any of this back then.

I'm beginning to think Dr Clay Durante is
right. I need to let them in, so they can finally be
free. I continue to look in the box, and from luck
or some twisted fate, I find something

extraordinary. It's the verse to THAT song that plays out of THAT music box.

The old Keevil bridge will not stay up,
Will not stay up,
Will just not stay up,
The old Keevil bridge will not stay up,
Trapping us inside....

I began to get cold chills, so I took a look around the room because it started to feel like I was not alone down here anymore. Then out of nowhere, a piece of paper fell from above me and landed in my lap. I see my mum and dad's old address written on it, but this was the house they lived in before I was born. They welcomed Talia to the family whilst they lived in this house. But underneath the address, I see a drawing that looks like a child has created it. It is scarily similar to Talia's picture of BEEBLEDOSH. It's a man, burning from his waist down, only this picture differs from Talia's because, in this one, he's hanging from a tree in the back garden. Then underneath the man, it clearly says the word....

BEEBLEDOSH

Followed by a different verse of THAT song that
plays out of THAT music box....

> **The old Keevil bridge will not stay up,**
> **Will not stay up,**
> **Will just not stay up,**
> **The old Keevil bridge will not stay up,**
> **Trapping us inside....**

> Beware now Beeble Dosh will come for us,
> Will come for us,
> He will come for us,
> Beware now Beeble Dosh will come for us,
> Nowhere to hide....

What on earth is this? How does a piece of
paper from centuries ago have my parents
information on it? Could this be the very place that
BEEBLEDOSH met his end, and is this how
Talia ended up making friends with him? When
they moved to our house, did BEEBLEDOSH
come with her? I can't help but wonder what would
make him hang himself? Or worse, was he hung? A

thought plagues my mind, is it BEEBLEDOSH that connects my parent's old address and THAT song? Why is this information being stored in this church? Does this mean BEEBLEDOSH died in my mum and dad's old house? Was this BEEBLEDOSH'S house?

Then an unwelcome scary idea comes into my head, THAT song is about keeping the old Keevil bridge up. THAT Elder was cursed to walk this earth for all eternity because he let it fall....

Is BEEBLEDOSH....

Elder Achlys Mallory Armaros?

Does this mean my family's old house was once THAT Elders house?

BEEBLEDOSH'S house?

If he is BEEBLEDOSH, then Talia is in danger, but wait, is she? I mean, he was her friend all that time. She even told him she did not want to see him anymore, and she's been just fine. As far as I'm aware, he's never actually hurt her. But THAT

Elder was pure evil. How can someone so evil have
been following Talia around all this time? If the
curse did not stop him and he had a chance, Would
he actually harm her? I need to tell her all of this as
soon as possible. There is a massive hole in this
idea though, why would he be known as
BEEBLEDOSH if he was an Elder? It makes no
sense.

A strong instinct develops, insisting I turn the
page over and there lies the scary truth. I almost
don't want to believe it. I find myself looking at
another drawing. The Elder is being hung and set
on fire with children stood around him singing
THAT song. The words are next to them, making
it clear what they are singing. There is also some
other writing, but I can barely make it out.

I stare at it for a moment whilst I wipe away
the dust, and I'm only just able to read what it
says….

This name is now bound to you for eternity,
and you will be doomed to remain in purgatory
with no way out insight. You are now,
BEEBLEDOSH…. It means the space between
the LIGHT and the **DARK**. You are forever
cursed to be stuck in-between. You don't get to be

LIGHT, and you don't get to be **DARK**. You're not alive, but you're not dead either. You are no one, and you are **MARKED**. You will roam this earth with no escape because now you are **NOTHING**!

I'm left entirely speechless, and I feel like I'm going crazy **AGAIN**. Do I imagine all of this? I just seem to be getting answers to all my questions, one after the other. But something about this just doesn't feel right, and it seems far too easy. A drawing can mean different things through interpretation, so it's not solid evidence. I need some concrete proof. I wonder if any records go back that far and list who lived in what house all those years ago.

My time down here is coming to an end, and I feel like it's been very successful. If this has been real, that is, and I'm not back at home asleep, falling deeper into my dark insanity. I take pictures on my phone of everything, mostly to prove to myself later that this actually happened. I know I will need those pictures to do the right thing and tell this story. I can't help but feel that once I leave, all these documents will go missing. Or someone or something will destroy them because I have found out too much.

Now that I have all the evidence photographed, I pack everything away and head over towards the stairs, but a folder catches my eye. It's my favourite colour, and this is why it has stood out to me. So I decide one last thing won't take a minute and I should be ok to look. I pick it up and open it, exposing the first page, and there's a name written in what looks like blood. I'm careful not to touch any of it as I try to make out the name....

The name is,

Rue Than

The more I stare at it, the more I notice this handwriting looks very similar to mine, how is this possible? I'm a firm believer in thinking everything happens for a reason, but what does this mean? I look towards the paper, and I see more writing underneath the name....

He led a mass riot against Elder Achlys Mallory Armaros. More commonly known as **BEEBLEDOSH***, to make him pay for the pure*

EVIL crimes he was guilty of committing. Rue Than and a group of villagers followed **BEEBLEDOSH** *home and hung him from his very own tree in his garden while the kids sang the song of the old Keevil bridge and then set him on fire.*

Rue Than wanted and got revenge on **BEEBLEDOSH***. The reason for this was because* **BEEBLEDOSH** *had personally made Rue commit terrible crimes. The job that* **BEEBLEDOSH** *commanded Rue Than to do was the most heinous of all. His role was to trap the souls inside the bridge and make sure they didn't escape. This was for one purpose, and one alone, to keep* **BEEBLEDOSH'S** *bridge up. Rue Than's dying wish was to expose this terrible secret and expose* **BEEBLEDOSH***.*

But most of all, he wants to tell the Amista's story because he was so full of regret. Ever since he trapped the two small children inside that bridge, this was and always will be his biggest regret. Rue could not live with what he did, so he went to their

*home to deliver his message and apologise to let them
know he was truly and eternally sorry. He told them
he would prove it to them, so Rue went to The Old
Keevil Bridge. Where he built himself in to make
sure he suffered in the exact same way that they did.
He was offering them the ultimate sacrifice in return
for forgiveness.*

*They say if you are lucky enough whilst you sit
on the bench at The Old Keevil Bridge, Rue Than
will come and sit with you and tell you his story.
But you better listen carefully, for he won't stick
around long.*

Because,

Beeble dosh will come for us....

I'm utterly speechless. Did I meet Rue Than?
Did this man sit with me? Did this happen to me?
But he did not seem like an **UNSEEN**. He was
real, I know it. I saw him in the daylight. He walked
up and sat there right next to me. How can all this
be? How does this happen? Just when I mention
that I need solid proof, I find this letter confirming,

Elder Achlys Mallory Armaros is BEEBLEDOSH? I need to go outside and walk all of this off, but not before taking a picture of this. Maybe this is all happening because I need to show myself it's all genuine and has occurred. But most important of all, I need to tell this story. This tragic event has been hiding away for far too long, and they deserve better.

Chapter Twenty Five

Unseen Let Me See, And Set You Free

I find myself wandering through the church's graveyard. After that insane experience in the archives, I think that maybe this is all happening around me, and I'm not crazy after all. I should stop fighting it and embrace it. I must now listen and follow the wise advice Dr Durante has given me. I suddenly feel inclined to stop where I stand and look at the gravestone, but it's no one I know. I walk a bit further into the graveyard, and then, there, right before my very eyes, I see Xander Mika's grave. It means he was an actual person, so what does this mean for the letters and the fate of

BEEBLEDOSH. Is he genuinely PURE EVIL, or is he, in fact, a victim of someone far worse? Are we all just players that are part of a far bigger game?

Now eager to find the rest of the graves, I continue searching.

I finally FIND THEM, but they are spread out across the graveyard. How have I never looked here before? I found the Amista family, Seth, Raylene, Zuri and Keefe. I also found Rue Than and Dr Alfred Zavier. When I discovered the grave of THAT monster, Elder Achlys Mallory Armaros, I noticed that his grave also had BEEBLEDOSH carved into it right across his name. It appears your crimes follow you in life and after your death.

I sit down for a moment and watch the mist floating over and in between the graves. I continue to watch, hypnotised by the beauty of its elegance as it reaches up to the sky, spreading an ominous feeling as far as it can reach. I decide that enough is enough, and this ends TONIGHT.

I jump to my feet and run all the way home. I run forwards, and I don't look back. I head straight through the village, and I don't stop until I reach our front door. Once I arrive, I go straight to the kitchen draw, pull out the phone book, and look under the letter, M. I need to find a medium because I know that what I'm about to do, no one should do alone. I call three mediums and have no luck. Should I take this as a sign to give up or try one more number?

Tap,

Tap,

Tap,

Tap....

I suddenly hear THAT all too familiar tapping, and I now believe it's a clear sign. So while doing my best to ignore the warning, I close my eyes. I spin my finger around in the air four times before putting it down to the page. The name my finger lands on reads....

Mr Laurel Cedar.

I immediately called him and quickly explained a short version of everything, and he seemed very interested. I didn't even get to the price when he said never mind a fee because he was coming just based on what I told him. He said he's never heard of anything so interesting. I hope he's not a fake. Either way, I won't be alone for this, and it needs to happen.

Tap,

Tap,

Tap,

Tap....

It feels like the **UNSEEN** know that I have found out everything, so now they plan to torment me or possibly even try and stop me.

Tap,

Tap,

Tap,

TAP....

The old Keevil bridge will not stay up,
Will not stay up,
Will just not stay up,
The old Keevil bridge will not stay up,
Trapping us inside....

The old Keevil bridge is no longer up,
Is no longer up,
Is just no longer up,
The old Keevil bridge is no longer up,
Without them inside....

THAT song began to play out of THAT box. I run into the living room, and there it is, right where I left it. To my horror, I see the winder turning as it plays THAT song. I slowly reach in my bag to grab PIPPY, and then I run straight outside. I go over to the opposite side of the street to be as far from the house as possible. I decide to sit on the edge of the road to wait for Laurel because this way, I will see him arrive. I felt a strong presence in our house, and it was almost as if I was stood right before pure EVIL.

THAT tree is swaying in perfect rhythm with the gentle breeze that blows through Keevil. The eerie mist creeps through the streets, hiding the roads as it climbs up to meet the beam of LIGHT that's reflecting down from the moon. The stars are oddly bright in the sky tonight despite the mist that plagues the village.

I sit here looking at the house, but it seems somehow different now. Before, I would look at our home, and think of all our happy memories, so much laughter at Christmas and happy times. I would even think of all those sleepless nights I laid there in fear of being tortured by the UNSEEN. But now, when I look at this house, all I see is an awful tragedy unfold before my very eyes.

When people move into a house, they create a home and live out their lives, but what has this house witnessed? What would the walls tell you if they could talk? Can a house ever truly belong to one family at a time, or is there more to it? Are we sharing our homes with all the other families who also call that house their home? I pull PIPPY in close and hug him tight, and I whisper to him how I just want this nightmare to end.

A dark blue car pulls up outside the house, and I see a man step out. He grabs a bag out of his car boot, walks up the path to the house, and rings the doorbell. To my utter surprise, the door creeks open. I notice the man jumps a little, but then he leans forward to move his head to take a look inside the door. I hear him shout my name, and then he waits patiently in silence, but he gets no response. I can see him analysing what he's up against already. He's waited long enough, so I stand up and shout over to him. He abruptly turns around and begins walking towards me. He asks me why I'm over here and not inside. I explain to him that I can't be in there alone for a moment longer, knowing what I know.

Laurel suggests we go inside and that I should explain everything to him while he sets up his equipment. I begin to tell him the whole long story, not missing out on a single detail, so he fully understands. But whilst I explain, I can't help but watch him set up his machines because I find it fascinating. Once I get to the end of my explanation, I immediately ask him what all this stuff is and what it does. He explains that it's to measure any frequencies and signals in the house and record anything unusual with the video camera. He also says that some devices will pick up any abnormal sounds that would usually remain undetected. He thoroughly explains that the equipment is nothing to worry about and it's all very safe.

I ask him if he's ready to begin, he responds to me, letting me know that he's more than ready. I'm not even entirely sure that this is going to work. I've never had the UNSEEN become SEEN in front of anyone else before. They usually vanish when other people interrupt them. I immediately get an overwhelming feeling of despair because I have invited this medium in. What if I prove nothing more than the fact that it's me who needs help, and I AM on a deep, dark and dangerous road to insanity?

It's too late to go back now. It has already begun....

I grab THAT skull,

I grab THAT music box,

I make sure I have PIPPY,

I make sure I have the TORCH.

Then we lock the back door with a key and leave the front door shut, but unlocked, in a state of easy access just encase we need to leave the house in a hurry.

We turn off all the LIGHTS and run straight up the stairs to the top hallway. I gently push Talia's bedroom door, and it slowly swings open, revealing her room just as it was left. Laurel Places THAT skull on the table, who we now know as Elder Armaros, or maybe BEEBLEDOSH if that paperwork I found is authentic. We then drag the table into the middle of the room and place THAT music box next to THAT skull.

I then realised we needed Talia's drawing of BEEBLEDOSH because I felt like everything must be as it was. So this means we need to place the picture back under her pillow, but it's downstairs on the table. I say to Laurel that I need to grab that drawing quickly, but he's already spooked and says that I can't leave him in this room alone, not even for a moment. So I suggest we both go downstairs to get it. I turn the TORCH on, and with caution, we take one step at a time. We safely get to the bottom of the stairs, so I grab the picture from the table.

As I hold the picture in my hand, it catches my eye. So I look at **BEEBLEDOSH**, and I notice he's raised both of his arms this time. It seems like he's pointing towards us as if he knows that we are both here. I get butterfly's in the pit of my stomach and begin to shiver with a chill, so we head back up the stairs. I let Laurel go ahead of me, and then I take one step, followed by another, and then another. But then, as I place my foot on the next stair, I get an overwhelming feeling like someone is stood right behind me, breathing on my neck. So I decided to run, but as I lifted my foot, it wouldn't move. It felt stuck where I stood. I take a look behind me, but nothing is there. Then I proceeded to run up the stairs, but as I ran, something grabbed my ankle, it was only for a second, but something had me.

I walk into Talia's room and begin to regret this whole idea. Am I putting us in real danger?

Laurel sits on a chair and says, what now? I explain to him we turn the LIGHT OUT, and then we wait!

I place Talia's drawing under her pillow and begin to set up THAT music box. I rotate the dial in a clockwise direction, around and around until it won't turn any further. Then I get Laurel to hold it, so it can't start playing THAT song just yet. Then I walk over to the LIGHT switch, turn the TORCH back on, and I finally count to four,

One,

Two,

Three,

Four....

And,

Click, the LIGHT **is OUT!**

I walk over to Laurel and take THAT music box from him, placing it next to THAT skull. I

hold the TORCH and shine it over towards
Laurel, and I ask him if he is sure he's ready to do
this. He responds to me with a yes, of course.

Click the TORCH **is OUT….**

> **The old Keevil bridge will not stay up,**
> **Will not stay up,**
> **Will just not stay up,**
> **The old Keevil bridge will not stay up,**
> **Trapping us inside….**

> **The old Keevil bridge is no longer up,**
> **Is no longer up,**
> **Is just no longer up,**
> **The old Keevil bridge is no longer up,**
> **Without them inside….**

> Beware now Beeble Dosh will come for us,
> Will come for us,
> He will come for us,
> Beware now Beeble Dosh will come for us,
> Nowhere to hide….

> **The old Keevil bridge will not stay up,**

Will not stay up,

Will just not stay up,

The old Keevil bridge will not stay up,

Trapping us inside….

The old Keevil bridge is no longer up,

Is no longer up,

Is just no longer up,

The old Keevil bridge is no longer up,

Without them inside….

Beware now Beeble Dosh will come for us,

Will come for us,

He will come for us,

Beware now Beeble Dosh will come for us,

Nowhere to hide….

As THAT song plays, we sit and wait. My eyes have not adjusted yet, and all I can see is total darkness. Laurel has his night vision camera on, so he's keeping an eye on that while I'm just sitting here, waiting. We agreed to remain silent unless it's vital to speak, but despite the fact I know Laurel is here, I can't help but feel like I'm alone. I call out to him to make sure he's still here. Thankfully I hear a response confirming that Laurel is still in the room. He also states that he has never felt this scared in his whole life. He said that he senses a tremendous pain in this house, but he can't make out if it's current or from the past.

The old Keevil bridge will not stay up,
Will not stay up,
Will just not stay up,
The old Keevil bridge will not stay up,
Trapping us inside....

Tap,

Tap,

Tap,

Tap....

THAT branch, from THAT tree, began to tap on THAT window. It began to become more intense, TAPPING louder and louder. Laurel yelled out to me, begging me to move closer to him. Then, there it is, THAT long, bony, old pointing finger shows itself, it points directly towards us. Then THAT face begins to emerge out of the darkness, making sure that all of its features become more and more evident by the second. I stare at it with all my might trying to be brave. But THAT look on its face feels all too familiar. It seems like forever since I've been in its presence. It manifests such an evil, sinister look and just stares straight into my soul with such ease. I've become frozen with an intense feeling creeping up on me. I sense someone standing right behind me, but no matter how hard I try, I'm unable to turn around. All I can do is stare into THAT face.

I've felt this feeling many times before, and there is nothing I can do. It suffocates me with isolation and entrapment. I once again find myself unable to move. Then a dreaded thought forces its way into my mind. I have no bed in here this time, so I have nowhere to hide from THAT thing. Will it still seek to grab my right ankle in its desperation to lock its entangled fingers around my skin, taking me prisoner once more. Or will it be different this time? Will it stay away because Laurel is here with me? The UNSEEN has not yet been SEEN in the presence of another.

My eyes have finally adjusted to the darkness. I look over towards Laurel and see him looking into his camera. I notice he has a complete look of horror on his face. What is he seeing? I manage to take the camera from him, and all he tells me is that I'm right, that they are coming and that I am in grave danger. I look directly at the screen on his camera and point it towards THAT window, next to THAT long pointing finger. I almost drop his camera. I feel my heart beating so hard that it hurts my chest, but I know I must take another look and be brave, so I point it towards the window once again....

Was THAT face just a shadow in the nothingness? Was THAT long pointing finger nothing more than a small child's imagination? Somewhere, somehow, they have manifested into something undeniable. Right before my very eyes, I see THAT shadow slowly turning into human flesh. I also see THAT long pointing finger made up of nothing more than darkness turn to pure bone.

I find myself taking steps backwards until I accidentally fall onto Talia's bed. As I remain sat here, I pass the camera back to Laurel, then I close my eyes and repeat the same four words over and over in my mind,

This is not real,

This is not real,

This is not real,

This is not real**!**

I hear a scream,

Aghhhhhhhhhhhhhhhhhh,

HELP**!**

My eyes spring open because that's Laurel's voice. I immediately respond to him to ask if he's ok, but I get no response. My eyes finally adjust to the darkness, and I see Laurel led on the floor clasping onto his camera. I move my eyes down towards his feet to see if he has tripped over something....

But it's far worse!

Wrapped around his right ankle, THAT thing's long, bony, old fingers are entangled around his foot, connecting and locking into place. I want to look away, I feel my very soul forcing me to run, but I know I brought Laurel in here, so I must get him out. I wanted this, so now I have to face it. I force my eyes to look at THAT thing with everything I have, and I tell myself that I have no other choice than to finish what I have started.

I grab the TORCH and hold it out in front of me as if it's a weapon that will protect me from the enemy. I convince myself that I'm ready, I force my head to remain still and look. I start by looking at Laurels foot, and I slowly move my eyes up….

THAT thing is right there….

I just can't accept this.

It's NOT REAL!

How can it be?

THAT thing looks so old and genuinely evil right to its core. Why is it smiling? Why has it grabbed Laurel? Does it think He is me? Or does it know what it's doing? Is it, in fact, more intelligent than I'm giving it credit for after all of these years? Does it **WANT** me to see this? To witness from the outside exactly what it did to me for all those years.

I take a step backwards because it's evident that Laurel has passed out. I slowly lean down, bending my legs at my knees, keeping my eyes locked onto **THAT** thing, and I slowly reach forward and take the camera from Laurels hands. I move the camera towards my face until it's level with my eyes. But then I realise that my fear is beginning to take over, so I look up to the ceiling and count to four....

One,

Two,

Three,

Four!

Somehow I gained the courage to look into the camera, in the direction of THAT thing. I immediately see A FRAIL OLD LADY. She appears to be very aged and extremely skinny. As I look towards her, she begins to laugh hysterically like someone who just escaped from an asylum. Her head jilts upwards, and she suddenly springs up, releasing Laurel. I felt a relief sweep over me as she released him, but what does this mean for my fate. I drop the camera, and as it crashes to the floor, she flies towards me in one fast gust of wind. As she reaches my face, she lets out a yelp and silently blows up into thin air before my very eyes.

I'm frozen where I stand, and my breathing is undeniably erratic. The darkness feels like it has slipped into some more profound level of nothingness, creating an endless void where everything falls out of focus.

I decide enough is enough. I'm utterly terrified as it is. Therefore it can't possibly get any worse. Can it? I know my priorities have changed, and I need to get Laurel out of here, no matter what else happens. I suddenly remember something Dr

Durante and Zavier said to me. They told me that the dark road to my insanity ends here. Real or not, I must do something....

I AM THE **FIRE** IN FORTITUDE,

UNSEEN **Let me** SEE**, and set you** FREE....

I begin to feel weak. I fall to my knees and develop this undeniable need to sit down, but I make sure I sit as close to Laurel as I can get. I cross my legs, ensuring my feet are securely underneath my knees and safely placed away from anyone or anything. I hold up the TORCH and point it into the corner of Talia's room....

Click the LIGHT **is** ON**!**

Chapter Twenty Six

You Can't Fight Fate

I look deep into the LIGHT, and I hear a strange voice talking to me, but it does not sound the same as if someone was here next to me. It's as though whoever is speaking to me is doing so straight into my ear, but not externally. It's internal and coming from inside my head, but I am not producing it. I do all I can to block it out, but it just continues getting louder, I keep my eyes on the LIGHT, and I begin to see something….?

I suddenly change my mind and decide to listen instead of shutting it out because THAT voice WILL NOT STOP….

Deep in my mind, I hear someone say….

You asked to see,

So we can all be free,

This could all be undone,

Yet you still run.

Then out of nowhere or somewhere? I SEE THEM....

Seth, Zuri and Keefe are walking through the forest. The sun is shining, and the LIGHT is gleaming through the trees, reflecting off the leaves. It appears to be a beautiful day. But wait, who is that I see up ahead? Seth runs over and starts to well up. Tears stream down his face, and simultaneously, the two children scream out as if they were hurt. But wait, they are in pain....

Oh no, is this Raylene? Why am I here? I don't understand. I did not ask to see this.

I see Seth caress his wife as his children cry out in despair. They cry and cry, but time shall always pass. They sit on their knees, holding her and praying so hard for her to return to them. I hear Seth yell out, why her? Why her? The children weep for their mother, tears of the broken-hearted.

I see an old lady walking towards them through the trees. Wait, can it be? Is it her, THAT thing? Why is she here? What does she want with Seth and his family?

I can do nothing but stand here and watch them as she approaches. They have no idea she's even there because they have become so lost in grief. She kneels next to the children, reaches out towards them, and grabs their ankles with her long bony fingers. She tells them not to fear her because she has come to warn them. I hear her say the town is hunting them down because they didn't attend the meeting regarding the old Keevil bridge. Elder Armaros has decided that they are all sentenced to death. She goes on to tell them that they must hide, that they must have FORTITUDE and forget their grief, or there will be four deaths today instead of one. She tells them of a cottage where they can stay, to hide until the Elders calm down.

She tells them to make haste and not worry

because she would take Raylene to the church and see to it personally that she has a proper burial. Seth and his children run off in a different direction to the old lady, and I find myself suddenly following her. She keeps looking back at me as if she feels like someone is behind her. Can I not be SEEN? Her body language suggests that she knows someone is following her. She suddenly stops, I fall through her, and simultaneously she shudders as if she got a cold shiver. Then she develops a look as though she knows someone's there. With Raylene on her shoulder, she unintentionally drags Raylene's feet along the floor as she runs to the church without stopping. I find myself running alongside her, and I catch her eyes looking towards me every so often.

The old lady keeps her promise and lays Raylene to rest, but in the meantime, we see Elder Armaros tear the village apart, looking for Seth and his children. He gets to the point where he will stop at nothing to find them. I stand helplessly watching as every child in the village is taken by order of Elder Armaros. He sends them inside the church and yells out to the village, at the top of his voice, to let everyone know he will not give these young ones back until Seth, Zuri and Keefe are handed in.

I don't know why I do it, but I walk up behind him and whisper **BEEBLEDOSH** in his ear. He flinches, turns around and looks right into my eyes, but he does not see me. I proceed to walk straight through him, and he also shudders with a chill. What is going on here? Am I now their **UNSEEN**?

I walk into the church and see all the children sitting there looking scared. So I decided to walk to the front of the church, stand there, and yell out....

BEEBLEDOSH,

BEEBLEDOSH,

BEEBLEDOSH,

BEEBLEDOSH,

BEEBLE DOSH,

BEEBLE DOSH,

BEEBLE DOSH,

BEEBLE DOSH!

I suddenly find many different verses to THAT song flowing through my mind. I have no control over my actions, and I don't even know why I'm doing this. There is nothing I can do because I can't stop myself from singing THAT song....

The old Keevil bridge will not stay up,
Will not stay up,
Will just not stay up,
The old Keevil bridge will not stay up,
Trapping us inside....

The old Keevil bridge is no longer up,
Is no longer up,
Is just no longer up,
The old Keevil bridge is no longer up,
Without them inside....

Beware now Beeble Dosh will come for us,

369

Will come for us,
He will come for us,
Beware now Beeble Dosh will come for us,
Nowhere to hide....

The people of Keevil build it back up,
Build it back up,
Just build it back up,
The people of Keevil build it back up,
Trapping them inside....

The people of Keevil are now stuck inside,
Are now stuck inside,
Are now forever stuck inside,
The people of Keevil are now stuck inside,
Nowhere to run....

The old Keevil bridge is now finally up,
Is now finally up,
It Is now finally up,
The old Keevil bridge is now finally up,
Letting us outside....

The people of Keevil are now falling
asleep,

Are now falling asleep,
Are now forever falling asleep,
The people of Keevil are now falling
asleep,
Watching no more....

The old Keevil bridge will not stay up,
Will not stay up,
Will just not stay up,
The old Keevil bridge will not stay up,
Trapping us inside....

I see the children looking around, so I know they can hear me. I feel it in my heart, so I sing THAT song louder and louder. To my amazement, they begin to sing it, out loud and in time with me....

BANG!

The church door smashes open and hits the brick wall that sits behind it. Elder Armaros struts in, and at the top of his lungs, he yells out, SHUT UP. He tries his hardest to get the children to stop singing.

I become lost for words. These children sing louder and louder, with more and more force in their voices as the verses go on. But then Elder Armaros grabs one of the children by their arm, and I hear him say,

IF YOU DON'T ALL SHUT UP, YOU WILL NEVER SEE YOUR FRIEND AGAIN.

Complete silence fell over the church. All of them were silent, but one. It was as though this small child was looking right at me for courage as he spoke out, I heard him say, loud and clear to Elder Armaros....

BEEBLEDOSH, you are nothing but a coward. You will never feel satisfied or complete. Let us go!

Elder Armaros abruptly moves his hands to grab this small boy by his neck, but **THAT** old lady grabbed the child first in an attempt to stop any more hurt being caused. She says to Elder Armaros that she knows the location of Seth and his children. She forcefully tells him to let these innocent children go. They all proceed to rush out of the church and run home. The old lady makes one request in exchange for Seth's location. She somehow gets Elder Armaros to agree that she has permission to go to Seth first, and the two children are to remain unharmed and free.

I immediately find myself following her. I just can't believe she would hand Seth over like that. She runs to the cottage that she previously advised them to go to so they could hide, and she says to Seth, your wife is at peace, and the deal is accepted, just as we agreed. Seth responds by asking THAT old lady to do her best to make sure they spare his children. The old lady tells him that she promises to do all she can, but they must make haste now if he still wishes to return to his home before they come for him.

I walk through the forest alongside them. Seth acts as if nothing is wrong, just as any father would, but his children cannot hide their pain, and it's evident that they are still grieving. It is clear how much they appreciate their dad, and this suddenly reminds me of my dad. I know he would do anything for our family. A fathers love for his children is a bond that not even a force of pure evil can break.

Seth and his children return to their home just as promised so that they can have one last evening as a family. I stand at their window and look in, to watch them. It truly is mortifying to feel the way I do right now. I know his fate and I can't do a single thing to stop it. I can't do anything to save them. I walk into his home, and I walk straight through him. He does not alter! No shudder, no shiver, and I get a different feeling from him. It's like a shimmering warm LIGHT beaming onto your skin through a window on a hot summers day. Seth truly is an angel. He is so pure of heart, so why does he have such a dark fate?

I sit on one of his chairs and I just enjoy the happiness he's creating with his children. It's been a long time since I felt these feelings. Watching Seth and his children reminded me so much of my family, my mum, dad and Talia when we would laugh, play and enjoy PIPPY at the door. How could anyone walk in here and tear this apart?

CRASH!

I feel a sharp, intense and painful tear in my heart as Elder Armaros gets what he so truly desires on his fourth attempt to find Seth and his children. This perfect moment has instantly become a living nightmare. As I stand here, all I can do is watch as Seth and his children are torn from their home, and all I can feel is my heart breaking into a million pieces.

I follow them to the bridge, and so that he's not alone, I stand right next to Seth, and I remain with him because their fate is doomed to unfold. His children get forced into THAT bridge, and the bricks get built up before their very own eyes. But for as long as they could, they watched out across the water, never breaking eye contact with their father. Seth remains entirely still, and he does nothing else but looks to his children to show them that he will stay here with them, and always be there for them no matter what happens. Seth has no choice but to watch this heinous act as it takes place. Trapped and imprisoned, all he can do is watch. I stand here, and I whisper into Seth's ear....

There is more than just this life, you will be with your children once more, and you must tell your story.

I walk over to the bridge, and I somehow get through the wall. I just walked right through it, but it felt like it wasn't even there. I see Zuri, and she is just sitting there with a blank look on her face. She looks empty as if her soul has already given up and left her vessel. I speak into her ear, and I tell her that I will never forget her, and you must find peace to be free. Then I walk to Keefe, and I say the same into his ear, but I don't know if they can even hear me, but I say it anyway, just in case. I go back to Seth, sit on the bench next to where he stands, and stay with him. I watch him, and he just continues to stand firm for his children, showing such FORTITUDE.

THAT old lady shows up and begs Seth to forgive her. She pleads with him, explaining that Elder Armaros promised her that Zuri and Keefe would not be hurt. I continue to watch as I become utterly shocked to hear Seth so effortlessly say to her,

I forgive you, now go, you must protect the other children of this village.

I speak into Seth's ear one last time, and I tell him we WILL meet again! Then I follow the old lady back to the village. She goes into Seth's house, my house, and simply sits there on the floor in Zuri and Keefe's room, mine and Talia's room. I find it odd how our room was almost identical to how Seth's children have theirs arranged. She sits down in THAT same space, THAT same area on the floor where THAT THING sat for all those nights tormenting and torturing me. Sleepless nights spent lying awake in the nothingness, in the darkness. She puts her long bony hand over the bed and walks across the sheets with her fingers to reach a small teddy bear. She grabs the bear and wraps her bony fingers around it, and tears begin to fall from her eyes as she rocks back and forth. She cries and cries, whilst saying in a quiet, soft voice how sorry she is.

THAT tree then begins to tap on the window, just as it always has, for all eternity. I watch as the old lady begs Seth and his children for forgiveness every single day. She cries out to them, explaining how she can't live with herself. She never knew what the Elders were going to do. She never knew they were going to sacrifice his children. Elder Armaros gave her his word that they would remain safe.

To my absolute horror, I see her fate unwind right before my very eyes. What she did, and the choices she made continues to tear her up inside. In the end, it becomes too much for her to bear. So she gets up and walks outside with a rope. She swings it up over THAT branch and ties a noose. Then she turns a bucket upside down and stands on it whilst putting the rope around her neck. She pulls it tight and once more says sorry and begs for forgiveness. She elegantly swings herself off the bucket, knocking it over....

SNAP....

As I stand here helpless and unable to stop her, I see a black shadow floating away from her body. Is this her soul? Has she left her vessel to find peace, finally? This shadow heads upwards towards the sky and fades away into nothing.

She is dead!

She hung herself from THAT same tree that torments and tortures my very being. But on this particular night, THAT branch has no other option than to **TAP** and **TAP** on THAT window. It's her weight pulling IT downwards as her limp, dead, cold body swayed in the wind. THAT tree branch instantly becomes doomed to **TAP** on THAT window every night for all eternity to open her door and force her to return. I now finally understand why she grabs my foot at night. It's not to hurt or harm me, but because she honestly believes that she's still alive and is here, holding onto that bear. She now remains stuck inside the in-between, trapped in despair and madness, trying to ease her pain.

I feel a severe emptiness deep within me because of this terrible fate caused by a bitter regret from an inability to accept forgiveness.

I find myself walking back over towards the bridge. When I arrive, I sit next to Seth, noticing that Elder Armaros is standing on the top of the bridge. He is looking out across the water, watching Seth. As I sit here, I notice Seth is changing. When I first saw him, he was wearing pure white robes, and he had such a LIGHT soul, but now he's turning black. He has an outline that's becoming **darker** and **darker** as time passes. Could this be his aura? Is this what Zavier meant by an aura? Is Seth turning black because he's becoming excessively drained and exhausted? Or is it more to do with the fact that he is utterly heartbroken?

As I sit with Seth, I see him fall to his end, but something different happens. I see a black shadow leave his body. It maintains an upright posture and stands tall as Seth drops to the floor. I tried to catch him, but he fell straight through me.

Why does Seth have a black shadow?

Is this him?

Has he become the darkness?

I then notice two other black shadows rising from the bridge. They immediately turn and float across the water towards me. Before my very eyes, Zuri and Keefe manifest from within the dark shadows and become what looks like the same two children who haunted my childhood. I now understand! Their looks of torture and despair were the result of pure pain and heartache. How could I have got this so wrong? They stand before the black shadow that came out of Seth's body, and they remain immaculately still as they wait. I wonder what they are waiting for, so I continue to watch intently. Seth's black shadow begins to manifest into THAT exact black figure who stood between the children in the darkness, in the nothingness. I thought he was evil and trying to hurt me, but he was just protecting his children.

Seth is pure of heart and showed such FORTITUDE to his very last breath. It does not make any sense. Why is his soul so full of darkness? Has his soul turned black because of the way he died and his struggle to the very end? The pain he endured used every last bit of energy he had. He made sure he never took his eyes off his children and always kept his head up to remain strong for them. But then, in death, their souls reunite, and they live out their eternal lives in MY house because it is THEIR house.

IT IS OUR HOUSE!

I look up towards Elder Armaros and look him straight in the eyes because I want him to know that I saw him. I want him to know that I'm entirely aware that he just watched all of this and didn't even flinch. I decide to walk up to the top of the bridge. I now stand face to face with the monster that is Elder Armaros, and I suddenly realise that I have no idea where I got this courage from or what happens next.

As I stand here before him, I do nothing else but stare straight at him, but I find that I don't feel scared or threatened. I just feel an overwhelming sense of sadness for him. I can't help but feel like I wish I could turn back time and help him be a better version of himself. He is releasing such a strong feeling of loneliness, and he's so bitter and twisted. But I see it in his eyes that maybe, just maybe, if he had opened himself up to love, he may have walked down such a different road.

I suddenly find myself walking right towards him, and no matter how hard I try to stop myself, I get closer and closer to THAT monster. To my horror and inability to do anything else, I immediately cover my face with my hands as I walk straight into him. But this time, I don't come out.

He's not like the others!

Why was I unable to walk through him?

I feel his intense darkness and his desperate yearning for revenge. It's so powerful and overwhelming. I can feel it doing everything it can, trying to draw me in and contaminate my mind.

I begin to see the bridge, I'm not sure of the day, but I can tell this is the construction of the original bridge. I suddenly hear a man yelling out with extreme panic in his voice, saying,

STOP, HE'S STUCK!

HE'S STUCK!

HE'S STUCK!

STOP!

STOPPPPPPPPP, HE IS STUCK!

But despite the man's cries, Elder Armaros

demands the construction must continue. The next day, I have no choice but to stand and watch, as the man's body is dragged out of the bridge in two pieces as the consequence of Elder Armaros's ignorance. This man's body has been torn right through the middle. Elder Armaros commands that he gets taken to the church and put into a grave.

I stand here and watch as this man is lowered into the ground to rest in peace. I see a few of the other Elders bring out his gravestone, and once this man had reached his final resting place, they began to fill his grave with soil. I find it odd how no one else is here for this man, only me. Did he not have any friends of relatives? Or was no one else aware that he has passed on? Did Elder Armaros seriously not inform this man's family?

Once his grave was complete, the Elder's place his stone at the head of his grave....

I can't see what the writing on it says from where I stand, so I walk over to it, getting close enough to read it.

It reads....

Here Lies, Xander Mika....

Could it be that the first man Elder Armaros sentenced to death is the very entity that cursed him?

Everything suddenly becomes black. All I can see is darkness. Am I now in the nothingness? Has the darkness of Elder Armaros consumed me?

I see a LIGHT, and it beams down on Elder Armaros. He is holding four letters, and he's gripping them, clinging onto them as if his life depends on them. But he and I both know that out of some desperation to keep himself alive, he knowingly sacrificed and punished others to keep himself in this world. His selfishness has led him down a dark road to desperation, revenge and loneliness. But he only has himself to blame.

Then Elder Armaros returns to his home (my mum and dad's old house). He just goes and sits in his back garden without a care in the world. He has no conscience at all for anything he has done. Or any of the hurt he has caused the people of this village. As he remains sitting there drinking some water, I hear a strange noise. It starts in the distance and seems to be a low tone, but it becomes much louder and more precise as it gets closer. People are yelling and shouting out in an aggressive manner as they head towards the home of Elder Armaros.

As I remain unable to do anything or intervene in any way, a swarm of people, adults and children suddenly circle Elder Armaros, trapping him in the centre.

I hear them shout out.

This is for Seth and his family.

A man grabs Elder Armaros and strings him up on his own tree. He does not even fight them. He just lets them do what they need to do. As he stands with a noose around his neck on an upside-down wheelbarrow, I can't help but notice the irony. Ironically he's dressed in pure white. They dropped him as fast as they strung him up. But I stand right in front of him and look straight into his eyes. As he falls and his neck snaps, I don't see evil in his eyes. All I see is a sad, lonely man yearning for a way out. As his cold dead body blows with the wind, the children set him on fire, and as the flames rise, they dance around him singing THAT song.

I then hear a man suddenly begin to shout....

My name is Rue Than, and this man who hangs here before us all forced me to bury many people, adults and children, into **THAT** bridge. But the ones I regret most are Zuri and Keefe Amista. So this is for them, may every soul **BEEBLEDOSH** took,

NOW REST IN PEACE.

I see a white LIGHT, but it's so bright that I have to block my eyes.

I then hear a voice call out....

BEEBLEDOSH, I am Xander Mika. You know me as the author of your letters. But where you do not know me from is The Old Keevil Bridge. During its first construction, there was a day when your workers were yelling out to you, asking you to stop, do you remember? Well, you should, because I am the man you killed that day and all of this has been

your test and has led up to this exact moment....

BEEBLEDOSH, you had many opportunities to save your soul, more than you deserved. Did you risk your own life to repent for all the pain you have caused your fellow human beings or remain on the selfish path you have led yourself down? You chose a dark road and for what, to spend a lifetime alone anyway, all because you cared more about power. You cared more about your reputation than an actual mortal soul, so I tested your loyalty to humanity. Would you sacrifice yourself for them? If you had said NO, to any more death, you could have saved your immortal soul, but you chose darkness, and by doing so, you have chosen your own fate.

One day Rue Than shall tell this story to one chosen mortal soul because he will remain forever locked in a sea of guilt because of you, BEEBLEDOSH, and the truth must and will be told. But it won't be your story that lives on, for it is Seth Amista who has suffered the most. The people of this village will eternally remember Seth and his family because of what

you did to them here in this village.

I stand here looking upon two Pure white entities, but why would a man of such evil be white. To my complete surprise, Xander Mika looks straight at me and nods his head as if he's making a gesture to say his work here is done. As I watch him fade away into nothing, Elder Armaros, now BEEBLEDOSH, just stands there. After some time passed, he walks right through the villagers as he walks into his house and stands in the doorway. BEEBLEDOSH looks out towards me and stares straight through me. Is he looking past me, or can he now see me? I continue to watch him mainly because I suddenly remember that I don't belong here on this side of reality. I need to go home and get back to my family, but it seems my only way home has something to do with BEEBLEDOSH.

As I continue to watch him, his pure white glowing essence begins to change into a deep jet black. It starts at his feet and ripples through him to the very tip of his hat, completely absorbing all the LIGHT around him. He closes his eyes, remains completely still and does not move. But suddenly, I have to shield my eyes because all I can see is a wave of intense burning flames. I manage to compose myself, open my eyes and hold my breath as I slowly walk backwards.

BEEBLEDOSH is on fire. I know deep in my heart I have seen him before. If I'm honest with myself, I know I've seen him a few times by this point. He IS part of the UNSEEN. I know this now because I just watched him die. It also means Talia is his chosen one! She's entangled and forever stuck in his curse. Once BEEBLEDOSH decides he needs to end his suffering, what is her fate? Will, he let her die?

I figure my only option is to leave. I will just walk to the bridge and try using my aura to get home because I know I do not belong here. Just as I'm about to go, I catch BEEBLEDOSH move out the corner of my eyes. He is coming towards me at an immense speed. I look straight at him, but his eyes are gone. He is just a complete black entity consumed in roaring flames. He stops abruptly, leaving a gap between us,

Then, all I see are....

BIG RED EYES,

All I see are two deep **RED** eyes glaring back at me but just as quick as he opens his evil **RED** eyes, he vanishes into thin air.

As I walk towards the bridge, I see the church up ahead, and I have no explanation why, but I have a yearning to go inside. As I stand in the basement, I make a quick note about what I know, trying to include absolutely everything. But I realise **BEEBLEDOSH** has followed me and manifested himself in the corner of this dark, dusty room. I see a black shadow and those peering **RED** eyes just staring at me like I'm his next victim. Does he want to trap my soul in **THAT** bridge too? I begin to get a strong feeling of dread. I see him. I know he's there. But I can't help feel an emptiness in the pit of my stomach, and a sensation at the bottom of my spine, almost like someone has knocked the air out of me, but I can still breathe. I quickly finish writing what I know on a few pieces of paper and shove them on top of a box that sits up high so no one will discard them,

And then....

I RUN!

I run straight to the bridge, and I don't look back, but I suddenly find myself walking out of BEEBLEDOSH. What is this? Did time just catch up to itself? I'm back exactly where I began. I look towards him, but we are no longer face to face. He just continues to stand there looking out towards the water. Then out of nowhere he begins to fade away along with the bridge and everything else. I find myself once again sitting here on Talia's bedroom floor, pointing the now dim LIGHT from my TORCH into the corner of the room.

I immediately look to my side, and Laurel is still unconscious on the floor. I suddenly become very aware that I'm now alone in the dark. I know HE'S watching me, THAT evil man, who for all these years made me suffer and think I was being haunted by evil entities who are, in fact, just stuck here and are in pain themselves. But now I know that in reality, it is him, BEEBLEDOSH, who is the EVIL one, and he has been following Talia all this time. If his curse is real, it means he still watches over her even now. But it's time all of this stopped. She needs to know everything....

I'm frozen where I sit, and I find myself unable to comprehend anything that has just happened, so I close my eyes and count to four,

One,

Two,

Three,

Four!

I jump to my feet whilst I grab PIPPY.

Then I run over to the LIGHT to switch it ON....

Nothing!

The room is empty!

It's just us in here.

I run over to Laurel, and I shake him to try and wake him up, but it does not work. Then just as I thought I would have to call an ambulance and perform CPR on him, he comes around. He asks me what happened. I began to explain that he got spooked and passed out. But he says he can't remember anything, so I respond to him to let him know that he would not believe me even if I told him. We decide enough is enough and pack away the equipment, and head downstairs. Laurel suggests that we check the camera before he leaves just in case we caught anything. So we plug it into the television, and it's just white noise, fuzzing away. However, just as we were about to turn it off, we heard some children singing THAT song, but it was very faint.

> The old Keevil bridge will not stay up,
> Will not stay up,
> Will just not stay up,
> The old Keevil bridge will not stay up,
> Trapping us inside....

Is this the proof I need to finally convince myself that this is real and not my dark road to insanity? Laurel decides to write it off as an abnormality, and he then lets me know it's been an experience. He also explains on his way out that he knows something happened and that it's ok that he doesn't remember. He says to me that this was more about me and my demons than him trying to prove ghosts exist, and as long as I got what I was looking for, tonight has been a success.

Once Laurel left, I couldn't help but think about what he said....

MY DEMONS,

When I was a child, would I have agreed with that? I tell myself the answer is yes because I would have. But after everything I've just seen, I can't say they are demons because I know they are not. They are lost souls who have suffered immensely. So next time I lie there in my bed and fear the dark, I will tell myself, that it does not matter how scared I am. Because the real question is, how scared am I making THEM feel? For who is the UNSEEN? And who is REAL?

Are they the UNSEEN, or is it us who allow ourselves to be SEEN....

Chapter Twenty Seven

Face The Fear And Rise

Despite the circumstances, I'm excited for Talia to arrive. She's finally coming over, and I can't stop thinking about how excited I am to see her. I've missed her so much. I haven't seen her in forever, and it makes me sad that I have to tell her about all of this today. I suddenly find myself thinking about last night. Once again, I try to convince myself that this is all real. I need to accept this. I know I heard the children singing on that video camera recording. However, I can't help but wonder if it was all just a dream. Did I fall unconscious too? Were we both just asleep that whole time?

No....

I have to stop doing this to myself. I know in my heart what is true, and this **IS REAL!**

I'm now completely aware, what the lost verse to THAT song means. BEEBLEDOSH will come for us, because he's cursed to walk this earth forever. In life, he will come for you to keep his beloved bridge up. But in death, he will come for you because he must now do the opposite and keep you alive. He is doomed to care forever, but this also means he **MUST** always watch, or both BEEBLEDOSH and his watched soul will perish. Will he ever grow tired of watching or has he finally learnt what matters the most, and he won't ever let the one he cares for die? No one can hide from a curse, Not even BEEBLEDOSH. The only way he can finally end this is if the one he watches and cares for understands absolutely everything and sees him for what he is. Then and only then, they must freely forgive him with their whole heart.

Creeeeeeaaak,

Knock,

Knock,

397

Knock,

Knock....

I run towards the door....

It's Talia,

I run towards her and hug her so tight because I don't want to let her go. Whilst I hug her, she whispers in my ear that I'm lucky she came because this house gives her the creeps. I finally let go of her and grab us both a bottle of water from the fridge. Talia asks me about the pieces of paper on the table. I explain to her that all will become clear. We walk towards the living room, and as we walk in, Talia passes THAT skull and says aloud how it's always freaked her out, but it's kind of cool at the same time. I take this opportunity to tell her that I have a lot to say to her. But to my surprise, she explains that she finally has some stuff she wants to say to me after all these years.

Talia, it's important I tell you everything. A lot has been happening around here since I've been home, and there is some stuff you **NEED** to know. I'll let you know everything first, and then you can say what it is you need to say. If you think I'm crazy partway through, please bear with me. **YOU MUST HEAR THIS**. But remember that I love you very much and will do anything for you.

I met with a neurologist called Sebastian Wyatt. He managed to get me an appointment at a nearby research centre, to have the aura with migraine I suffer from looked at in a bit more depth. They have helped me more than they realise. I began to understand a lot more about myself. However, I noticed that one of the Doctor's had the same name as a medium I met the other night at an event held in the Church of the Holy Spirit. His name was Zavier, and he hosted the event. But when I went back to the church to try and contact this medium, Pastor Indigo told me he had no memory of any event taking place that night. Or any night, in fact, over these last few years. But to make a long story short, I've found out that....

I might hold the power that's needed to open doors to alternate realities.

Talia, I'll be completely honest with you, I think I'm slowly slipping down a very dark road. I have been falling deeper and deeper into the darkness. Feeling crazy has led me into very lonely places. Sometimes I see and hear strange things. But most of all, unusual stuff is happening around me, and there is no record of any of it. I said to myself, enough is enough, so I went to the church archives, well, what they call archives anyway. I went down to the church's basement with permission, of course. I found the answers I was looking for, so I searched through the phone book for a medium and found Laurel Cedar. He agreed to come to our house and help me. We were in your room, with your drawing of BEEBLEDOSH, THAT skull, and we played THAT song....

Then....

I saw it all!

I left this place that we call reality and crossed over into what I can only describe as uncharted territory. I was somewhere that I did not belong. I had no option other than to stand and watch many terrible, heinous crimes unfold right before my very eyes.

Talia....

BEEBLEDOSH was the leader of the Elders of Keevil back when it was known as Eivele! I had THAT skull tested, and the institute has traced it back to him. I even received a letter with the results, and I made sure to keep it. I've put it out there on the table. There is no denying it Talia, it's HIS skull. I also know how he finally met his end. The people of Keevil, or Eivele, were led by a man called Rue Than. They went to BEEBLEDOSH'S house and hung him from his very own tree.

But, the bad part is that his house is Mum and Dad's old house, and you lived there as a baby Talia. BEEBLEDOSH protects you from the UNSEEN because you are his best friend. You are the one he cares about, and he truly believes that if he does not keep you safe and watch over you until the end of time, then someone or something will take you from him and this world. He has done many bad things in his lifetime, and this is the price he has to pay for all the terrible, despicable crimes he's committed. **BEEBLEDOSH** is forever cursed!

A long, long time ago, **BEEBLEDOSH** used to be called Elder Achlys Mallory Armaros. He had a task to build a bridge that would allow the people of Keevil to be free to see the world. During the construction of the bridge, a man died because of a decision **BEEBLEDOSH** made. He had every opportunity to save this man, but he cared more about completing his bridge than saving a life. A man named Xander Mika was the one who wrote to **BEEBLEDOSH**, commanding him to build the bridge in the first place. Xander Mika volunteered to help with the bridge's construction because he genuinely believed everyone should be free and that a few chosen Elders should rule no one.

That day when Xander Mika went to help at The Old Keevil Bridge was his last, because of **BEEBLEDOSH'S** selfish decision.

One selfish decision cost **BEEBLEDOSH** his eternal life. Xander Mika wrote three more letters to **BEEBLEDOSH**, offering him a chance to repent for what he had done.

BEEBLEDOSH sacrificed two innocent children and forced their father to stand and watch as one of the workers was commanded to trap the two children inside the bridge. He built bricks up around them to lock them inside, creating an eternal tomb with no escape. This man was called Rue Than, and he could not live with himself, so he led a massacre on BEEBLEDOSH, hanging him from his own tree, Mum and Dad's tree. But as BEEBLEDOSH'S body turned lifeless in the wind, the children of Keevil set him on fire. They wanted to show him that even in death, they wanted to force him to suffer the same way he made the Amista children suffer. They made sure he was choking alive, suffocating with no hope in sight and feeling trapped with no way out. Then as the flames blew up in the wind, the children sang THAT song. You know it well, THAT exact song that comes from MY music box.

Rue Than sat with me at THAT bridge and told me Seth's story. Rue explained his part in it and how he had no choice over his actions because he had orders from BEEBLEDOSH to continue to sacrifice people to THAT bridge. But what he regrets the most and what led him to take his own life was Zuri and Keefe Amista. Rue Than locked the Amista children into the old Keevil bridge, one brick at a time. Whilst Seth had no choice but to stand across the water and watch helplessly as this terrible event unfolded. All of this was the result of orders given by **BEEBLEDOSH**. The UNSEEN are not what I thought. They are not the bad ones. They are the lost souls who are suffering eternally because of **BEEBLEDOSH**.

As soon as he left his lifeless vessel, Xander Mika cursed Elder Achlys Mallory Armaros to be eternally known as **BEEBLEDOSH**. Talia, your childhood imaginary friend, is doomed to walk forever in purgatory. **BEEBLEDOSH** is as real as you and me. Some might even say you are his imaginary friend because he can SEE you. But you are UNSEEN by the others. You are invisible to all the lost souls who run from him, hiding in the nothingness, in the darkness of the night. He is doomed to keep the one he cares about alive until the end of time, and this is his price to pay, for he, too, will survive, existing forever in eternal pain.

He must watch forever, just like Seth had to watch his children die. **BEEBLEDOSH** will be stuck in purgatory forever, nothing more than a watchman making sure the one he cares about is safe. He is forever cursed to feel the guilt in death that he should have felt in life. He had no conscience and took the souls of so many innocent people when he had no right. He is cursed to become attached to any child who enters his home.

There is a lost verse to THAT song, I found it when I was in the church, and it means he will come for you, but at the same time, it's saying that he must watch you, Talia, or you will both perish. He is dangerous even in death because he is a selfish man under a curse, meant to punish HIM, but he still holds the power to harm others should he choose to give up and stop watching. Xander Mika has held onto the power of FORGIVENESS and hopes that BEEBLEDOSH will listen to his guilt through his attachment to you. But you must understand that he must suffer for your life to remain safe, forcing BEEBLEDOSH to let himself finally commit a selfless act.

No one can hide from a curse. The only way he can be free is if the one he watches completely understands what he is and still forgives him. Talia, that's you! You're the only one who can finally end this and set him free. You are the key to ending his eternal torture, and, in doing so, you will also free the UNSEEN. They will no longer need to hide from each other or BEEBLEDOSH. But most importantly, they will no longer need to hide from US.

But does he even deserve to be free? Has he suffered enough in return for what he has done? Is it even possible to measure how much someone is suffering? How long does his pain need to last before he can make up for the heinous crimes he's committed and even begin to make any of this fair? Will he ever deserve to be free? I wonder how many people he has possibly saved along the way since his demise. Maybe he scares people in the deep darkness of the night to get them out of danger, making them move at certain times to keep them safe. Or does he still, even now, only act out of selfishness to keep himself in existence through people's fear.

You have a choice to make, Talia. I just hope you make the right one. He's only free if you truly forgive him in your heart. You know him more than anyone, but you have not SEEN the things

I've **SEEN**. You must understand what he is, and it won't work if you're only doing it to save yourself. A selfish act won't cancel out another selfish act....

Talia then hugs me and tells me it's going to be ok, and she's sorry for never letting me keep the LIGHT on, but it did not come from a selfish place as she had no idea what I was going through. She then says that she has some stuff she needs to tell me....

She begins....

BEEBLEDOSH told me long ago that the **UNSEEN** think they are alive. Alive or not, they live side-by-side with us. I could never see them, so I thought **BEEBLEDOSH** was messing around, but now it makes perfect sense. They see the world as it used to be, but we see it just as it is. Two worlds collide, but which one is real? Who knows. As you said, we might be their **UNSEEN**. In the same way, that they are what we call the UNSEEN. But no one could possibly know unless someone like you comes along with something special. You open a door allowing all to be **SEEN**

from both sides. You create a way for both realities to merge and clash into one. Allowing the UNSEEN to see each other, but not as you and I see each other. The darkness creates a scary projection of the entity. We immediately develop fear against it because it should not be there. You are the definition and explanation why only some people can see these entities known as ghosts, or as you call them, the UNSEEN.

BEEBLEDOSH also told me that your aura and migraines produce the perfect frequency that's needed to open a door allowing us all to be **SEEN**, just as you have been told. Although I have never seen them, the UNSEEN have always been here. According to **BEEBLEDOSH**, it's us who have invaded their reality, and we are the **UNSEEN**. But we view them as a threat because we naturally fear what we can't understand.

BEEBLEDOSH said he visits me to protect me and prevent the UNSEEN from harming me. He says they are not our friends because they want to hurt me to punish him. I used to think he was just lonely and didn't want to lose me as a friend, but as time passed by, he became meaner and more forceful each time I saw him. **BEEBLEDOSH** knew you had the key, the frequency and the correct aura to cross realities and be **SEEN**. He said he was counting on your ability to see the UNSEEN to keep the door open so we could be friends forever. He knew that lack of sleep would lead to a build-up of harmful toxins in your brain that you can't clear without sleep. He was all too aware that your lack of rem sleep would cause the significant changes needed in your aura to allow fate to take its course. **BEEBLEDOSH** never mentioned that he is cursed or that if you don't keep that door open, he and I will both perish.

BEEBLEDOSH told me that everyone begins with a colourful aura. But entities only turn **BLACK** if they become drained of energy. He planned to make you seem like an evil **UNSEEN** to scare off the OTHERS, so he could keep them away from me, to protect me from THEM. He convinced me that they were after me to punish him. I'm so sorry I knew all this and did not tell you, I thought I was helping, but you were scared and alone. I want you to know that once he revealed all of this, I no longer wanted to see him or be friends with him. It's why I would get mad whenever anyone would bring him up, I thought that if I made him leave, it would all stop for you, but I was wrong. It seems it only got worse.

I don't know what to say!

All this time,
All these people,
All the lives that have crossed and intertwined with each other.

But all that's come of it is so much suffering and pain.

What is the price to pay.
You can't fix pain with more suffering?

Talia....

Where does it end?

I decide to give Talia some space to think about what she wants to do with all of this.

I can't help but continue to think about everything. Suppose it's me who crosses the realities and not Dr Alfred Zavier. In that case, I must have manifested Zavier because I needed to know everything he told me. Everything that has happened must have been for a reason and led us to this exact moment. Is this our only road to end all of this suffering and the void of darkness, keeping everyone stuck inside? Meaning none of this has happened by accident. All of this was supposed to happen, exactly as it has.

One question remains in my head, and I can't shake it because the paperwork at the church has revealed the truth about the UNSEEN. The UNSEEN also took me on a journey I'll never forget, revealing the brutal reality of the dark secret past of this village. But who is the last soul, the one who I have SEEN? He was that breeze of air that blew on my face. He was the man who would pace up and down next to my bed. But he was not SEEN last night or mentioned in the church archives. Could he have passed through a different door created from another frequency, reality or world altogether? Is he something completely different? Was he lost? Or was he also there for a reason?

Talia says she needs to go and clear her head.

She wants to take a walk around the village and have a think about everything. I tell her to go via the church and look at the gravestones to see the names we mentioned because they are all there. While she goes for a walk, I go into the kitchen and gather all my paperwork, placing it into a pile. I then take a slow walk through the house until I reach the stairs. I gaze up at them, and out of nowhere, I begin to see ghost-like versions of us as small children playing on the stairs without a care in the world before all this started. Maybe once it's over, if it's ever over, I might feel that way once again.

I'm overwhelmed by a warm fuzzy feeling. I think I'm finally accepting that this is all REAL. I'm not going crazy, and there is hope for this house. But we're not done yet. The UNSEEN are not at peace, and a curse still traps many souls in the in-between.

I run up the stairs just as I always do. Especially after last night, once I get to the top, I look into Talia's room. It feels different somehow like all the negative energy has left, gone or moved on. That eerie, ominous feeling has lifted. The sun shines in with a ray of LIGHT beaming onto the window and reflecting off the glass. I walk down the hallway to my room, push open my door, and place all the papers away in a draw because I don't need them anymore. I now know what happened here in this village, and I WILL tell THEIR story. I WILL help them find PEACE....

I look out the window as I stand here winding the dial on THAT music box to play THAT song. I place it on my desk and stand it upright, leaning on the wall to play aloud for all the UNSEEN to hear. But as I stand here listening to THAT song, I suddenly realise I need to go and look for Talia because I think I know what we must finally do....

Chapter Twenty Eight

Talia

I find Talia knelt at **BEEBLEDOSH'S** grave. She has tears rolling down her face, and she explains that she feels terrible for what he did to all those people, but she can't help but feel sad for him because he was her best friend for so long. He was kind to her, and they did share so many good memories before **BEEBLEDOSH'S** fear of losing her consumed him. Talia then said how this burden has been with her for all these years, and she feels guilty for it, but she wants to forgive him and set them both free.

As I stand here next to her, I get a strong sense that she is feeling relieved to know that **BEEBLEDOSH** is genuine and not imaginary after all this time. I suggest to Talia that we go to the bridge because it seems like he's been struggling to find her since she moved house. It's most probably where he's waiting for her. I'm just not sure if we will find him or if he will hide. I don't even know if the door is still open, but time will tell. She wipes her face and responds to me, letting me know that we should head over there now. The sooner, the better.

As we walk to the bridge, I think hard to myself about what she will do. Is she going to forgive BEEBLEDOSH and set him free, or will she condemn him to continue to walk this road forever locked in eternal pain?

I can see The Old Keevil Bridge up ahead, and it's clear, nothing and no one is there. We walk over and sit on the bench. Whilst we wait, we talk and look out towards the bridge. Talia asks me if we can go and see the walls that the children were trapped behind. I respond to her and say I guess it will be ok. After all, it is Keevil's bridge.

We walk around the bridge to get to the stone brick walls, we find ourselves standing in front of the right pillar. I immediately feel sick to my stomach as I stand here before the very tombs that started it all. Talia places her hands onto the stone wall and says she is sorry to the Amista family for what she has to do. But it is the only way, and it is the right thing to do. I then place my hands onto the wall and tell them that I'm sorry for what has happened, I could **NOT** help you back then, but I CAN and WILL help you now.

We decide that maybe we should head home because **BEEBLEDOSH** is nowhere to be SEEN. But then, just as I turn around to begin walking home, Talia asks me to open the door! To think of him and channel him. She begs me to shout out loud, to just shout for him!

I begin to think about him with everything I have, and then I shout out. Quietly at first, but then I find myself yelling out to him.

BEEBLEDOSH,

BEEBLEDOSH,

BEEBLEDOSH,

BEEBLEDOSH,

BEEBLE DOSH,

BEEBLE DOSH,

BEEBLE DOSH,

BEEBLEDOSH!

I look towards Talia for guidance to see if she wants me to shout again, but she interrupts me and tells me to look up!

As I raise my eyes to the top of the bridge, I freeze in horror. I see HIM. BEEBLEDOSH is standing at the edge of the bridge, staring right at us. I ask Talia what happens next. She responds by saying she has to do this next part on her own....

BEEBLEDOSH, You listen to me NOW!

You have been in my life for as long as I can remember, you have been my best friend, my worst enemy, and I've even called you my family. But as I stand here before you today, I know what you are, and I know what you have done. Your choices have led you down a dark path, one that you can't escape. You have put your fate into someone else's hands, and in doing so, you have also cursed me.

Forgiveness is a voluntary process that no one can force. You have made me feel so many different emotions towards you over the years. But recently, I can't control my feelings, and I've had a change of heart towards you. I have overcome my negative emotions, and I no longer want vengeance upon you. I no longer resent you.

I know you once had a WHITE soul. You were once pure of heart, but the choices you made, impacted so many others and yourself in the process, and now your soul is **BLACK** because you let go of the LIGHT. You lost faith in yourself because you hold a constant weight on your shoulders, and you can't escape the burning fire that constantly reminds you of your eternal pain. Your constant fear of ceasing to exist has caused you to become exhausted, fatigued and drained. You need to channel our energy in order to be **SEEN** because you have depleted any power you had left, I know you're tired, and I know this has to end.

You had a choice to choose the LIGHT or fall into the darkness. BEEBLEDOSH, you chose your path, and you went down a long road to darkness with no end in sight. The more you tried to drag yourself out, the deeper you became. BEEBLEDOSH, you need to find peace within yourself. You need to accept responsibility for your wrongdoings and mend all the hurt you have caused.

I am your best friend!

BEEBLEDOSH, I FORGIVE YOU....

I completely and utterly forgive you, and I have and always will see you as my friend.

My best friend who once made me smile and laugh with joy....

Talia turns around and looks at me as if to say, why is he still stood there? Why has this not let him move on? If it was all true, he should have found peace. She forgave him, and there is no doubting that. I can see it in her eyes, the tears she shed as she spoke to him from deep within her heart. It was not easy for her to get past all his darkness and see his LIGHT. Why does he remain up there standing immaculately still, staring at us whilst he yearns for help, for an escape from his immortal prison?

Talia then says something very concerning to me. In a broken, quiet worrying voice, she explains that maybe it's me! That I must forgive him because he used my aura and my energy. She says that because he's been with her for as long as she can remember and he followed her from his own home to our new one, it means he has also been around me since I was a baby. But I respond to her, explaining that the curse says BEEBLEDOSH will form an unbreakable bond with any pure soul who goes into HIS house. I've never stepped foot into Mum and Dad's old house. Talia then says as she looks straight at me, that I have been there! When I was a tiny baby, our mum and dad had something they needed to sign for the new owners. We both went with them, but we waited in the kitchen because I was in a car seat at the time.

I don't know how I feel about this. I have not come here today prepared to forgive

BEEBLEDOSH.

I had no choice but to stand and watch as it all unfolded in real-time before my very eyes. I felt every emotion, every strike of pain that Elder Achlys Mallory Armaros inflicted upon the people of Eivele. I stood there and lived through it all with them, each painful moment, and I don't know who's choice it was, but somehow, this village became named after this bridge of death, this grave as it has become. It's thanks to THAT music box and THAT child's song that the secrets of Keevil have made it to the surface. Setting all of this in motion to create the steps needed to lead us down this path to the final destination that we have found ourselves at, right here, right now.

Talia was the one he cared about, but he knew that I would not be far from wherever she was. But he didn't consider the fact that we would grow up and live our own lives. We outgrew him and this village, which is why he still watches, despite us living our own lives.

We walk back to the bench, and I feel BEEBLEDOSH following us with his eyes the whole time. I stand there with Talia, and as I feel the wind blowing past my face, I turn and look out across the water, and I stare straight at HIM.

I stand in the exact place where Seth stood and watched his children die. As I stand here, I see them repeatedly, those poor children as they get dragged to their graves, and I feel all the pain and suffering that Seth felt.

I stare at BEEBLEDOSH....

I glare at him, staring deep into his RED eyes, and he does not alter. As I stand here, I see everything playing over in my mind. I think about the pain he has caused everyone, even me. All those sleepless nights that I lay awake terrified of the UNSEEN when they were just begging for help. I think about how BEEBLEDOSH used me to continue his selfish mission even in death.

Then I think about what Dr Clay Durante told me,

I AM THE FIRE **IN** FORTITUDE!

What is fire? It can burn and hurt, but it brings LIGHT along with it to help us see. Is it BEEBLEDOSH'S fate to harm people and commit unforgivable crimes in order for us to SEE and learn what LIGHT is? Is it from Seth Amista's story that we understand how we must have **DARKNESS** to measure LIGHT?

BEEBLEDOSH was once set on FIRE, and now he burns eternally, but is he doomed to forever burn because he is, the FIRE in the **DARKNESS**.

There has been one other with a WHITE aura. Was this BEEBLEDOSH? Was he once LIGHT? Is this why we are connected? Is he the proof that even the purest souls are not safe from becoming victims to the **DARKNESS**? Or do we all start our journey with a WHITE aura, and then the choices we make, and the lives we lead dictate how we end up. For Seth was the purest, and the fate that BEEBLEDOSH sentenced him to turned his pure soul **BLACK**.

So much pain.
So many wasted lives.

But now I must show, **THE** FIRE **IN** FORTITUDE and face my **DEMON** once and for all.

BEEBLEDOSH....

HEAR ME NOW, ONCE AND FOR ALL....

Darkness is LIGHT, and we can't have one without the other. You made your choices, and you have paid the price whilst condemning everyone in your path. But to finally be free from you, others still have to sacrifice.

Where does it end?

Everyone should be free to choose, LIGHT OR **DARKNESS**!

BEEBLEDOSH you have to,

Let it all go, Let the UNSEEN go, Let everyone go....

Face your fear and rise!

As I stare into his eyes, I think about how we should all be free to decide our own fate. I notice that his fire starts to calm, becomes smaller, and then disappears. Then BEEBLEDOSH starts to turn transparent and fades out to nothing. My trance brakes, and I fall to my knees.

On my knees, I look out towards the water. I see Seth and his family very faintly in the distance. Seth holds hands with his wife and two children and walks towards the bridge. But then I notice Seth turns his head, looks towards me and lifts his hat as if he is gesturing to say thank you. Then he turns back around and the **DARKNESS** that had consumed him lifts away, and I see a sudden beaming WHITE LIGHT as they fade away into the nothingness.

Talia asks me if it is finally over?

But I can't give her the answer she desires because, in all honesty, I just don't know. I wanted to forgive BEEBLEDOSH so badly, but I became at war with myself, and now I'm unsure if my energy depleted or if he is finally FREE....

At the start of our journey, I asked you to join me if you **DARE**.... Well, you joined me and witnessed actual pain, loneliness, struggle, sacrifice, commitment, and loyalty. But most of all you have witnessed fear, a **FEAR** so real that you feel it deep down to the dark depths of your very core.

Now you know the deepest darkest places a lost soul can take you.

How do you feel? Will you now live and not just survive....

My mum and dad returned home from their fantastic holiday, and all is just as they left it. They unpack and get ready for bed. It's just my mum and dad in the house tonight, so they sit down to watch a movie on the television after having such an amazing holiday.

They fall asleep on the sofa due to being exhausted from all the travelling. But my mum wakes up for some reason. She doesn't move because my dad is leaning on her shoulder as he sleeps. My mum remains sitting there thinking about how much of a good time they have had,

....Then, out of the **DARKNESS**, there stood in front of the glass cabinet. A **black** figure stands tall, burning in deep WHITE and BLUE flames....

The Old Keevil Bridge

The old Keevil bridge will not stay up,
Will not stay up,
Will just not stay up,
The old Keevil bridge will not stay up,
Trapping us inside....

The old Keevil bridge is no longer up,
Is no longer up,
Is just no longer up,
The old Keevil bridge is no longer up,
Without them inside....

Beware now Beeble Dosh will come for us,
Will come for us,
He will come for us,
Beware now Beeble Dosh will come for us,
Nowhere to hide....

The people of Keevil build it back up,
Build it back up,
Just build it back up,
The people of Keevil build it back up,
Trapping them inside....

The people of Keevil are now stuck inside,
Are now stuck inside,
Are now forever stuck inside,
The people of Keevil are now stuck inside,
Nowhere to run....

The old Keevil bridge is now finally up,
Is now finally up,
It Is now finally up,
The old Keevil bridge is now finally up,
Letting us outside....

The people of Keevil are now falling asleep,
Are now falling asleep,
Are now forever falling asleep,
The people of Keevil are now falling asleep,
Watching no more....

The old Keevil bridge will not stay up,
Will not stay up,
Will just not stay up,
The old Keevil bridge will not stay up,
Trapping us inside....

The old Keevil bridge is no longer up,
Is no longer up,
Is just no longer up,
The old Keevil bridge is no longer up,
Without them inside....

Beware now Beeble Dosh will come for us,
Will come for us,
He will come for us,
Beware now Beeble Dosh will come for us,
Nowhere to hide....

My name is Melissa Scott,

In 1988, I was born in the City of Bath in England, and as I grew older I moved to many more places.

I joined the British Army in 2007, where I enjoyed a long and rewarding career serving my country. But then, I decided to take on a new challenge, so I joined the Royal Air Force in 2015. I enjoyed pushing myself to new heights whilst learning a lot about myself in the process.

But in 2019, I just knew it was time to move on. Something inside me was pushing me to take the next step, take on new challenges and invest more time in my family and other areas of life. I felt like I could not go any further in the military and I was ready for what came next along my path into destiny.

Since then, I have begun studying for my degree in Geography and Environmental Science and I've also finally wrote my story. Writing this has been the most significant goal I have ever set myself, and now I get to share my story with the world.

My story, while it is a complete work of fiction, is based on true events that took place in the City of Bath. I have based my story on the village of Keevil because I would go there with my dad and sister when I was younger, and I always found it to be a very mysterious, ominous and creepy place.

I would like to personally thank you for reading my book. I hope you enjoyed my story, and I appreciate you coming along with me on my adventure.

Kind regards,
Melissa Scott

If you would like to contact me regarding anything to do with my story, please don't hesitate to get in touch.

you can reach me at:

melissa-scott-novels@outlook.com
www.afairytalewish.com

A Fairytale Wish

✦ Hope Conquered Fear... and they lived happily ever after. ✦

Lightning Source UK Ltd.
Milton Keynes UK
UKHW051309140222
398647UK00004B/26